MW00623568

GHOSTS
and Other Unpleasantries

GHOSTS

and Other Unpleasantries

by

C.S. Sahu

J.W. Sheahan & Company
Alhambra, California

"Mean Mister Mullins" originally published in *Alfred Hitchcock Mystery Magazine,* September 1997.
"The Book of the Servant" originally published in *Alfred Hitchcock Mystery Magazine,* November 1997.
"Honey" originally published in *All Hallows 26,* February 2001.
"You Should Have to Live with Yourself" originally published in *Aquainted with the Night,* Ed. Barbara and Christopher Roden, Ash-Tree Press, British Columbia, 2004.

This is a work of fiction. Names, characters, businesses, places, events, and incidents are either the products of the author's imagination or used in a fictitious manner. Any resemblance to actual persons, living or dead, or actual events is purely coincidental.

Copyright 2016 by C.S. Sahu
All rights reserved

ISBN 978-0-9975785-0-8

Library of Congress Control Number 2016907802

Cover art by BespokeBookCovers.com

Cover photograph: Joseph Hall, New York, New York, 1906

sewn and glued binding
Printed in the United States of America by
Thomson-Shore, Inc.
Dexter, Michigan

In memory of my sister, Jeanie:
a great ghost-story teller.

Table of Contents

The Book of the Servant

"So your old fella died, eh?" Mrs. Benninghoven asked of the woman who had just sat down in her office. They were waiting for a fresh pot of coffee to finish brewing. "What a shame. He was a very nice old man."

"Yes, he was," replied Elsie Spry, a neat, middle-aged woman, chubby and perhaps a bit homely, but cheerful and pleasant – a housekeeper by trade, and employed by Benninghoven's Caregiving Services on a case-by-case basis. They were discussing her last client. "But it was more than time for him to go," Elsie continued with philosophical regret. "Ninety-six he was, believe it or not, and very tired those last few weeks. He would just sit in his chair, watching the leaves fall –" She fluttered her fingers poetically downward. "Lost his desire to eat, and didn't like being wheeled outside for his walks anymore. He used to enjoy them so much! I think he was just as glad to go."

"The nurses told me you were a great help to them in lifting the patient and so on. And they praised your cooking to the heavens," said Mrs. Benninghoven.

Elsie smiled a bit self-complacently.

"Now let's see what I have available for you next," Mrs. Benninghoven continued, opening her schedule book. The coffee had finished brewing, and Elsie got up and poured them out two cups, hot and black. She had stopped by the bakery on her way in and now brought out, from a pink box, four oversized, plump blueberry muffins sprinkled with big crystals of sugar.

"Oh, how nice. Thank you," said Mrs. Benninghoven, taking

the blueberry muffin Elsie handed her on a napkin. "...I have nothing open right now," she said slowly, nibbling. "But a young couple expecting their first baby will be needing someone... though the due date is in early November, and of course there's no knowing when exactly."

"That would add up to several weeks of unemployment for me," Elsie put in, "this being only October – which would be a little hard. Don't you have anything sooner?"

"Well, something might come in any day, of course. Especially if we get an early snow. We always have a few slips and breaks call in when the freezing weather begins."

"But it's looking very mild," objected Elsie. She leaned over and peered into Mrs. Benninghoven's schedule book. "What about that one, there?" she asked, pointing to a note scribbled in last Thursday's square, the one for September twentieth.

"Oh, that," Mrs. Benninghoven frowned. "I was planning on ignoring that one, to tell you the truth. Mr. Parsloe. He's looking for a housekeeper only, no nursing involved, which suits you. But he's really too much trouble."

Elsie leaned back, laughing dismissively. "You and I have both dealt with plenty of those before, Mrs. B. If I refused every troublesome client, I'd be standing in the welfare line this very minute."

"Oh, I'm not simply saying that Mr. Parsloe is crabby or demanding," said Mrs. Benninghoven, a bit ruffled by the implied aspersion against her toughness. "I wouldn't have gotten where I am today if I weren't able to deal with that sort of thing quite effectively, if I do say so myself. But last year we had a different kind of problem. This Mr. Parsloe called in saying that one of our girls had stolen money from him."

"Oh, dear. And had she?"

"I never knew the girl very well. This was the first time we used her, though she had very good references. And I didn't get the chance to question her because she ran off after that, which does point to her having been guilty. But I found Mr. Parsloe very unpleasant to deal with. He accused me of hiring people off the street! And, when I suggested that he should have contacted me first before confronting the girl, and that at any rate, the police would have to be notified, he became very angry. He cursed me and threatened to sue."

Elsie murmured shock and disapproval.

"Now, after several months, he calls me back again, requesting another girl! But besides that," continued Mrs. Benninghoven, "there's something about that man. He's... *creepy*. He lives alone in a big house, very old – pre-Revolutionary, I believe. It's been in the family for generations. And they were all very odd people. He's the last of the line and, it seems to me, the oddest. They say he writes books on his family's history, on local history... and the history of witchcraft."

"Oh, how exciting!" said Elsie gleefully. "The perfect place to spend Halloween."

"If you like that sort of thing..."

"And I do," replied Elsie. "There's nothing I love better than a good ghost story or, for that matter, a tale of witchcraft. And I do need the work. Let me have the assignment, Mrs. B., and I'll be grateful to you."

"Well, if you insist," said Mrs. Benninghoven, looking doubtful but picking up the phone.

Mr. Parsloe seemed more than amenable. In fact, he came straight over. He picked Elsie up from the Agency, drove her to pick up her luggage at the location of her previous assignment, and took her back home with him, then and there. He seemed eager to dispel any bad impression he may have given the Agency originally.

And this would indeed be a good place to spend Halloween in, Elsie thought, as Mr. Parsloe sped his little Karmann Ghia up a long, shaded drive to a clearing where stood a two-storied house, large and square, with a great, peaked roof and several many-paned windows. The clapboard siding was in need of paint, and there was no shrubbery - the yard around the house was bare except for a few spindly, unhappy-looking trees whose dry leaves scuttled over the bare front porch. Not a very welcoming aspect, she said to herself; but maybe we can do something about that before the children arrive.

"Do you get a lot of children here, Mr. Parsloe?" she called to him as he lifted her suitcases out of the trunk.

"Children! What do you mean?" he demanded, looking around him quickly.

"I mean for Halloween. Do a lot of children stop by here for Trick-or-Treat?"

"Oh!" he laughed nervously. "No, not many. None at all, in fact. We're a bit set apart here."

"Well, we'll just have to work harder at attracting them, then. Once they taste my sugar cookies, word will spread, and we'll have the whole town here Halloween night."

"How lovely," Mr. Parsloe grimaced. Then he said briskly, as if to change the subject, "Well, Elsie, I want you to make yourself at home here. Feel free to do what you will, and make use of things as you see fit. You don't need to tell me anything about your arrangements," he continued, fitting the key into the front door lock. "Just take whatever you like." He peered down at her for a moment through the tiny round lenses of his spectacles, looking for all the world like an owl about to swoop. But he only nodded his head several times for emphasis and, stepping aside, let her in through the front door.

Elsie spent the next few days settling into a comfortable routine. It was a very easy assignment, really: Mr. Parsloe ate his main meal in the evening, having no breakfast, not wanting much lunch, and not being fussy about what was put before him. In fact, he always had a book in front of his face at the dining table and hardly seemed to notice what he ate. Elsie would cook up a nice juicy roast or broil a good cut of steak, dressed with helpings of potato and green and yellow veggies, and he would eat it without comment. She suspected he would have eaten a peanut butter and jelly sandwich the same way, without noticing the change. It was somewhat off-putting. Elsie felt a bit unappreciated.

The housework took almost no time. Though there were several rooms in the house, they were very lightly furnished. Dusting and vacuuming were over quickly. So, after quite a bit of heavy-duty scrubbing the first day or two to get the kitchen in proper shape, and a bit of work getting her bedroom clean and cozy - Mr. Parsloe had offered her a second-floor room but she felt more comfortable above, in the garret – she was free to spend the rest of her time as she liked.

Many women would have become bored, but Elsie made a

game of adapting to the frequent changes in environment which her profession required. She could always find something interesting to do. Soon she was in the habit of walking the mile or so into town every day, to do a little shopping and visited the lending library. Sometimes, she talked to the children she saw or stopped to chat with old Mr. Jonas, retired from the post office, who sat with his friends on a bench outside the market when the weather was kind enough to allow.

It turned out that Mr. Jonas and his friends didn't like Mr. Parsloe. "He has a very bad reputation in this town," Mr. Jonas piped in his high, creaky voice. "No one likes him! And I wouldn't trust him with any woman of mine, not for a minute."

Elsie laughed. She had put down her bag of groceries and books to give her shoulders a rest while she chatted. Now, she picked up the bag again, preparatory to moving on. She did not like to listen to gossip about the man who was employing her.

But before she could leave, Mr. Jonas reached out a thin arm and grabbed her by the elbow. Raising his other arm and making a fist, he said dramatically, "If he gives you any guff, Elsie, you run straight over here to me. I'll give him a taste of *my* cooking!"

Elsie laughed silently all the way home, imagining a showdown between the feeble but courageous old man and the thin bookworm who jumped every time the wind rattled a windowpane. She didn't know which one she would bet on to win. And what would be the prize? She herself, the damsel in distress! Elsie burst out with a laugh so loud she scared all the crows back into the trees.

As for Mr. Parsloe's day, well! That was another matter: he had no visitors, rarely went out, and spent most of his time upstairs, either in his bedroom or in his study across the hall. He stayed up very late. A few times, when Elsie had occasion to get up in the middle of the night to get a cup of cocoa or make doubly-sure she had turned off the stove, she would see the light still burning under the door of his study down the hall and hear him murmuring to himself, sometimes quite loud, in some uncouth but sonorous foreign language. Mr. Parsloe, in fact, must have been in the habit of lighting a fire in the fireplace, because the light she saw falling upon the carpet in the hall had a red glow, and it flickered. Elsie couldn't be sure of this, though, as she had never actually been in Mr. Parsloe's study. He had directed her not to clean it: he would do it himself, as he didn't want his books displaced, he said.

Some evenings, as Elsie paused on the stair and listened to Mr. Parsloe's voice as it rose and fell – sounding quite foreign and odd; sometimes angry, sometimes wheedling – she would notice a shadow pass and pass again, blocking out the square of red light upon the carpet at rhythmic intervals, as if he were pacing or even *dancing* slowly around the room.

No wonder he had a reputation! Elsie thought, starting back up the stairs again. It was really something straight out of M.R. James.

One morning, while Mr. Parsloe was still asleep, Elsie, standing in the kitchen with her mid-morning cup of coffee and looking out the window, took notice for the first time of the little side yard directly below her. It was enclosed by a stone wall, five or six feet high all round, and had probably been the kitchen garden, though nothing but weeds grew there now. A low hut or shed, fashioned of uncut stones, and windowless, stood at the far end; its original use might have been for storing dairy or smoking meat. The doorway was not much more than four feet high.

The yard had a rustic charm – and the garden could be brought back. That would make the view from this window cheerful and pretty, Elsie mused, instead of dreary, as it was now.

No sooner thought than acted upon. Elsie scrounged up a few rusty but serviceable digging implements from inside the garage and spent the next few hours digging up and turning over the hard but workable soil. Good exercise! and next spring she would be able to just step outside for her fruits and vegetables – if she were still here, of course. If not, someone else would bless her for her labors.

Finally, she straightened up and looked around her. That was enough for today; she had cut quite a swath. Picking up her shovel and fork, Elsie thought of the stone hut again. She might keep her tools in there until tomorrow. But when she ambled over to see about it, she found that the wooden door was shut up with a large, heavy padlock.

Making a mental note to ask Mr. Parsloe for the key, Elsie trudged back into the house. Tomato soup and corn muffins would be nice for lunch – and maybe a sandwich made from that beautiful cut of beef Mr. Parsloe had hardly touched last night. A nervous constitution, and no wonder, with his lifestyle – the sun past its meridian, as her father used to say, and he, Mr. Parsloe that is, still in bed. She pulled off her sweater and beret and carried them into the front hallway, to the closet where they were kept.

There she noticed something lying on the floor: a twenty-dollar bill. It had evidently fallen out of Mr. Parsloe's coat at some time or other - though she hadn't noticed it when she took her sweater out that morning. But then, the coat hangers had been tangled together, and she had had difficulty getting her sweater out. Maybe she herself had knocked the bill out of one of his coat pockets. At any rate, it definitely wasn't hers. She picked it up and placed it on the hallway table.

"Ha ha!" laughed Mr. Parsloe that evening when Elsie mentioned the twenty dollar bill, laying on the hallway table still. "I didn't have any idea I had lost it. I have so much money, Elsie, and my wants are so few, as you can see. I don't know what to do with it all, and certainly never miss it once it's taken – I mean, lost."

"You should put it in the bank, then," replied Elsie. "It's not right to be careless with money. You might need it someday. And besides, you might put some poor soul in the way of temptation."

"Temptation! You don't believe any of that Ten Commandment stuff, do you, Elsie?"

"Of course I do, Mr. Parsloe," Elsie replied in a grave voice, and refused to say anything more.

But through the ensuing week there were many more occasions on which Elsie could have delivered the same lecture – and would have, had she felt it would fall on anything other than deaf ears. Mr. Parsloe seemed to be an inveterate money dropper, a sort of shedding King Midas. She found everything from half-dollars on the stairs to rolls of bills tucked into old flower vases. And there were other valuables, too: a pair of gold earrings lying in a candy dish, and a very valuable-looking, antique cameo brooch under a sofa pillow. Even more surprising, every time she put the money

15

or whatnot on the hallway table and told Mr. Parsloe at dinner that night about it, instead of thanking her, he seemed displeased. In fact, he became more and more irritable about the whole thing, as if it were her fault that he was so careless!

Finally, she stopped telling him. When she found money or anything else where it shouldn't have been, she just dropped it into the large Chinese vase that sat on the table in the hall and didn't say anything about it.

Certainly the character of her employer added a piquant flavor to her otherwise gentle routine. One morning, when Elsie was outside digging, as was now her daily custom, in the kitchen garden, she heard one of the second story windows being pulled up, and saw Mr. Parsloe leaning out, waving one hand, in which he held a book, and shouting at her in an agitated manner. Soon he came down, looking very odd, with his clothes disheveled, as if he hadn't even gone to bed yet, and demanding an explanation of just what exactly she was doing there.

Determined to appear calm and reasonable, she told him she was just preparing the soil for a few vegetable seeds, which would come up nicely in the spring, and by the way, could he give her the key to the stone shed against the wall there? That would be just the place to store her tools.

Here Mr. Parsloe took several slow, deep breaths, as if making a great attempt to control himself. And then he said, his voice shaking: Under no circumstances must Elsie go anywhere near that stone shed. It was unsafe. Loose stones might tumble down onto her head. At any rate, he had lost the key to the door. And as for the digging, the ground was practically frozen now, and he really must forbid her to come into this yard any more – not until spring, at least.

Really, thought Elsie as she trudged back to the garage, Mr. Parsloe was as touchy as a cat. She had never worked for such an odd man. But then, looking on the bright side, he really did give her quite a bit of freedom, generally. And he was right: the weather was turning a bit frosty. Winter was coming on – tomorrow was Halloween, as a matter of fact.

Well, most of her digging-up was finished; there was plenty of room for the corn, beans, and other vegetables she planned, and

Mr. Parsloe would never know if she quietly threw a few seeds down. She went back inside and set up a cold lunch on the dining room table for Mr. Parsloe, who was now nowhere in evidence, thank goodness! Passing quietly up the stairs so as not to disturb him, wherever he was, she retrieved her library book from her room, then put on her good coat and went out for her walk to town.

It was good to get out of the house – good to hear the birds and to see the townspeople, busy with their errands. At the market, she bought the few ingredients she still needed for her sugar cookie dough. She reminded the children she saw playing along the way to be sure to come see her on their trick-or-treat route.

In front of the market, old Mr. Jonas sat alone: his cronies, being "a buncha weaklings," did not show up unless the weather was warm. Elsie sat down on the bench beside the old man, showed him her groceries, and said she would make an extra dozen cookies to bring to him the day after Halloween.

But Mr. Jonas shook his head and looked skeptical about the town children coming onto the Parsloe property at any time, for any reason. "I tell you," he said, "Parsloe is not well-liked around here, to put it mildly. And some people are even scared of him. There've been two or three incidents where people who crossed him came to a bad end."

"Oh?" said Elsie. This *was* gossip, of course, but she could hardly get up and leave now without hurting poor old Mr. Jonas' feelings. And so she listened.

"He threatened 'em," Mr. Jonas affirmed.

"Oh, dear!" Elsie said, interested despite herself. "It sounds like something out of one of my horror stories!"

Two of Mr. Parsloe's enemies, Mr. Jonas continued, were missing and presumed dead: his old high school machine shop teacher and a girl who had gone out with him a few times and then dropped him. The more "simple-minded" folk thought it was a case of witchcraft, but Mr. Jonas believed the whole thing was mostly coincidence. "Both of 'em drank, and the girl was a real fool. She's probably in Hollywood right now, trying to become a movie star. Good luck with that one!" he chortled, rather mean-spiritedly.

So, he continued, Elsie should not take it personally if she had a lot of cookies left over on All Saints' Day. He'd be happy to help her finish them up, certainly. "And just be glad you don't have to worry about any kids soaping your windows or turning your outhouse over," he teased.

When Elsie got to the library, she was disappointed to find it closed: the library was not open on Fridays, and she had forgotten that Friday was today. She could keep the book she had, of course, but it wasn't very good. It was an anthology of ghost stories, but she had read all the good ones before, and the rest were just fluff. So she dropped the book into the return bin and started back home.

At home that afternoon, she disregarded Mr. Jonas' gloomy prediction and mixed up a quadruple batch of cookie dough. She wrapped it in wax paper and set it to firm up in the refrigerator for tomorrow.

It was not until she had finished the dishes and made herself something to eat that she realized she had nothing to read. Oh, that's right, the library had been closed! And Elsie could not really enjoy her solitary meal without a book in front of her.

There was a bookshelf in her room with a few old Harlequin Romances left by a previous occupant. Elsie went up the stairs towards her room. But on the way, she came across the book Mr. Parsloe had been waving at her that morning. It was lying, precariously balanced, on the ledge under the open window in the hall. She pulled the sash gently to and picked up the book. The binding held a Latin title. She had studied Latin in high school, many years ago. Now, brow bent, she read slowly: "*Liber Servi...* the Book... of the Servant."

Encouraged by this initial success, she took the book downstairs to read while she ate. It seemed to be some kind of history, quoting ancient writings on the summoning forth of spirits by various means and for various purposes – "a sort of recipe book!" Elsie thought. The frontispiece contained a woodcut illustration of a robed gentleman, a wizard of some sort. He was standing with arms raised above billows of smoke and flame, amidst which appeared the naked form, black and stooping, of a sort of medieval ghoul.

"This must be one of the books Mr. Parsloe studies for his history of witchcraft," said Elsie to herself. The book smelled very musty and moldy, now that she had it so close to her nose. Elsie turned the pages over. She found one marked by a ribbon and, after carefully wiping her fingers with a napkin, took up her sandwich and began again to read.

"*If a man has many enemies,*" Elsie made out, "*He is called unfortunate by those who do not know...*" (something she couldn't quite make out). "*But the servant will come to do his master's bidding, and the man will see his enemy's blood. In truth it is well for this man to possess many enemies, for each year those who have done true evil to his person or property may be marked and the servant called to them. But if there is no such enemy, then woe to the master, for the servant, though not called, will yet come.*"

Elsie finished her sandwich and closed the book. "Very interesting, but just that little paragraph took me fifteen minutes to translate! I wonder what Sister Bernadette would say to me now?" And, carrying the book upstairs, she put it back where she had found it.

Mr. Parsloe came down for dinner, but he was back upstairs again before Elsie, who had been in the middle of cutting up a chicken for marinading, could go in to say hello. The only thing she saw of him that evening was his shadow, crossing and re-crossing the red square of light upon the hallway carpet. He was talking to himself again, with an intensity that struck her as ridiculous. A grown man whining to himself in that way! she said to herself. Like a child nagging his father for treats. Who did he think was going to answer him?

The next day was Halloween. Coming back that morning from her usual trip into town, Elsie happened to glance at the stone shed in the yard, and noticed that the padlock was missing. How odd, Elsie thought. Here the man warns me against going in there, and then goes in himself and forgets to lock up again. He probably absent-mindedly put the lock in his pocket and went off with it. Elsie trudged over to the shed and grasped the door handle.

But what was that sound? Elsie seemed to hear something moving inside the shed, right behind the door. Not a skunk, hopefully! Better to leave well enough alone. She passed out of the yard and went into the house through the kitchen door.

And there she found a surprise: Mr. Parsloe, sitting slumped at the kitchen table, red-eyed and pale, but smiling. Elsie asked him if he had eaten his lunch; he replied that he had, but would like some more coffee.

"I'm feeling very guilty, Elsie," he began hesitantly as she filled the coffee pot with water, "about how I treated you yesterday... It was yesterday, wasn't it? When I shouted at you in the garden?"

Elsie told him yes, it was, but she hadn't minded at all. He did, though, seem a little nerve-wracked. Maybe he shouldn't drink so much coffee.

"I'll cut down," he said, waving his hand impatiently. "Let me say that I have been haunted by a deep remorse ever since that unfortunate incident. Though I still warn you – ask you, that is – to stay away from that garden and the shed. So many accidents happen in gardens..." he continued lamely, then grimaced. "I have become entirely too dependent on your skillful ministrations to allow any harm to come to you, you see."

"Why, thank you, Mr. Parsloe," replied Elsie, not knowing what else to say. She was about the mention the missing lock, but before she could, Mr. Parsloe went on:

"I think you told me, Elsie, that you sometimes suffer from arthritis?"

"My right knee has been giving me some trouble lately, yes," Elsie admitted.

"Well, let me give you this," said Mr. Parsloe eagerly, pulling out of his pocket a chain, upon which hung a heavy medallion with a large, dark red stone in the center. "The wearing of this stone was said by certain medieval practitioners to be a cure for arthritis. And I have, in my own studies, found that these medieval doctors are, more often than not, right on the money. Wear it continuously for twenty-four hours, and I promise you, you will feel a marked improvement."

"Why, thank you, Mr. Parsloe," Elsie said again, slipping the chain over her head. It was very ugly. She would wear it to humor him, but for twenty-four hours only.

"By the way, what's that on your forehead?" Mr. Parsloe asked. Elsie was standing quite close to him now and, before she could move, he had reached up a trembling hand and touched her forehead with one thumb. She felt something cold and sticky being smeared upon her skin. "Oh, dear, what did I do now?" said Mr. Parsloe with exaggerated chagrin as Elsie ran to the little mirror that hung beside the kitchen door. "I thought I saw a speck of something on your forehead, but look at my hand. I must have accidentally dipped it in something when I was taking out the medallion – there were some pots of salve in the same cupboard. I'm so sorry. Will it come off, do you think?"

Elsie got a paper towel and a little soapy water but couldn't wash off the bright carnelian smear that now adorned her forehead like a red dwarf star. She blotted at it with a paper towel, but this only seemed to rub the waxy stuff deeper into her skin. It would probably wear off in a few days, but what would people think in the meantime? She went to the mirror again: her image struck her as akin to some kind of heathen idol, a Hindu goddess of pots and pans.

Elsie was really beginning to feel a little irritated now, but she had to tell Mr. Parsloe it was all right, of course. He apologized a few times more as he gulped down his coffee, then rose unsteadily to his feet and made his way back upstairs again.

The morning had been bright, and Elsie had taken her daily walk downtown in sunshine, but now a cold wind had blown in, and with it came a troop of dark clouds. Elsie knew the best place to be in this type of weather was a kitchen, and the best thing to be doing there was baking. She took out her sugar cookie dough and set up her rolling pin, board, and bag of flour on the kitchen table. Then she took out her heirloom set of cookie cutters, which she carried with her from job to job, and selected the ones with a Halloween theme: a crescent moon, a witch on a broomstick, an arch-backed cat, and two ghosts: one big, one little.

The lamp spread a cheery, butter-yellow light over the table. And the oven, carefully pre-heated, made the room so toasty that she threw off her sweater. The color of her cheeks soon matched the blotch on her forehead.

She worked until nightfall and then sat back with a cup of coffee. A bright orange-and-black foil sign exclaimed "Happy Halloween!" to anyone approaching the kitchen door, and the porch light was on.

But Elsie waited in vain: no little ones came – no teenagers – nobody.

Hm. It looked like Mr. Jonas would be proved right. Oh, well. At least she had tried. She would have felt worse if she hadn't. And there was always next year.

Elsie moved to the living room, as close as possible to the kitchen so she could still hear a knock at the door, and curled up in an armchair. Opening *Ghost Stories of an Antiquary*, which she had gotten that morning from the library, she promptly fell asleep.

Several hours later, she woke up. She looked at her watch: it was past eleven! Halloween was almost over, and no one had come at all. Mr. Parsloe hadn't come down for his dinner, either.

She got up, stretched her stiff limbs, and climbed up the stairs to his study door, which was, as usual, closed. Counter to custom, though, there was no sound, no chanting. Maybe Mr. Parsloe had fallen asleep, too? Elsie knocked gently.

She heard a quick movement towards the door. After a second or two, she heard a hoarse voice, close to the panel, whisper, "Who's there?"

"Didn't you want any supper, Mr. Parsloe?" Elsie called.

"I'm sorry, Elsie, but I can't possibly open this door!" Mr. Parsloe cried, though she had asked him to do no such thing.

"But I just wanted – "

"No, I can't, I can't possibly open the door!" he fairly shrieked. "I have too much to do, please don't ask me, and please don't come knocking again!"

And so, for some reason, Mr. Parsloe had now taken to barricading himself within his study! Odder and odder, Elsie thought. She would call the Agency tomorrow and see whether they could send over a good doctor – a mental one.

Downstairs again, she looked around the kitchen: 11:30 already, and several plates of sugar cookies that would have to be wrapped up, not to mention a tableful of dirty mixing bowls, cookie trays, and the like. How lazy of her to have sat down to read without finishing the dishes first. It would not do to leave them till tomorrow, when the sugar dough would be hardened solid. She filled the sink with soapy water and began washing.

The minutes ticked away. She turned the radio on to country music, which she thought would have a cheerful sound, but it seemed all twang and whine tonight. The classical music station, which she turned to next, sounded desolate and dreary and out of tune. Mr. Parsloe's skittishness – not to mention the isolated circumstances here – was beginning to affect even her. Maybe when she called tomorrow, she would also ask for another assignment. Well, no use thinking about that right now. Tomorrow morning she might feel entirely different...

But what was that odd smell...? She had left the kitchen window up a crack and now could detect that something definitely unpleasant was outside. Maybe an animal had gotten into the garbage cans again. Tomorrow she would probably have a not-so-pleasant mess to clean up.

She reached over to pull the window down, and that was when she saw someone moving around outside near the kitchen door.

This was a Dutch door, the upper part of which had panes of glass. And, though she had already switched off the porch light, from the light of the window Elsie could see the outline of a small, childlike figure, bobbing and swaying, as with either impatience or indecision, upon the stoop.

A trick-or-treater? This late? Elsie asked herself as she wiped her hands and hurried to open the door.

Now, the attentive reader will perhaps, at this point, question the likelihood of Elsie doing anything so foolhardy as scurrying up and opening the kitchen door under those circumstances – and at "The Witching Hour," of all times. Without even mentioning the possibility of purely natural dangers, anyone would think that Elsie, being a voracious consumer of supernatural literature, should have known better than to just throw open the kitchen door like that. But the writer of this history begs to differ: I maintain that Elsie's behavior, from a psychological perspective, made sense. A person with an overactive imagination, who steeps herself in the supernatural, learns to ignore her fears. She could hardly get along in life without doing so. In fact, I contend that a person such as Elsie is actually more susceptible to the eerie – to the eldritch – than the average person who reads only romances or hot rod magazines and leaves the Poe and the Steven King very much alone.

At any rate, however it was, Elsie opened the door. The dark shape stood silent upon the stoop as she cried out gaily that it had startled her and how frightened she was. It really was a very clever costume, clever especially in its reserve of detail: most of the figure was shrouded in a dirty gray cloak, leaving nothing uncovered except the forearms and face.

But, as she looked more closely, Elsie became disturbed: either this was a costume the likes of which she had never seen before, or the child really was deformed. How did it stoop like that, with its back almost horizontal, as if perfectly capable of running away on all fours? And the hands, the fingers of which were impossibly long and thin – their movements so agile, so impatient. And that mask over the face – the eye sockets were deep and dark, but out of one of them, something was lazily crawling…

"Oh, my Lord, help me!" Elsie cried as she backed up against a chair and fell huddled into a corner.

The creature approached noiselessly and bent down over her, holding its face very near hers, breathing upon her a scent of rot, repulsive to an extreme. Elsie had covered her eyes with her hands, but she could feel the thing's bony fingers touch the medallion still hanging from her neck, lifting and turning it over. Suddenly, Elsie felt a sharp tug against the back of her neck, and she knew no more.

It was just beginning to get light when she awoke to find herself lying flat out on the kitchen floor. The door beside her was still ajar: through it, the raucous sound of early birdsong came. Before she even got up, Elsie knew it was best not to think about what had happened last night, or to try to go upstairs to see if…

She got to her feet and tottered out the door, down the driveway, and onto the main road to town.

The sheriff came to the Parsloe house later that morning, after Elsie had made her report. (Her sister, a farmwife in a neighboring state, was already on her way over to take Elsie back home with her.)

Entering through the open kitchen door and mounting the

stairs, the sheriff found the door to Mr. Parsloe's study open, with no signs of forced entry. There was no sign, either, of Mr. Parsloe himself, or of a crime having been committed. Everything looked perfectly normal.

Normal, that was, until, going out to check if Mr. Parsloe's car was still in the garage, the sheriff noticed the little stone shed. Just for the sake of thoroughness, he pulled opened the low door and peered in. He stared into the darkness for several seconds, then got out his flashlight.

There was a bundle thrown into one corner which, upon closer scrutiny, bore a striking resemblance to Mr. Parsloe. The sheriff noticed only one difference: the face of the Mr. Parsloe he knew had always worn a superior little smirk, and this face was frozen in an attitude of great fear.

A thick red smear of blood marked the center of the forehead, and the head lay in unnatural relation to the chest, upon which the sheriff's flashlight caught the glint of a heavy gold disk with a dark red stone laying over a broken chain.

Mr. Parsloe sat slumped in this most uncomfortable manner upon a couch of old, gnawed bones.

The Watercolorist

U.S. Highway 395 starts at the Canadian border, just above Spokane, and travels south through Washington, Oregon, and California. Unlike the better-known and much busier U.S. 101 and U.S. 5, the 395, though also a north-south route, keeps its distance from the coastline and stays well inland, traveling down through the three Pacific states close to their eastern borders. In California, it passes Lake Tahoe, Yosemite, and Mammoth Mountain before bee-lining through the middle of the Mojave Desert and ending at the Cajon Pass, one of the gateways into the Los Angeles basin and its spaghetti bowl of crowded local freeways. Apparently, the 395 will have none of this smog and congestion and will only travel where it can get its fill of lonely mountain vistas and desert air.

The lower section of the 395, just south of Mammoth and north of the Mojave, runs through the Owens Valley, a long strip of high desert, 75 miles long and squeezed up, on its eastern side, against the Inyo and White Mountain Ranges and, on its western, by the high Sierras.

Most of the time there, a warm wind blows. You stand among dried brush and boulders on the high desert floor and squint up to see deep snow on jagged Mount Whitney, the tallest peak in the Continental United States. You stand there and find it very odd to think that, less than a hundred miles in the opposite direction, to the east, over the rolling Inyo Mountains, lies Death Valley, the lowest point in the U.S. – named, some say, by the 1849 wagon train of prospecting families, many of whom died in an ill-advised attempt to find a short-cut from

Salt Lake City to the gold fields of California.

This is a land of contrast. But the towns along the 395, especially in the north Owens Valley, are moderate and pleasant little venues, with shady, well-paved roads. Each claims a population of a few hundred people. Turn-of-the-century wooden houses, sitting in prim gardens girt by picket fences, alternate with grassy acres where horses run, with diners and bakeries, fishing supply stores, and pillared stone buildings with wide front steps, the seats of local government.

In one of these little towns, there is a bed-and-breakfast: neat, quiet, and very recommendable. The food is good; the rooms clean and cozy. Its hand-drawn brochure boasts that the house was built in 1903 – which is old, by California standards. The owners, a hale and happy couple named Andy and Jeanie Ince, are quick to provide you with any reasonable comfort. And if you're... oh, let's say, a writer, looking for something to write about, Andy will talk to you for hours, telling you old tales of early explorers (like the Death Valley wagon train mentioned above); of rattlesnake bites and other accidental deaths; of eccentric old hermits whom "you could never find anywhere else but in the desert"; and of bloody wars between the miners and the Piute Indians. In his enthusiasm, he'll hustle you off that comfortable front porch rocker – yes, sure, you can bring your plate of pie and ice cream with you – through the back yard, to higher ground, where he will point out to you the very pass from which those Indians braves descended, and the hollow where that prospector's camp once stood.

The most unusual story he has to tell, however, is the one Andy tells most rarely: he saves it for people who are good listeners, who show respect for the stories. It has nothing to do with pioneers and Indians. If things aren't too busy in the kitchen or at the front desk, and if the subject happens to come up over a bottle of Napa Valley white he's consented to share with you – which doesn't take much coaxing – Andy might tell the story of how he first came into possession of this house of his. It's an odd little story, more of a sketch really, part of the charm of which is hearing it told by the man himself. But, that given, the story's intrinsic interest, I think, still warrants its commitment to paper.

Many years ago, Andy and Jeanie and their four children were living in a tiny stucco bungalow, cramped, badly built, cold all night and hot all day, that sat upon the middle of the valley floor. They had inherited it from Jeanie's grandfather and, though they didn't like to look a gift horse in the mouth, they would have moved out in ten minutes if anything better had been available and affordable. But with four little ones, just keeping up with monthly expenses was difficult. The dollars in their savings account, as Andy says, came and went like strangers through a Greyhound bus station, with hardly a nod and a wave to remember them by.

He was working as a handyman, driving up and down the valley on calls which were not too frequent and did not pay very well, since people around the valley, descendants of the original pioneers, are self-sufficient and mostly make their own repairs. Andy talked about moving to an area where work might be easier to come by, but they had strong family ties here and Jeanie didn't want to leave unless their financial circumstances made staying completely impossible.

Their situation was thus when, one July morning, Andy got a call to take care of a plumbing problem up in town. The house, right on Main Street, as that stretch of the 395 is called, looked to be a cross between a Victorian mansion and a barn, with gambrel roof and gingerbread siding, washed white many years ago, now gray, and not unpleasant to look at, except for its painful state of disrepair. It was isolated at the time in a yard which extended out towards empty lots on either side and ran quite a way back towards the foothills, where mountain boulders of all shapes and sizes sat placidly sunbathing. Ivy grew up along one side of the house, shading the plank front porch and pulling up roof shingles. When Andy drove up, the elderly lady who had called him was standing there waiting.

"I think there's something wrong with my pipes," she said without greeting, repeating the words she had used to describe the problem over the phone. "They make a noise. A clanging sound." She stood looking at him, arms crossed over huddled chest, mouth pursed with grim anxiety.

Andy was used to these maiden ladies who panicked over the slightest household glitch. "That shouldn't be too hard to fix," he said confidently, pulling his tool box out from the back of the truck.

"You should be worrying about that ivy, though. It'll ruin your roof, like an iron crowbar. When you turn on the water – is that when the noise comes?"

"No. It comes and goes at all hours. It comes from somewhere under the house." Slowly she climbed off the steep porch steps and led him to the south side of the house, to a ventilation hatch. She stood there, arms crossed, waiting, her shiny print dress blowing in the hot desert wind. "You need to go down there and see what's wrong," she said pointedly.

Andy stood there for a while looking into the dark hole at the base of the house. Obviously, the hatch led to no real cellar, only a crawlspace. The opening was three feet wide but less than two feet high: he'd have to get on his back and shimmy just to get through it.

He'd hated this ever since he was a kid, helping his dad with plumbing jobs. Being small and wiry, it had always been his job to go under the houses. All manner of little animals like to live in the cool space between the ground on which a house stands and the subfloor. Possums, skunks, even snakes – they didn't bother Andy out in the open, but suspecting they were close by when there wasn't even enough vertical room to get up on your hands and knees was a whole 'nother ballgame. And earthquakes – there are few experiences more likely to bring on an attack of claustrophobic panic than lying underneath floor joists while an earthquake rattles the house above you. Just looking at that crawlspace hole made Andy's heart pound sickeningly.

But Amanda, his oldest daughter, wanted ballet lessons, and that money had to come from somewhere. Jeanie said ballet lessons meant leotards, shoes, one of those funny skirts... He thought of his little girl dancing in her nightgown on the carpet at home, arms outs, balancing on her toes. Her little brothers always tried to tackle her and wrestle her down, but she just slipped away and started dancing in another spot.

He didn't know what could be causing the noise that the old lady was complaining about – noises like that should come only when the water was on – but it was certain she wouldn't be satisfied until he crawled around underneath the house and got all sweaty and dusty. She'd feel she was getting her money's worth then. Andy pulled off the chickenwire-and-wood frame that covered the opening and, lying down on his back, pulled himself, head first, under the house.

The space opened up a little once he was through the hatch, and there was enough light to see with from the vents – which was a good thing, because he now realized that he'd forgotten his flashlight. The air was nice and cool, ten degrees lower than outside, easily. Like standing in front of the refrigerator door, Andy thought, except no cold beer to grab, unfortunately. He turned over onto his stomach and, raising himself to a half-crouch, started exploring the hot and cold water lines that ran along the floor joists just above him.

Everything looked okay. He did see a few small gray mud tubes running up the concrete foundation walls on one side – those would be caused by subterranean termites. He made a note to tell the old lady about it. She'd probably freak out again, he thought, moving quickly along. No snake holes to be seen. He would be out in another five minutes, barring complications. All he had to do was keep calm and work efficiently.

Then, crawling around the chimney foundation toward the north side of the house, he noticed something strange: a large patch of yellow light, with no discernible source, shining out from the middle of the ground.

Andy lay there and reconnoitered. It might have been sunlight from a large vent or even a hole in the flooring above, shining down into the crawl space. But this was light from a bulb – not sun, not even a flashlight. It was coming out from behind a concrete lip or sill that ran several feet along the southern side of the house. He couldn't see over the sill.

This was odd, but odder yet were the sounds that now came to his ears – Andy says he didn't hear them until after the light appeared, and that, as he watched and listened, the light became a little brighter and the sounds increased in volume, like when you keep your finger on the volume button of a remote control. There was a scrabbling – a rustling of paper or cloth – then, the tinkle of glass and metal knocked gently together – and, last to reach his ears and strangest of all, a murmuring, a tuneless humming.

Andy readily admits to being nervous at first, but the humming, though certainly out of place, reassured him. He dismissed from his mind the odd way the light and sound had first appeared, and noticed now that the sill was the top wall of a partial cellar, dug out from under that part of the house. A section of stair was just visible, and ducts and piping, probably from a heating unit installed there, ran in and out of the hole. And somebody was down there working.

Andy crawled to the sill and looked down into a little room not more than six feet by ten. The wooden steps he had seen apparently led up to the interior of the house – the trapdoor at the top of the stairs was shut right now. An ancient furnace and an old water heater took up most of the cellar, but jammed up against a corner was an small wooden desk – a piece of children's furniture, rickety and stained. A bare bulb, the source of the light Andy had seen, was suspended above it.

An old lady sat hunched over her work at the little desk. Not the woman Andy had talked to outside – that one had been thin and angular. This one was rounder, heavier, her clothing of a more delicate hue, her silver hair arranged in braids that crowned her head in the old Swedish style. Before her on the table were big pickle bottles filled with water; brushes, pencils, pens, and inkpots; rags and sponges; and tea saucers smeared with liquid color, thick blue blending into watery green on one dish, rose passing into pink and then to cream on another. She looked large yet dainty sitting at the little desk, on a tiny wooden chair that hardly held her width. A board rested on her lap, balanced against the edge of the table. Upon the board was a thick piece of paper, downy white, fastened all around by a frame of masking tape, and on this the lady was drawing minutely with a fine, soft pencil, crooning to herself while she worked.

Over her shoulder, Andy could see the subjects of the picture: a horse and rider. And he could see without study that the man and horse had traveled many miles without rest, without water, and had all but lost hope of ever finding either. By his get-up the man was a scout, gone ahead of the settlers to find water – upon his skill and luck depended the lives of all the families in the wagon train he had left behind. Andy marveled at the story the picture told – he himself, with his talent for storytelling, knew the number of carefully chosen words it would take to describe the desperate situation this scout was clearly in. Here, on a square of paper, the old lady had done it wordlessly.

Equally surprising to see was the background, in which sat prominent the very mountain peak that Andy himself saw every morning and evening through his tiny kitchen window – *his* mountain, identifiable, unique, though he didn't know its name.

"I know that place!" Andy cried, still lying there in the dust above the concrete sill, stretching out one arm to point. "That's not a half-mile from where I live!"

"Oh!" the lady cried, throwing up her hands in gentle fright.

"Sorry to startle you, ma'am," said Andy, recalling himself. "I'm just the plumber, checking the pipes. Didn't know anybody was down here but me."

"Neither did I," the lady replied with a nervous but pleasant laugh. "This is my little workroom, as you can see. Please, come right in. It's nice to have a visitor – though I'm so ashamed – I have nothing to offer you."

Even by Andy's rough concept of etiquette, this was a little odd. Most old ladies didn't entertain in their cellars, did they? But he crawled over to the stairs, lifted himself over the sill, and sat down on the stairway while the old lady fussed, moving things around to try to create a little more room – clearly a physical impossibility.

"Nice and cool down here," Andy commented.

"Oh, yes, isn't it?" the lady replied. "In fact, it's temperate here. I expect it's very hot outside? But hot or cold, it's always about the same down here. I'm just as glad to be out of the heat. But the feel of the wind, that's something I do miss."

They talked about the weather a bit more. The lady was garrulous, full of things to say. She told him her name – Karen Olsen – and that she was a cousin of the lady upstairs. Her father had come out west to mine, as her husband had. There was no money left when either of them died, and she had come to live here with her cousin. She spent her days doing watercolor now, the passion of her life.

"Well," began Andy, offering her a stick of gum (she took it gratefully, a "rare treat") and coming to the point he was most curious about. "You must know your own business," he said, "but most of the painters I've seen do their painting outdoors, or at least in front of a window. I've known artists to expedition out into the middle of Death Valley and set up an easel, right in the middle of nowhere, and then sit there waiting until the sun falls *just right*," – forming his fingers into a frame and squinting through them with an expression of artistic persnickety – "to get the shadows just where they want them. But this place seems more fit for a darkroom than an artroom."

Karen shook with mirth, hand over mouth, at Andy's perplexity with her arrangements. For several moments she laughed silently, enjoying her own merriment. Andy didn't mind. They were friends already.

Finally, her blue eyes wet with tears, she became thoughtful. "That's a good way of putting it," she replied. "That's exactly the description that serves. You see," she went on carefully, her plump hands spread out upon her lap, "I'm not much on new inventions – tell me if I get it wrong – but a camera is like an eye. You take it to a place, open the eye, and catch the photograph. Isn't that right?"

Andy nodded.

"But then what do you do? Do you open the camera right there, in the sunlight, where you took the picture? No, the photographic paper would be flooded with light – ruined – no memory would be retained. Instead, you take it to a darkroom to be developed. In darkness, the memories separate and sort out. And that's how my watercolors work. Would you like to see?"

Karen bent over and pulled out an orange crate from under her worktable. In it, carefully sandwiched between odd pieces of cardboard and scratch paper, were dozens of paintings, in style and execution identical to the one Andy had seen her working on when he first chanced upon her. They all depicted life in the Owens Valley, but many years previous to the present – Andy judged that this was how things had looked around here fifty, maybe even a hundred years back. The subjects formed a catalogue of pioneer lifestyles. There were rich cattlemen on horseback; common cowboys riding among the steers; miners crouched over their cradles at the riverbank, sifting for gold, their faces revealing something halfway between hope and disgust. Men played poker in rough saloons and drank whiskey alone at the doorways of tiny log cabins among the pines. They hunted game, shot it, and spitted it over an open fire. Pack mules carried ore out through the mountains and hauled water tanks into the desert, long, dusty miles.

And there was fast action, too: outlaws on horseback sprang out behind rocks, drawing guns upon stagecoaches; men fought, sometimes with fists or knives, mostly with guns, barrels glinting, eyes sparking. Even the details on the firearms, their shape and make, were accurate, Andy saw with admiration. Mexican vaqueros paraded in silver and black, just passing through. And there were many scenes of Indian life: Piute children bounding and splashing in a mountain pool, men relaxing in their sweat houses, women preparing food in front of their wickiups. The white women and their daughters also labored, inside their farm shacks, baking, washing and sewing, stern-faced and old before their time from too much work and worry.

"I just wish my grandfather could see these," Andy said after several minutes of rapt examination. "He used to tell me stories, such stories, all about the things you've shown in these pictures. He was a great storyteller. People say I have his gift." Andy looked up at Mrs. Olsen. "People must say the same thing about you, too."

Karen flushed happily. "You are very kind."

"No, really!" Andy replied. "You should frame these and put them up, try to sell them or something."

She laughed. "If my cousin could hear you talk!"

"Well, doesn't she tell you the same thing?"

Karen just smiled.

"If she doesn't, she's jealous, and I'd tell her so to her face," Andy said, hard-jawed. "I have my own bone to pick with that woman. Here she had me crawling on my belly under this house like Satan after the Fall, and all along I could have walked down these stairs here. That reminds me, I better check the water heater."

Andy got down on his hands and knees to check for leaks, then got up and checked all the lines and connections. Karen went back to sketching upon her board, humming to herself tunelessly. Andy had to admit that it would get on your nerves after a while.

"Well, nothing wrong with these pipes that I can tell. I'll go back up and tell your cousin – I expect she handles all the repair arrangements around here?"

"Oh, yes," Karen replied. "I'm too old and scatterbrain to sort out such complexities."

"I would have thought," said Andy, wiping his hands with a rag from his back pocket, "that you and her were about the same age."

"No, oh no! She is more than twenty years younger than I."

Andy was puzzled at this testimony. The other old lady had looked to be about seventy-five or so. That would make his friend Karen here... but it would be impolite to question the matter further.

"Well, I'm going up now. Thanks for showing me those beautiful pictures," Andy said, starting up the stairs.

"That door is locked," Karen called after him, fluttering nervously.

"What in the heck for?" asked Andy, surprised.

"My cousin, you see," she replied quickly, "has a very nervous constitution. She's a good woman, but there's a bit of choler in her temperament, if I may put it that way. It makes her nervous having me pop in and out of the door at odd moments. It ruins her baking – makes her drop things. So she locks it when I'm down here."

"You mean she locks you *in?*" questioned Andy, disbelieving. "Don't tell me she's the one who makes you come down here in the first place."

"My humming makes her nervous, too," Karen smiled, anxious to placate. "I can't blame her for that, can I? It's a habit I can't seem to break."

She picked up an old wooden chair leg and began to rap with it against one of the pipes overhead. "When I need to come up, I just do this," she said, "And my cousin comes and unlocks the door."

"I can't believe this," Andy said, sitting back down on the stairs with his head in his hands.

Karen kept hitting the pipe with the chair leg, but several minutes passed and nobody came. Andy would have to crawl back out the way he came. Karen apologized repeatedly. "I don't want you to think we don't get along. She's very good to me. She took me in when I had nowhere else to go."

"I understand you, Karen," Andy told her. "But someone needs to have a talk with your cousin."

He muttered angrily to himself as he made his way back through the crawlspace. When he pulled himself up and out into the hot daylight again, he saw the cousin way over in the back of the yard, fussing with something growing along the fence. He didn't see why she would be out there – the whole yard was nothing but weeds. Her face was turned from him. He decided to go in the house first and open the cellar door.

It took a while to find the door. It should have been in the kitchen, but wasn't. He looked around in the hallway and other rooms but couldn't find anything like a cellar door. Finally, he went back to the kitchen, and there it was – he had missed it the first time because part of the kitchen stove and a baking cupboard stood in front, blocking the lower half.

This was unbelievable! Setting aside the question of cruelty to your kinfolk, that cousin must be a Samson in kneehose to move that furniture back and forth from in front of the door every day. But, Andy knew, there was no limit to what a spiteful relation could do.

He pulled the cupboard over into the middle of the room and, grunting, shoved the range farther along the side wall. Then the real surprise – nailheads running at odd intervals along the door near where it fit into the jamb. Someone had done a poor job of it: half of the nails were bent or driven in crazy directions. But their positions surely indicated an intent to *rivet the door shut.*

Andy says that, at the time, he didn't think much about it. Otherwise, he would have realized that the door couldn't have been nailed up and reopened in this manner every day. But he was too mad to think. He got his hammer out of the tool box and pulled out the nails embedded in the jamb. Finally, he pried the door open.

There was his friend, standing at the bottom of the cellar, looking up at him with shining eyes.

Andy had already decided he would take her down to the police station and have charges filed against the cousin. Karen didn't seem to want anything done that would reflect badly on her cousin, so he wouldn't mention his intentions until she was safely in the truck cab. So, wordlessly, he descended a few steps into the cellar and put out his hand to her.

She took it, that much Andy knows. He remembers the touch of her soft, cool fingers. He was holding onto the door and looking backward to watch his step while pulling her gently up the stairs. But as he brought her up into the bright kitchen, the feeling of her hand in his "faded." He looked back, thought he saw her for a second, but then realized she wasn't there at all. It was akin to the sensation, Andy says, when, glancing into a dusky room, you're startled to see someone standing there; but then, looking a second time, you realize you're all alone.

No light was coming from the cellar now, either.

Forgetting his hammer, leaving the cellar door wide open, Andy went outside to his truck and climbed in. Seeing he was leaving, the cousin ran out from among the weeds.

"Where're you going?" she cried.

"Home."

"Did you fix the problem?"

"Yeah."

She smiled. Andy found the look self-satisfied, as if she were thinking he had forgotten to charge her.

After he turned the truck around, he called out the passenger door: "I saw your cousin. I let her out of the cellar."

And, before driving away, he saw the smirk fall from the old lady's face.

People who drove through town that afternoon say she was out in her yard all day – not in the back where Andy had seen her, but in the front, standing there holding onto the fencepost that bordered the highway. She looked up absently as cars passed by but did not acknowledge her neighbors' waves. No one saw her past sundown, though, when the quick-gathering desert cold must have driven her inside.

Someone checking on her the next day found her lying on her bed, fully dressed, eyes open, looking toward the door – but she was no longer living.

The next time Andy entered the house was during the estate sale, when he bought the orange crate full of odd scraps of art paper. He took the watercolors to the county historical society, where a man who knew about such things agreed that they were worth quite a bit. Eyewitness drawings of the old times were hard to come by, and were often more valuable to historians than photos, which were usually carefully staged with the subjects woodenly posed. In addition, these watercolors were really very well done. The execution was that of a very talented amateur with a very good eye for detail.

Andy sold about half of them. He got quite a bit of money, and when they auctioned off the old lady's house as a fixer-upper, he bought it.

He and his wife and daughters have made it into the place it is today. And, of course, at the end of the story he drags you out to the kitchen, where he opens the cellar door and points down to the child's desk, still cluttered with jars and dishes, and to the little chair – which, you're relieved to see, is empty.

"She's gone to a better place," Andy finishes. "Leastways," he said, glancing at the kitchen walls around him, "she doesn't *live* here anymore – though we suspect she may visit occasionally..."

And he straightens the little watercolor of a desert sunset, lovingly framed, and hanging on a nearby wall.

Wiggy

Oliver never planned on getting married.

He never planned on enlisting in the Navy, either. But, since his family didn't know what else to do with him, and he didn't care one way or the other, he spent six years in the service. After being honorably discharged, he took the Greyhound from San Diego to Los Angeles and got a job in an aviation plant.

But things were kind of intense at the plant. They expected Oliver to be part of a team, to get excited about projects, to work overtime on short notice. Pretty soon, he quit. He started picking up work repairing VCRs and small appliances for a fix-it shop in San Pedro. He came and went when he wanted to. The boss was a hang-loose kind of guy.

Oliver got an apartment – a one-room bungalow really, faded peppermint stucco – in one of those old-fashioned courts where eight or ten tiny houses are grouped together with only a few feet between them. Those court bungalows weren't in style anymore – everybody wanted to live in apartments or condos – and the place was a little run-down. But Oliver didn't mind that.

Every morning, he had his breakfast at the counter of a coffee shop on Gaffey, a few blocks from the fix-it shop. If the off-shore air flow kept the cloud cover from lifting before noon, he went to work. If the sun came out, he went to the beach and hung out, took a dip, did some people-watching, maybe played a few videogames in the arcade.

One morning, though, a woman came to sit at the coffee shop counter, two seats over to his right. He looked at her appreciatively, and ended up not going to work that day, even though the clouds never lifted.

She was from one of those islands in southeast Asia. She was very short, but wore heels all the time, which added another two or three inches to her height. She had black, curly, glossy hair, big brown eyes with long lashes, and long fingernails which she painted in different colors – red, orange, even purple. She was always dressed up, even when she worked – she was a clerk or a receptionist or something at an old people's home. She was talkative and vivacious and a good girl. They were married in Las Vegas a few days after they met.

She moved her things out of her sister's house and into Oliver's bungalow.

They got along fine the first few weeks: she was a good cook and, though she talked a lot, she didn't seem to notice if Oliver wasn't paying attention.

The problem came from an unexpected corner.

Oliver had been around, but had managed to stay naive about women. The few enlisted girls he met in the Navy had been pretty tough, competitive types, and he had stayed away from them. One thing he liked about his wife was her feminine ways. It never occurred to him to wonder what kind of mechanism was behind it all.

Now, living with her, he found she cluttered up the bedroom with her make-up and brushes and rollers, and the whole place smelled like hair spray. The smell put him off his food. He started smoking more cigarettes just to get rid of some of the smell.

She took over the closet, too. He had to move his stuff into the closet in the hall. He couldn't believe that one little girl could have so much personal junk.

Then, she started coming to bed at night with her head all bound up in a scarf, her skin and hands greasy with beauty cream, her body wrapped in an old bathrobe. She always wanted the light turned off as soon as possible because she had "taken all her glamour off." That was the way she put it, and it was a big disappointment. Oliver had married someone he thought looked a certain way and felt cheated that she couldn't look that way all the time.

But it was too late to complain. He coped by telling himself it was part of the feminine mystique. And she did try to hide the assembly process from him as much as possible. Those first weeks, if he accidentally opened the bathroom door while she was in there making herself up, she'd giggle and push him out again with a coyness that was kind of cute.

In the mornings, she'd get up early – she started work at seven – and spend about an hour in the bathroom. Oliver didn't get up until eight-thirty or nine, so that was okay.

But then, one morning, he opened the bathroom cabinet to get an extra towel and got the shock of his life to see a head, back behind the lotion bottles, with curly black hair, just like his wife's!

It took him a while to realize it was a wig stand. He pushed away the bottles and took it out. He felt the hair on top. Yes, that was his wife's hair, the hair he had stroked in the park that day she had gotten him to propose. His wife's hair – on a back shelf of the bathroom!

He was disgusted. It was one of those blank, styrofoam dummy heads that you see all the time in wig shops. Someone had stuck a pushpin in its face, where the right eye would have been, or just above that. He looked at the dummy. And it, in turn, gazed discreetly upwards, over his left shoulder, as if it were embarrassed for his sake.

He put the dummy in the bedroom, on the dresser. When his wife came back from work, she'd see it there and realize that he knew her little secret now. Hopefully, she'd have the decency to throw the thing out without a word and save them both the humiliation of having to talk about it.

He worked a little late that night, not really wanting to go home. When he came back, she was standing at the stove, frying something up. She gave him a shy little smile he couldn't quite read, and for once she was silent. Her hair looked the same as always.

He pretended to go to the bathroom. Then, on his way back, he looked into the bedroom.

There was the wig and its dummy head, looking at him with that slightly skewed, red pushpin eye, right where he had left it. Only now, next to it, sat another styrofoam head, bald – the head for the wig, undoubtedly, that she was wearing now.

She must have put it there.

Apparently she thought he had taken the first dummy out to show that he didn't mind seeing it, that she didn't need to hide it in the bathroom – that she could keep the wig stands in their bedroom from now on – *in their bedroom!*

The idea that now, he would have to actually watch her taking herself apart – that it would be part of their intimacy – was unendurable. And who knew what else would follow? False eyelashes, plastic fingernails – pretty soon, they'd all be lined up on the dresser there, like a display at the natural history museum.

The styrofoam dummy with the pushpin eye was soundlessly laughing at him.

A wiser man would have handled the whole situation better. A wiser man, with more knowledge of women, would have put his arms around his wife, told her she was beautiful just the way she was, and asked her to throw the wigs out for his sake. She probably would have done it. She might even have loved him better for it.

But Oliver was inexperienced, impatient. He had no wisdom of the heart. He felt all the emotion of a man caught in a bait-and-switch scam.

He lost his temper. He picked up the dummy heads, first one, then the other, and threw them against the wall. With one arm, he swept all the rest of the junk off the top of the dresser. Then he yanked out all the drawers and dumped them, too.

His wife was standing in the doorway, her little red mouth half open and her big black eyes wide with fright. He felt a twinge of guilt when he saw her face, but the question of how much of her expression was real and how much was make-up set him off again. He pushed her out of the way and stomped out of the house.

After a fast-food dinner, he took a walk along the bluffs above the beach. Soon, his anger gave way to weariness. He just wanted it all to be over when he got home – the house cleaned up, and all that junk put in the dumpster out back.

It wasn't. The place was clean, all right, but she had picked up everything and put it back. All the drawers full of toners, powders, and cleansers, her facial steamer – everything was back where it had been before. And the dummies still sat on the dresser, except their faces were turned away from Oliver, toward the other wall, like they didn't think he was even worth the trouble of looking at.

His wife was in the bathtub, taking a soak.

"Letty," he said, standing over her, "I want you to get up right now and throw all that stuff out."

"No. I won't," she answered.

"Letty, that's not a request. It's an order."

"No."

"This is my house, Letty."

"I pay half the rent!" she replied. It was true: she had offered and he had accepted her money; but considering that now only made Oliver madder.

"Letty, get up right now!" he shouted.

"No!" she shouted back.

Oliver never told anyone about that argument. Later on, he told the police that he had kissed his wife good night, closed the door to the bathroom behind him, and gone to bed. It was true, he had noticed the hair dryer, plugged in and precariously balanced on the dirty linen hamper, right next to the tub. It was a tiny, old-fashioned bathroom, not meant to be used as a beauty salon. He had told his wife many times that it was unsafe to leave the hair dryer plugged in. But, for someone so careful about her appearance, she was not at all careful about electrical hazards.

And he had been really tired from a rough day at work. He had gone right to sleep. He hadn't realized there had been an accident until just before dawn, when he woke up to go to the bathroom.

The neighbors had heard nothing. There was no sign of a struggle, no insurance policy recently purchased in the deceased's name, and no reason not to believe his story.

The funeral was almost over. His wife had looked beautiful in state. Oliver had instructed the mortician in the dressing and making up of the body. He had even taken one of the wigs out to be groomed by her favorite stylist, who did it for free – his wife had been such a good customer, she said. Relatives from as far away as New York came and cried over her, remarking how young and lovely she looked. They clicked Polaroid shots of the open casket.

After the church rites, Oliver stayed kneeling, almost crumpled up, his body draped over the back of the forward pew, his head buried in his arms. He figured no one would approach him in this posture, and if they did, he could pretend he didn't notice them. They would go away – they would decide to send him a note of condolence through the mail. Much easier that way for everyone.

The church was slowly emptying. Oliver, still crouched in the pew, could hear the sound of the altar boys clearing away the books and things; somewhere up above, the organist was closing up her instrument and chatting with someone about the horrendous price of sheet music nowadays. But soon the voices faded down the choir loft staircase and out the front doors of the church.

He was alone. The burial would be later in the morning. No one would blame him if he was too ill to attend.

The overhead lamps had been switched off and the church was enveloped in a twilight gloom, like a big, cool cave. A stand of votive candles winked and wavered to the right of him, below a statue of St. Rose of Lima.

The last few weeks, he was thinking, had been a nightmare, but now it was over.

Just as he was about to stand up and walk quietly out the side door, he heard the click of high heels in the vestibule at the back of the church. Someone was coming up the aisle. He bobbed his head down again and assumed the position.

The someone continued with short, sharp steps up the aisle, click, click, click, approaching him. A late arrival to the funeral, come to pay her respects? Probably. Whoever it was, she was coming right toward him.

He didn't move. The person paused at the entrance of the pew. Then he heard the rasp of expensive clothing and smelled a light, sweet, costly perfume, as she moved in and sat down right beside him. Someone come to pay her respects but not wanting to intrude on his grief. His grief... he was a widower. Oliver squeezed his eyelids together until the tears came – luckily, the tears of self-pity are indistinguishable from the tears of love lost – and he looked up.

She was turned toward him, watching him solicitously. She had a good figure; she was tastefully dressed in black, with a cute little hat perched above her dark, curly hair. And, when she lifted her veil, he saw her face was made of styrofoam and her one red eye looked slightly up and to the right, making her expression, as she leaned closer to him, difficult to fathom...

Her Father's Ghost

"Do you believe in ghosts?" Eleanor asked me as we drove down the highway to her parents' house.

I started to laugh, but one glance at her face told me she was serious – anxious, even, to hear my reply.

"I don't know," I finally replied, honestly. "Do you?"

"I don't," she said firmly, looking ahead. And she didn't say anything more.

What an unusual girl, I thought to myself, admiringly. You wouldn't get bored with her around. But what made her think of a question like that, under these circumstances?

Said circumstances being that we were driving out to check on her recently-bereaved mother, who was behaving strangely after her husband's recent demise.

I am a social worker at our local community hospital. One of my duties is to counsel relatives when a patient dies. This is not really the best way to meet girls, but that's the way I met Eleanor.

That very afternoon, just a few hours before, I had been walking into my office with a tray of spareribs from the hospital cafeteria. I had paperwork to catch up with, but on Sparerib Day I never miss lunch. My office used to be a supply closet, and is, consequently, very tiny. As I came hurrying through the door, with my mind on work, I saw, or rather ran into, her. She had been sitting in front of my desk, which is very close to the door. And when she stood up to greet me, I barreled into her, accidentally knocking her back into her seat, where she sat staring at me. The tray of spareribs landed on my desk, right in front of her. Bits of barbeque sauce splattered all over, onto my papers and onto the faded sweatshirt she was wearing. It was a red one, thank goodness.

Even though I'm a counselor, I don't find it easy to make small talk, especially with girls. And when I looked into Eleanor's big, brown, alarmed eyes, I found myself absolutely speechless. What a nice-looking girl, I thought. But that's not something you can just come out and say.

I didn't noticed that there was another person in the room, tucked into the corner near the file cabinet, until he began speaking. Luckily, I remembered him: Mr. Edelman, a friend of the family whom I had met last week, and who was there the day Eleanor's father had died.

"This is Mr. Thomas' daughter, Eleanor," he was saying in his hesitant way. "She's just come from school, and she wanted to know more about her father, and the whole... you know, so I brought her here to speak to you."

As it turned out, I should have been listening more carefully to Mr. Edelman's words. But as Eleanor stood up again, very close to me now, I felt as if I were in a daze. Brown eyes, brown pony tail, and a pretty, upturned nose were all I could take in at the moment. She was young, probably still in college, and dressed to run off and play volleyball. But she stood with an air of self-assuredness that I in my coat and tie couldn't match.

"Hello!" I said stupidly, still holding my tray. "Please sit down. Ah – would either of you like some ribs?"

Eleanor shook her head solemnly.

"My! Those do smell good," Mr. Edelman said, adding regretfully, "No thanks."

As I still stood there, Eleanor gently gestured to my chair and placed the tray of food close to it, then sat down again, nodding at me as if she were humoring an idiot – which was certainly the way I felt. Taking her cue, I sat down and tried to recover my professional aplomb.

"I guess I came here because I'm still having trouble believing it all happened," Eleanor began. "I know my father died suddenly, of surgical complications..."

"Yes," I replied. "Pulmonary embolism. It's not common, thank goodness, but when it does happen, it happens very quickly. He didn't have time to suffer. Still, it's very traumatic for the family."

I could place the event now. As Eleanor paused, head lowered, I recalled the disheveled room, crash cart equipment lying everywhere, and the doctor standing over the bed as he made the death pronouncement. The body was that of an old man, slight, frail. I had never seen Eleanor's father alive, but I remember remarking at the time how his skin now oddly matched the color of his gray eyes. Not exactly something I could share with the girl in front of me, and there was little more to say.

"It was quite a shock to me, let me assure you!" Mr. Edelman blurted out. "I wish I hadn't come to visit him at all that day. But he had wanted me to bring him some candy. Those were his last words, by the way, Eleanor," he added momentously, "'Bring me back some peanut brittle if they have it.'"

"Well, it was lucky that you *were* there, Mr. Edelman," I said, suppressing a smile. I turned back to Eleanor. "Your father didn't tell the nurses that he had any relatives at all." It was true: there had been nothing in the chart about who to contact in an emergency. Luckily, I was at the nurses' station finishing up some paperwork when I saw Mr. Edelman knocking on his friend's door. He had had quite a shock seeing the body, covered with a sheet, lying there. I had jumped up and broken the news to him, and he in turn had contacted Eleanor's mother.

"I don't know that it was such a good thing, my being there," Mr. Edelman mumbled. "I just hope nobody blames me for anything."

That was a singular remark, but singular remarks seemed to be Mr. Edelman's specialty. At any rate, Eleanor didn't react to it.

"I think Dad didn't consider that sort of thing, emergency contacts and all, to be important," she said. "He was always an optimist, always sure that things would roll his way. And – well, he and Mom had not been getting along. I think he was bitter about it. They didn't part on the best of terms."

"That must be difficult for your mother," I said quietly. "How is she handling all this?"

"Not too well, I'm afraid," Eleanor replied, looking pensive.

"Is she blaming herself for not being there?" I asked gently. "That would be a very natural reaction."

Eleanor hesitated. "At first, I think, she was feeling awfully guilty, as much as she could feel anything through the shock. But now..." she trailed off. "Now, she's behaving oddly..."

"Oddly?" I echoed inquiringly.

"She doesn't seem upset at all. In fact, it's bizarre, but she's almost... cheerful."

"Anita always did have a stiff upper lip," said Mr. Edelman admiringly. "No use crying over spilt milk and all that."

Despite this useful observation, Eleanor remained worried, and she didn't strike me as a girl who was easily alarmed. I waited, and she went on: "In the last few days, she's started making strange comments about how I shouldn't worry, how my daddy is with us in spirit, and how she'll soon be with him."

I took a deep breath. "I don't want to worry either of you," I said, "but that sounds somewhat like suicidal ideation." Eleanor gasped, and Mr. Edelman took his eyes off the spareribs and fixed them on me with a startled stare. "Where's your mother right now?" I asked.

"At home. She was sitting in front of the TV, quilting, when I left. But she didn't seem to be paying attention to the talk show she was watching. She was smiling and nodding to herself sort of, even though it was one of those typical, gruesome topics. Oh oh...," Eleanor trailed off.

"What's wrong?" I asked.

"The show's topic was, 'Assisted Suicide.'"

"I think we'd better go check on your mother right away," I said. Soon, Eleanor and I were heading out of the office for the parking lot, with Mr. Edelman trailing behind to give one last, longing look to that untasted plate of ribs.

So here I found myself and this lovely girl, with the big brown eyes and brown ponytail that swung when she walked, driving down the highway, she and I in my Ford Taurus while Mr. Edelman came along behind in his VW Beetle, the car they had come up in. Eleanor and I were alone together, but under such circumstances as rendered it impossible for me to express my romantic inclinations. This was probably just as well, I thought. Even under ideal circumstances, I probably would have blown it.

After her comment about ghosts, which I've already quoted

above, we drove in silence. Eleanor was understandably preoccupied.

"My mother must feel awful," she finally said. "You see, Mom stayed home with me all the years that I was growing up, while Dad traveled, worked, did all sorts of interesting things. When I went away to college, Mom decided it was her turn to do some traveling. She always had an interest in meditation, spiritualism, that sort of thing, and she had always wanted to go to India and spend time in an ashram – you know, those places where they teach meditation – sort of a retreat house where you can stay as long as you want. Dad, on the other hand, wanted to buy a camper and 'see the good old U.S. of A.,' as he put it. They fought about it. Dad forbade Mom to leave, so she did."

"Your mother was in India when your father died?" I asked.

"Yes, and I was away at school. During the time she was away in India, Dad sent Mom letters demanding, pleading that she come home. He wrote how much he missed her, how much he needed her. Mom gloated over those letters, saying that it served him right for taking her for granted so many years."

"It must have been a horrible shock for your mother to find out your father had died," I said.

"Yes. She started back right away. But, of course, it took her several days to get here. And it took me a while to get the news, too. Edelman forgot what state I was going to school in." She grinned. "He knew it started with an 'A,' but that was it. Actually, I was in Atlanta..."

As she was speaking, we drove out of the city and into the low, brown foothills. Clouds had come in and the sky was now a darkening gray. Eleanor directed me down a dirt road to a big, dilapidated old farmhouse, where a few raindrops were falling on the peeling asphalt tile roof and on the weedy front lawn. The whole effect was one of gloomy isolation.

But there was a yellow light shining in the window and, as we got out of the car, a middle-aged woman in a diaphanous Indian-type silk outfit came floating out, all purples and greens, and smiling graciously. This was Eleanor's mother.

"Oh, good! We've got company," she beamed after Eleanor introduced me. "Come in the house before you really get wet! I see Edelman driving up now. Let's go in and have a tea party!" She held onto my arm as we went up the front porch. "There's nothing more cozy than a tea party in the rain, don't you think?"

I stayed for tea, and for supper that evening. We didn't sit down until eight – Mr. Edelman had suggested Eleanor's mother make spareribs, and when she heard I had missed my lunch, she insisted on cooking them for me. "My husband always said: as human beings, we have an obligation to correct injustice wherever we find it," she said grandly. "You shall have your ribs!"

The conversation had been lively all afternoon and through dinnertime, with Eleanor's mother doing most of the talking, but I was no closer to being able to evaluate her emotional stability. She avoided our questions about how she was feeling, joking that she hoped we didn't think she was too much of a "merry widow." When Eleanor pursued the subject more directly, her mother rushed back into the kitchen, insisting that we let her alone to concentrate on her cooking, and saying Mr. Edelman should entertain us with his card tricks – a commandment which he obeyed to the best of his abilities.

Over dessert – home-baked banana bread topped with vanilla ice cream – I decided to make one last attempt at finding out how she was feeling. "Mrs. Grey..." I began.

"Please," she interrupted. "Call me Anita. It feels as if you're a friend of the family already. I hope you and Eleanor see a lot of each other from now on. You know," she warbled, "life is short! We're here today and gone tomorrow!..."

"Anita," I interrupted in turn, feeling my face turn red. Out of the corner of my eye I saw Eleanor grinning at my discomfort. "I like your daughter very much, but that's beside the point. I'm here to see how you're coping after your husband's death. Eleanor has been very worried about you."

"Oh, dear Elly," Anita cried, getting up to sit near Eleanor on the sofa and putting her arm around her. "Why would you be worried about me?"

Eleanor grimaced. "Oh, mom, you're just so – happy!"

Anita looked surprised. "But why shouldn't I be?" She blinked. "Oh! You mean because Daddy is dead? Elly dear," she said sweetly, patting Eleanor's cheek, "death is not such a terrible thing – it's just a passage to another state of being. Besides, it won't be long until I see Daddy again."

"You're going to kill yourself!" Eleanor cried reproachfully, the tears starting up in her eyes.

Anita looked shocked. "Of course not! Why would I do a silly thing like that?" She stared at us both, amazed. "Oh!" she laughed suddenly. "I see. All my references to seeing your father again soon... Oh, no, no."

"But Mom," said Eleanor, "it's just not normal to be so happy after your husband has died."

"Yes, but you've forgotten one thing –" Anita said mysteriously, "– my spiritual powers."

Eleanor and I stared. Mr. Edelman was rocking in the rocking chair, trying to look like he wasn't listening.

"Yes, dear, I know it's hard for the uninitiated to believe," continued Anita, her voice very matter-of-fact, "but I am in direct contact with your father's spirit!"

Eleanor looked like she was just about fed up, and I didn't blame her. This was a little hard to take: we had our choice between a diagnosis of suicidal ideation or psychotic delusion.

"Your father didn't want me to tell anyone," Anita continued. "He said it would be very dangerous. But I know now that he would want you to be reassured. And your friend here," she turned to me, smiling graciously. "I'm sure we can trust him with our secret. Edelman already knows."

Edelman rocked harder, studying the ceiling as if he had a test on it tomorrow morning. Eleanor and I still stared.

"You don't believe me?" Eleanor's mother exclaimed, wide-eyed. "Well, we'll soon fix that!" She got up and started clearing the dining room table.

"What are you going to do, Mom?" asked Eleanor, completely nonplussed.

"We're going to call up your father," Anita replied. "A seance, I think, would be the best way right now."

Soon, we were gathered at the dining room table, huddled over the Ouija board. At Anita's direction, each of us rested a few fingers on the little platen that supposedly would be moved over the letter-board by the spirits. We had built a fire and the lights were all on, but Anita had also placed candles around the room because, as she said knowingly, "There might be disturbances in the electrical field."

She was now sitting with eyes closed, summoning her psychic powers. I was feeling calm and, actually, quite interested, professionally. After a death of a loved one, I knew, many people sought help from mediums or other people who could be termed "folk psychologists." Generally, we discouraged this, because there was often financial fraud involved. But there was no such worry in this instance, since Anita was making the "connection" herself.

And the setting was Hollywood perfect: all was quiet except for the continuous patter of rain on the roof and the occasional crackle and wheeze of the well-dried eucalyptus logs in the big, open fireplace. Eleanor and Mr. Edelman sat motionless, their eyes on Anita's face. Anita herself looked completely calm, almost drowsy now, as if she were passing into a dream state. She swayed gently from side to side, just like in the movies, but clearly, she was completely serious about all this. Her subconscious self would, I thought, move the platen around the board while her conscious self would be unaware of any duplicity.

She began to speak: "Ever since I came back from India," she murmured, "I could feel his presence about me, all around, all around... He is here now. His spirit hovers above us. But I think it best not to call for a visual manifestation. It will be more – delicate, shall we say, to talk to him first through the medium of letters." Then she said, raising her voice, "Grey, are you there?"

The indicator lurched, hesitated, then moved to YES.

"Oh, good. Welcome, darling. Do you mind that I told Eleanor about you?"

The indicator moved again, this time sliding smoothly to NO.

"And this nice young man from the hospital?"

NO.

"Do you have anything to say to us?"

The indicator moved up to the letters, spelling out slowly, GREETINGS TO ALL.

"Eleanor, why don't you say something?" Anita whispered.

"Hi, Dad," said Eleanor awkwardly.

HI THERE, the spelling continued, HOWS SCHOOL.

"I'd like to say something," Mr. Edelman put in. He seemed to be warming to the experience. "Grey," he called loudly. "I just wanted to apologize for not getting that peanut brittle to you on time."

THATS OK PLENTY WHERE I AM NOW.

"Oh, that's a relief," sighed Mr. Edelman. "It must be a pretty nice place."

YES.

"Grey," put in Anita, "Eleanor has been worried about me, and this nice young man from the hospital here seems to think I'm crazy." I blinked. Despite appearances to the contrary, Anita was a very perceptive woman. "If you were to manifest yourself in a more tangible form," she continued smoothly, "I'm sure that they would believe me."

NO, the platen squeaked as it moved quickly across the waxy board.

"I know you think that it's dangerous, darling," Anita continued adamantly, "but really, I'm no amateur at these things. You don't have to worry. Everything will be fine."

The platen trembled above the word NO still, then moved away to spell BAD IDEA.

"Oh, come now, Grey," Anita continued. "Trust me."

The platen now began rhythmically spelling over and over, BAD BAD BAD BAD....

"That's enough," said Anita firmly, taking her hand off the platen. She stood up and announced, "He always disliked being told what to do. But I really do think it's necessary that you see him for yourself. This is the only way."

"Hold hands!" she ordered as she began to wander around the room, waving her arms in the air and calling out in a foreign language – Latin? Sanskrit? I had no idea. We all just sat there, watching her. Eleanor looked like she didn't know whether to laugh or cry.

After a few minutes of this strange chanting and dancing around, Anita suddenly shouted out five or six sharp syllables of what seemed to be some form of command. She went to a dusty upright piano, theatrically pulled off the old Mexican serape that covered it, sat down and played a few bars of something I didn't recognize. "That was our theme song," she told us parenthetically, getting up again, "'Town Without Pity.'" Next, she grabbed a hand bell, the sort you used to see at sickbeds, and shook it for several seconds. Then she stopped, listening intently.

The bell, though small and high-pitched, rang loudly in my ears and seemed to fill the whole house with its noise. When it stopped, there was nothing unusual to be heard or seen, although our eyes all darted nervously around, imagining movement where there was none.

After a minute or so, Anita rang the bell again. Once again, the metallic din faded into nothing but the sound of fire and rain, and a wind that seemed to be blowing down from the hills.

Suddenly, the lights went out. All three of us tensed as we continued holding onto each other's hands. My eyes met Eleanor's in the semi-gloom. The electric lights only had gone out, not the candles or the firelight. Was it a coincidental power outage? How could that be?

"He's coming," Anita whispered. She seemed to have heard something. We continued to wait in silence; I found myself becoming unnerved. I had to fight the impulse to laugh, to stand up and shout that this was ridiculous – that it was clearly a practical joke.

"He's coming," she repeated, with confidence now, and *gravitas*. "I have called him back, and he is coming."

We waited. And soon, above the crackle of the fire, I could hear another sound, somewhere inside the house. It repeated – a knocking or creaking somewhere. I could see both the kitchen and hallway doors from where I sat, and I watched them nervously.

Anita, standing motionless in the middle of the room, hissed at us urgently, "No one move, no one say anything! We don't want to frighten him! It's a very difficult transition."

It was then that I noticed the presence of someone else in the room – or rather, in the doorway that led off from the unlit hall. It was too dark to see anything other than an outline, but it seemed to be a man, leaning forward, hovering frozen in the doorway, as if hesitant or unwilling to enter.

Eleanor saw the form at the same time I did. "Daddy?" she called out hoarsely.

Immediately, the figure blended into the darkness and was no longer there.

For several seconds, no one moved. Silently, the lights flickered and then came on again. I got up – a little too late – and looked around the doorway where the figure had stood. "There's nobody there," I told them.

"Oh, dear!" cried Anita, throwing up her arms. "You can lead a horse to water but you can't make him drink. And Grey always was as stubborn as a mule. Well," she sighed, "at least I got him to show up, even though he wasn't very sociable. I'm sorry, Elly, but your father apparently thinks it's best that he doesn't materialize before you right now."

Eleanor's face was as white as a sheet, but she said grimly, "I'm going to find out what's going on here if it takes all night. Let's search the house."

We did – thoroughly – but we found no one.

By the time we finished searching, it was after midnight, and raining hard outside. Eleanor's mother insisted that I stay the night. I didn't have to work the following day and so accepted the invitation gratefully.

Edelman had gone home and Mrs. Grey was already in bed when Eleanor and I said goodnight. I was to sleep in the attic – which, oddly enough, was the best spare room in the house: all the others were being used as a meditation space, or an art studio, or a stamp collection sorting and display room, or else they were just filled with junk. The attic had been used by Eleanor's father as a study when he was alive. "The sofa in there is long enough to sleep on comfortably," Eleanor told me as we parted at the stairs. "I'm sorry to have gotten you involved in all this – and I bet you're not even earning overtime," she said, smiling wanly.

"Please, consider me a friend of the family," I said formally. "Like Mr. Edelman."

She couldn't help grinning at that. "Poor Edelman, I think he has a crush on Mom. By the way, before I forget, he and I got my father's belongings from the hospital today, before we came to see you. But I checked just now and they gave us someone else's things."

"Oh, great!" I muttered. "Sorry!"

"Oh, it was an easy mistake to make. They gave us a Thomas Grey's things. My father's name is Grey Thomas. He had problems all his life with that name, because, you know, it sounds backwards."

"So you're name is Eleanor Thomas?" I asked.

"Yeah. Does that meet with your approval?"

"Oh, very nice."

"Thanks. I was worried." Grinning, she walked off down the hallway, ponytail swinging. "See you tomorrow!"

That was the closest we've ever gotten to intimate flirtation, I thought pathetically as I mounted the narrow stairs to the attic.

I soon found myself in a small, roughed-in room with one dormer window. It was furnished with the afore-mentioned sofa – lumpy, in a comfortable sort of way – a small desk, and a large, old wardrobe in the corner. The walls were lined with makeshift book-shelves. In these, and spilling out over the wood plank floor, were books and more books – novels, history, poetry, sociology. Electrical wiring ran along the ceiling joists – Eleanor's father had wired this room himself, she had told me. It may be a firetrap, I thought to myself as I got out of my suit and changed into an old pair of her father's pajamas, but it certainly has personality. I climbed onto the sofa, pulled an old quilt over me, and switched off the antique floor lamp.

I wanted very badly to spend some time sorting out the events of the day in my mind. I felt there was something I was missing in the whole situation. But I guess I was more tired than I thought, because I dropped off within seconds.

I awoke with the feeling that something was wrong. I lay there without moving, listening intently. Had I heard a sound?

I didn't need to remember where I was – the events of the evening didn't seem far off. I confirmed this with a glance at my watch: it wasn't yet two o'clock. If anything, the short sleep I had had seemed to have heightened the sense of puzzlement and mystery I had felt earlier, during the seance.

I listened: the house below me was quiet. The rain on the roof just above my head was a continuous, barely audible patter. What could I have heard that would have awakened me so suddenly, so completely?

I waited, listening.

Then I heard a movement somewhere in the house below, not far from my little room. A stealthy, scuffling sound. Rats?

Then, a heavy creaking – too big for rats!

The noises were now clearly audible on the stairway. Whatever it was, it was moving up here, to where I lay.

Slowly, a dark figure was rising out of the trap doorway at the top of the stair. Seconds after, it was standing hunched in the middle of the small room. I must honestly admit that for the life of me I could not have moved. If anyone laughs at me for that, I can only say, try lying awake in a strange attic in the middle of the night hearing something creeping towards you in the darkness and see how you like it, and whether you handle it any better than I did.

After an endless moment, the figure moved forward towards me, with one arm outstretched as if to touch me and the other raised as if holding a lantern, though no light was visible. There was an odd smell in the cold air as the figure seemed to peer at me intently, studying me. It leaned towards me, closer – closer still – I felt it touch my arm!

I sprang up, vaulted over the back of the sofa, and stood crouching between it and the sloping attic roof, my heart pounding. The thing drew back, then drew itself up again and moaned in sepulchral tones: "I am the spirit of Grey Edward Thomas. Thou hast trespassed upon my resting place. Begone!" Then it lunged toward me, waving an arm menacingly.

I would have begone immediately, as suggested, except for the thought of Eleanor. Along with the mystery, she had never left my mind. And, if this was her father, it wouldn't do for me to run away, even if he was a little surly, and dead. I remembered Eleanor, and yes, the fact that I had a job to do. As a Licensed Clinical Social Worker, it was my responsibility to see this matter through to a documentable ending. I couldn't very well chart that I had come to the house, met the ghost of the deceased, and run off without taking a history. The mind works oddly at times like these, and it occurred to me that I'd better remember to pull the proper chart: Thomas, not Grey.

Then something clicked. As I stared into the eyes of the spirit of Grey Edward Thomas, everything suddenly fell into place. The mix-up with the last name... the fact that the ghost before me was a brawny man, whereas the corpse had been small... Mr. Edelman's odd comment about hoping that no one would be angry with him... and, to clinch it all, an odd smell that I had just noticed in the room – *the smell of spare ribs.*

Still crouched in my corner, I reached over and switched on the light. The specter was a large, strong-looking man with ruddy cheeks and nose and flowing, iron-gray hair. His wool pullover and polyester pants were sopping with rain, and he was holding a plate of what seemed to be leftover spare ribs in his hand. He stared at me, not quite sure whether the jig was up or not, ready to brazen it out if given half the chance.

"This is not very funny, Mr. Thomas," I said sternly.

"I'm not trying to be funny," he answered. "You are sleeping on my resting place – my couch, that is."

"You know what I'm talking about," I said. "Your wife and daughter think you're dead, and you're obviously not. What's all this about?" I asked narrowly. "Some insurance scam?"

"Oh, of course not, of course not," Eleanor's father said hastily, sitting down beside me. "Let's keep our voices down, shall we? Let me just slip into something dry and I'll explain the whole thing."

I climbed back over the sofa and settled down to listen, which was all for the best since, despite my stern and commanding demeanor, I was still shaking.

Mr. Thomas took off his wet outer clothing and, in undershirt and boxer shorts, wrapped a multicolored blanket around himself – the Mexican serape that had draped the piano, as it turned out. "It's all I could find downstairs," he explained, chummy enough now. "I can't very well go into my own closet at the moment. I must remember to return it tomorrow morning before anyone notices."

"But how did you get in here?" I asked. "Have you been here all along?"

"I've been spending most of my time since my death up here, yes. That little bell of Anita's would summon me from my nether world," he waved his hand to indicate this attic room, "and into her presence.

"Normally," he continued, "when I heard the bell, I'd climb down, use the fuse box in the hallway closet to turn off the lights, and appear before Anita in the living room. Tonight, of course, I wasn't prepared to find all of you there. You see, I had flattered Anita that, because of her unusually strong psychic powers and the sincere love that we bore each other, she was the only one who should see me clothed in what I called my 'psychic flesh.'

I made her promise to call me only when we could be alone together. I wasn't expecting to see all of you there, gawking at me! When I did, I hurried to the back of the house, then climbed out a window, skedaddled it across the yard, and spent the rest of the evening – while you were presumably searching the house – in the garage. I came back for these," he said, taking up a spare rib and biting into it.

"But how did you make the Ouija board move?" I asked.

He hadn't known anything about the Ouija episode, as it turned out. I explained how, at first, I had thought it was Anita herself moving the platen. But then, when the writing refused to allow him to materialize, I had changed my mind: it seemed unlikely that Anita herself could have been responsible for that message, even subconsciously.

"That must have been Edelman," Mr. Thomas finally concluded. "He was reluctant from the start to go along with this business. But he couldn't inform on me without implicating himself. It was all his fault, you see, telling everyone I was dead. The only way I got him to go along with all of this in the first place was by playing on his natural timidity – and, he had one other ulterior motive," continued Mr. Thomas, shaking a second rib at me. "He has a terrible *penchant* for Anita. He thinks I don't deserve her, and he hoped that this might give him a chance to win her from me. Told me about it straight out – I have to admire him for that. 'Fair enough,' I said," He chuckled. "Edelman thought my playing dead meant I would soon be out of the picture. Little did he know it would turn out to be a second honeymoon for Anita and me."

"So you planned this whole thing out?" I asked, shocked. "Pretending to be dead so you could make your wife appreciate you more?"

"Oh, no! Of course not," he said quickly. "And keep your voice down. No, it was all serendipity. You see, when Edelman came to see me at the hospital that day, I was down at the end of the hall, in the shower room. Maybe you've gathered already that Edelman is somewhat absent-minded. Well, he mixed up the room numbers. He was standing outside the wrong room when you approached him and told him I had just passed away. Then, he was too timid to go into the room. He never did see the face of the man who was actually dead."

"And it was my fault too?" I asked. "I got the names mixed up?"

"Not necessarily. You probably said to Edelman something like, 'I'm sorry, but your friend, Mr. Grey, is dead.' Edelman and I go back a long way. We went to high school together, and he's used to teachers and other people calling me Grey sometimes as well as Thomas. It didn't occur to him to correct you."

I thought about it: We have a tagging system to warn hospital personnel when two patients have similar-sounding names. But it's usually a matter of the same last name. And the unit secretary was new – she probably didn't realize that juxtaposed names needed to be tagged, too.

That explained how the confusion first arose, but...

"When you came back from the shower," I continued, "why didn't you tell anyone about the mistake?"

"No one asked me," Grey replied. "I didn't know there was a mix-up. I was discharged routinely from the hospital that day and drove myself home. And I didn't see Edelman for several days. By that time, it was too late."

Grey himself had not known anything about his supposed demise until, waking up from a nap one afternoon, he wandered into the dining room to find Anita, home from India, engaged in some sort of ritual to contact him in the netherworld. After she had seen him, fainted, and been revived, she still couldn't believe he was really alive.

"And, yes, I took advantage of that, telling her I was a spirit now, and that she had called me back. It was perfectly innocent, really," he hastened to say. "I'm sure that, on some level, Anita knows I'm not dead. It's just a little game we've been playing. I mean, who would be so gullible..."

He noted my disapproving glare.

"You still don't think this is quite right, do you?" he asked. "You don't think my behavior has been quite ethical?"

I shook my head.

After thoughtfully examining the tangerine stripes and electric blue zigzags of the serape for some time, he asked, "Have you ever been married, young man?"

"No," I replied.

"Well," he sighed deeply, "The problem with marriage is, a man can't win for losing. Take the predicament I'm in now. I love my wife; my wife loves me. But, while she thought I was alive, she ignored me – treated me worse than the cat. But now that she thinks I'm dead, and that she's calling me back from distant voids, she can't get enough of me."

"This could have turned out very badly, though," I interjected. "The reason I came here in the first place was because your wife sounded suicidal. And your daughter – she was very upset, too. Didn't you think of her?"

"Of course, of course," Mr. Grey answered impatiently. "I tried to get a hold of her to explain the whole thing, but when I called the university, they said she was off somewhere, backpacking or some-such thing, whatever college kids do these days. Anyway, her mother got a hold of her first, and then she was *en route* out here. I decided to tell her when she came home..."

"Well?"

"Well, I haven't been able to find quite the right moment to tell either of them yet," he concluded, looking thoughtfully into the distance, as if he were contemplating a difficult putt.

A voice from the doorway interposed: "You don't have to worry about telling me, Dad."

It was Eleanor. Our voices must have awakened her. Her face was white and stern, but other than that, she seemed to be taking it well. "I don't know how you're going to tell Mom," she said. "If she has a heart attack, it'll be your fault."

The next morning, Eleanor and I sat at the sunny kitchen table, trying to gently break the news to Anita that she wasn't a widow after all. Finally, we brought Grey out of hiding and he apologized sincerely for all the trouble he'd caused.

Anita looked at him, then at us for some moments. Then, turning her attention to the Saturday Times, she said lightly, "I knew it all along."

We stared in disbelief.

"I was just going along with the joke," she added.

"Anita darling," said Grey with Shakespearean pathos, going down on one knee before her, "you forgive me, then?"

"I didn't say that," she said, throwing down the paper and

rising from the table. "Grey, you are low and despicable. You have a small soul."

She exited regally.

Surprisingly, Grey didn't seem depressed by this. "She's a bit piqued, but she'll get over it," he whispered to us, gesturing reassuringly. "Really, I can tell she's very pleased to know I'm alive. Now," he said thoughtfully, following his wife out of the room, "I just have to think up some new plan to get her to realize it..."

Eleanor looked at me exasperatedly. I couldn't help laughing, and after a while, she couldn't, either. "My world and welcome to it," she said. "At least it's never boring. At any rate, thanks for everything you've done, and for your patience with all of us. If it hadn't been for you, who knows when Dad would have reincarnated?"

This praise from Eleanor, and the acknowledgment that I had been of use to her, meant a lot to me. So, of course, I became completely unhinged. I was stammering something inane, and Eleanor was watching me with those beautiful brown eyes, enjoying my discomfort, when Mr. Edelman poked his head in the kitchen door.

"Edelman," called Eleanor. "There's good news and bad news. The bad news is, Mom knows about your part in misleading her concerning Dad's supposed demise."

Mr. Edelman's eyes widened and he started to back out the door.

"The good news is," continued Eleanor, "There's pancakes for breakfast."

Mr. Edelman hesitated, then came in. "Better to get it over with," he mumbled.

I could continue with the story from here: what scheme Grey cooked up to win his way back into Anita's affections; how Eleanor ended up asking *me* out; and whether or not Mr. Edelman was forgiven and given his pancakes.

But that's another story – this was the spare rib one.

You Should Have to Live with Yourself

"POLTERGEIST (German, "noisy ghost"): A mostly playful and mischievous but sometimes malicious and baneful spirit which haunts a particular dwelling place and manifests its presence by manipulating (moving, hiding, throwing) household goods, furniture, etc. In the case of the doppelgänger (German, "double-goer"), can take the form of a family member, servant, etc. (see also DOPPELGÄNGER)..."

BONG BONG, BONG BONG. The front doorbell was ringing. "Hey, Barbara! Someone at the door!" Kelty bellowed, and kept on typing. He was on a roll:

"The typical poltergeist haunting generally passes from the initial stage of fright to a honeymoon period of amusement and even boasting and exhibition by the family to neighbors and friends; then on to annoyance, irritation, and finally, grudging tolerance. Poltergeists are notoriously difficult to get rid of but very easy to raise. The following incantation..."

BONG BONG, BONG BONG. That bell again – that silly bell, unbelievably pretentious for a tract home of this size. The woman has no taste, Kelty thought irritably. He ran a grimy hand through his too-long, greasy hair, and yelled again, "The door! Someone at the door!" all the while drumming at the keyboard:

"The following incantation, accompanied by the proper offerings and candle burnings as described in the beginning

*of this chapter, will certainly give satisfactory results, even
to the novice."*

"Ha ha ha," said Kelty cheerlessly. "To the novice, maybe – not
to me. But as they say: those who can, do; those who can't, write
about it. Hell's bells, where is that woman? Barbara! SOMEONE AT
THE *DOOR!"* he fairly shrieked.

Barbara Widgway, several years farther into middle age than Kelty but still trim and attractive, thought she heard someone calling
her above the roar of the vacuum.

For some time she ignored it – she just wanted to finish this
little corner *here* – but finally, reluctantly, she switched off her
high-powered, commercial-grade upright, and heard now, rather
too clearly, her lodger, Kelty, yelling from his back room that someone was at the door.

She sighed, untied her apron and head scarf, folded them and
put them away in their proper drawer in the dining room. Then she
went to answer the bell, which had rung once again in the meantime with the pretty chime Barbara had chosen so many years ago,
while her husband was still alive, and which still gave her pleasure
to hear: four precise, discreet tones: *bong, bong, bong bong.*

She paused before the mirror, took her clip-on earrings out
of her pocket, put them on, checked her hair, and opened the
front door.

The girl on the porch had already started back down the steps,
but she turned and came up again with an embarrassed little laugh.

"Good morning, Ma'am," she said. She was quite young, in her
early twenties perhaps, slender but with a bit of a bulging tummy.
Her dress was modest and well-ironed, her hair well-combed. So,
when she introduced herself as Jennifer and timidly asked to come
in and show her a new line of cleaning products, Barbara agreed
to at least have a look.

"I have to warn you, though," she said, ushering the girl to the
sofa, "I probably won't buy anything. I have just about every cleaning product known to man."

"Oh, please, don't worry about that!" said Jennifer. "It's so nice
of you just to let me in. You're the first person who has so far." Then,

as if thinking she shouldn't have admitted that, she blushed, and hastened to add, "What a lovely home! and immaculately kept!"

"Thank you, dear," said Barbara, in a complacent voice that rendered unnecessary the addition of, *that's what everybody says.*

The company Jennifer worked for was a sort of mix between Avon and Amway, and sold every type of beauty and cleaning aid a woman could want. There was a pudgy little catalog, a copy of which Barbara accepted, and then several demonstrations of unique products just newly invented by their cutting-edge team of scientists who, one was almost led to think, were brilliant enough to work for NASA, but had decided they could do more good for humanity by providing a better fabric softener and a longer-lasting mascara.

In-between her sales pitch, Jennifer, who was something of a talker, let on that she was twenty-four; that she had a baby at home which her husband was currently watching (along with the football game on TV); that there was another baby on the way; that this was her very first week on the job; that she was hoping to make enough extra money to buy a second car; and that maybe, if she were as successful as her senior sales partner predicted, she just might win a Disney vacation, this being the prize for the Top New Salesgirl of the Western Region. Since there were four tickets, and neither of the babies counted yet, they could also bring along her sister and her husband –

"I wouldn't count my chickens before they're hatched," commented Barbara wryly.

"Oh, of course not," Jennifer recalled herself nervously. "Ahem. Now, I know you will want to see this," she said, obviously lapsing into a spiel which she had memorized word-for-word. "Our scientists have just come up with it: Magic Pol-Away, a new fingernail polish remover without the icky smell of the old ones. Don't you just hate that smell? I know *I* sure do..." As she spoke, she quickly took out a sample vial and twisted at the cap, which seemed to be stuck. "Oh, dear," she said, twisting harder, getting it open – and then fumbling it above the sleek surface of Barbara's Louis Quinze coffee table!

There! Jennifer caught it up before it could spill. But then, amazingly, and undoubtedly out of sheer terror at the look on

Barbara's face, she dropped it again. And now Louis's veneer was splattered all over with Magic Pol-Away!

"Oh, no!" Jennifer cried, frozen, while Barbara whipped a cleaning rag out of her pocket and started mopping the gooey stuff up.

"Look what you've done!" Barbara burst out. "My beautiful coffee table!"

Jennifer, trying to help, only managed to knock the vial onto the floor, where it immediately began to bond with the deep pile of Barbara's oyster wall-to-wall. "I have something that will clean that up, somewhere!" she cried, leaving the vial to drip on the rug as she rooted frantically around in her samples case.

That was it. Barbara let the girl have a piece of her mind, all the while wiping and blotting. "You little dummy!" she cried. "How dare you come into my house and do something like this!"

Jennifer stopped rooting and started crying, which only irritated Barbara further. "Stop that bawling!" she scolded. "I didn't ask you to come in here! Did I ask you to come in and make a mess on my rug?"

Kelty, hearing the commotion, ambled out to see what was going on. "Aw, leave her alone," he said, seeing the company's name on the girl's sample case and extrapolating what had happened from there.

Barbara, bending over the carpet, glared up at him angrily.

"I'm so sorry, really I am!" Jennifer cried, hastily throwing all her materials back into the samples case.

"Sorry won't clean my carpet!" Barbara replied, scrubbing angrily.

Kelty opened the front door and, taking the girl by the arm, gently led her out. "Here," he said, taking a twenty dollar bill out of his wallet. "Take this."

The girl protested, but he thrust the money into her hand.

"Just take it. Run along now! And don't worry, everything'll be fine."

"What did you give that girl out there?" Barbara asked, standing in the doorway of Kelty's room, arms akimbo.

She had finally finished cleaning up after the morning's fiasco.

Thanks to her quick thinking, the spills were only barely visible. But the rug and table would never be the same, and grief made her voice sharp.

Kelty tried to ignore her. He had been running over the Poltergeist Raising Incantation, South Apennine Method, just to make sure he'd written it out right. The proper candles were lit on his desk, the correct herbs were simmering in the brazier and, wand in hand, he was intoning, *"Asknaz shintab florund, mirabund zinder..."*

"Oh, *please,*" said Barbara witheringly. "You know what I'm talking about! You gave her money, didn't you?"

"...triundum mohum. Oh! spirits great and small, betwixt the light and dark; I, Kelty, thy master, call upon thee..."

"I can't believe your gall!" Barbara continued. "Here you are, behind on your rent, and you're giving money away."

"...that here shall be thy dwelling place until otherwise spoken. Welcome, thou..."

"Can't you knock that off for a minute? I'm talking to you!"

"...seeing, saying, speaking double, here shalt dwell for weal or trouble!" Kelty thundered dramatically. Then he paused, arms raised, shifting his eyes over the room.

"What are you looking for?" demanded Barbara.

"Nothing," Kelty sighed, putting down his wand. "Nothing at all. I told you, I'll pay you on the fifteenth, when I get the final check for *Strange Brews.*" He snuffed out the candles and the brazier and wiped his eyeglasses on his dirty pullover.

"I don't know why anyone would pay money for the nonsense you write," said Barbara. "It's a very strange way for a grown man to earn a living, that's all I can say. Spells and mumbo-jumbo, and none of them work, of course. Haven't your readers figured that out by now?"

Ouch, thought Kelty. That one hurt. "How is that your business," he asked sweetly, "as long as you get your money on the fifteenth?"

"Because you owe it to me *now.* And how in the world do you think I feel about you giving money to that girl who ruined my furniture –"

Kelty knew better than to reply. It was impossible to concentrate on his work while she stood there haranguing him, but he began typing again, not wanting to admit that she was getting to him.

"– and keeping this place like a pigsty," she was saying. "Expecting me to clean up after you. Really, you should have to live with yourself!" She started picking up some of the clothes that he had draped over the bookshelf.

"I've never asked you to pick up after me, and don't touch any of my personal belongings, *please.*" He muttered an incantation designed to drive away noxious pests.

And oddly, now, she lapsed into silence.

Had the incantation worked? Was there yet hope that she might walk away and leave him in blessed peace? Kelty threw a glance from the corner of his eye. She was standing, looking into a small plastic bag he had absent-mindedly left there atop a pile of clothes. On the outside of the bag were printed the words, *"Patrick's Pet Palace."* Oh oh.

"What's this?" she asked, drawing another bag out of the first one. "Wood shavings? Litter?" Her voice became hard. "Are you keeping some sort of animal in here?"

"Only a pair of white mice," he said casually, and brought the wire cage out from behind his desk – no use in trying to hide it now. "It's for something I'm writing about the transmigration of souls. Why mice, you might ask? Well, they live and die and breed at such an astonishing rate –"

"Just answer me one thing," said Barbara, raising a finger to stop him. "In our rental agreement, is there a clause about pets? And let me point out also: doesn't that agreement say, No Pets Allowed?"

"Well, I took that to mean, as any reasonable person would, cats and dogs and ponies, not two tiny furballs in a cage."

"Doesn't it say, NO PETS ALLOWED?"

Kelty sighed, massaging his eyes with his hands. "Yes."

"Do you think it's fair to me, to bring something like this into my home? If you were me, how would you feel?"

"I wouldn't mind."

"Oh, of course not! You wouldn't mind the mess, and the rule-breaking, and not being paid your rent money… I thought you said there were two mice in here?"

"Yes."

"I only see one."

"I'm sure there were two – "

"Kelty!" Barbara cried. "The cage door is open!"

"Let me tell you something, Kelty – you should have to live with yourself!"

It took an hour of crawling around to find the escapee, who had managed to get into one of Kelty's dress shoes in the closet. Barbara had nagged him the whole time, and now, as Kelty sat at his desk, staring in front of him, she was still talking. Perhaps she was going for a record.

"Really, you should!" Barbara continued, shaking out his bed-spread. He had told her not to make the bed, but she was doing it anyway. "You should have to live with yourself! And then you'd see what it's like!" She looked at him hard, as if she were saying something new that needed time to sink in.

And finally, something inside of him just snapped.

"If I've heard that once," he said, "I've heard it a thousand times. But today's the one that broke the camel's back." He stood up, facing her, tired, droopy, baggy-faced. "Barbara, you and I go back a long way. You were lonely after your husband passed away, and when I first moved in, you were good to me. Those were happy times, and I thank you for them."

She stared at him suspiciously. "I'm not going to – " she began.

He raised a hand to silence her. "We used to be friends, and more. But the last few years, you seem to have tired of my society, and I, too... Well, I know I'm not tidy, I know my writing hasn't paid off the way we both hoped it would, that I drink too much – so many things. But, believe it or not, you're not perfect, either!"

"Well!" Barbara cried. "If you think I'm going to stand here and listen to any more of this – "

"The time is ripe for a parting of the ways," Kelty overspoke her. "My mice, and my mess, and myself will find another abode."

"You?" Barbara snorted. "Where will you go? You can't afford to move."

"I've got friends," Kelty said. "I'll find a corner on a floor some-where. And you, I'm sure, will get along just fine without me. You don't really need the extra money, and no boarder could ever meet your stringent expectations. I certainly can't. So, I shall be packing my things, preparatory to moving out this very night. In the meantime... please leave my room!"

Barbara, speechless with shock and anger, did just that.

That night, she was all alone in the house for the first time in years – a strange feeling, but she would get used to it. More, she would learn to like it. She was determined to.

The question was, how had she managed to put up with him all these years? With his slovenliness, his lack of presentability?

Another boarder might be neater, but would undoubtedly have other faults that were just as irritating. No, she was better off alone.

Now, determined to enjoy herself, she sat in robe and slippers, with a bowl of popcorn, a glass of diet cola, and a packet of pre-moistened hand wipes, in front of the Old Movie Channel.

She loved these old shows – everyone so well dressed and well-mannered, the story lines so clear and predictable. You always knew who the good girl was by the way she dressed: stylish, but conservative, while the bad girl always wore too much jewelry.

And tonight there would be no Kelty coming in, making sarcastic comments about her taste in movies.

Yes, it was a little strange, knowing he wasn't there, not hearing the occasional cough, chuckle, or shuffling of papers from his room. She felt a pang of regret that she hadn't allowed him to leave a phone number and address where he could be contacted, in case she – well, of course she wouldn't want to get in touch with him! If anyone called or sent mail here, he could just as well pick it up himself. Let him find out what it was like to do without her.

Right before leaving, he had said that he wanted to "part friends." But she suspected he had really been hoping for an invitation back. If he had apologized, she might have done so. Now, she didn't even know where he was.

Doris Day, in a fuzzy pink babydoll nightie, was kneeling on a pink satin bedspread and giving Rock Hudson a piece of her mind over a pink princess phone when Barbara realized she was nodding off. She got up, turned off the TV, and brought the popcorn bowl into the kitchen. She rinsed it, squirted a little dishwashing soap into it, scrubbed it, rinsed it again, and left it to dry on the rubber drain mat. Ran the water and the popcorn kernels down the garbage disposal, washed her hands, wiped them with a dishtowel, and threw the dishtowel into the laundry basket. Looked into the laundry basket, counted: one, two, three items in there; when it got to five, she would do the wash.

She climbed the stairs to bed, went through her nighttime ritual and, lying neatly tucked into bed, saw by the bedside clock that it was 11:15. Thinking of how she would tackle the cleaning of Kelty's room in the morning, she went to sleep...

...only to wake up, off and on, repeatedly. There were strange sounds from all over the house – things bumping around downstairs, sounds of floorboards creaking. Even water flowing through the pipes, though she knew nothing had been left on. Undoubtedly, these were sounds the house made every night. She was just noticing them now because she was alone.

She nodded off, then woke again with a start – somewhere downstairs, a door had closed. Surely there was someone down there? Breathless, she listened for many minutes without moving a muscle, but there was no other sound.

Heart in mouth, she went downstairs and made a search of the house. Of course, everything was in order, the doors and windows locked up tight, the way she had left them.

She turned on the outside patio lights and the light over the driveway, then fixed herself a hot toddy, cleaned up after herself, and carried the toddy up to bed. After drinking it and flipping through *House Beautiful* for a few minutes, she nodded off. Thankfully, she didn't wake up again.

The next morning she felt a little groggy, and if her alarm hadn't awakened her at the customary 7:30 a.m., she might have slept in an hour longer. But there was Kelty's room to scrub down – better not to put that off! Who knew what kind of mess awaited her there?

She was already downstairs and cleaning up after her toast and coffee when she realized that she had forgotten the toddy glass that she had been drinking from the night before: it was still upstairs. She went up to get it, but was surprised to find that it was not on the bedside table, or anywhere around. She looked under the bed, thinking she might have knocked it off somehow, but it was simply nowhere in sight.

Now, that was odd. Barbara sat down on the edge of the bed and thought. It annoyed her when things just disappeared like that. She prided herself on her faultless application of the rule, A Place for Everything, and Everything in Its Place. Still, here was the toddy glass missing. Was it possible that she had already taken it down, either last night or this morning? She had definitely been feeling heavy-headed before her coffee.

Oh, well. She was feeling much better now, and the morning fog outside, that had contributed, perhaps, to her mental haziness, had lifted; the sun was shining. After washing up the rest of the breakfast things, she put the radio on – they were playing a medley of Broadway showtunes – and got out the bucket, brushes, and cleaning rags she'd need for her assault on Kelty's room. She licked her lips when she thought about those windows. She had been dying to give those windows a thorough scrubbing since last winter, and to give the place a good airing out after all that candle smoke, not to mention Kelty's strange-smelling cigars.

It was with something very like disappointment that she found, once she threw open the curtains and took a good look, that the room was really not in very bad shape at all. The windows were quite clean, actually, and Kelty had dusted and even vacuumed before he left.

Well! All along, she had begged him to be a little neater, and he hadn't lifted a finger until the day he moved out. Undoubtedly, he had meant to make some sort of point. Mean-spirited, she called it.

She picked up a corner of one of the curtains and sniffed. Nothing! No hint of smoke or soot or even dust. And the walls? They were clean also. Even the oil stain above the bedstead that had annoyed her so much was gone – scrubbed off completely.

Barbara sighed brightly. Clean, everything clean already! What a relief. Less work for her, and now she could attend to the rest of the house.

But, upon inspection, the rest of the house turned out to be spotless, too. Of course it was – the house couldn't have gotten dirty in one day. Everything, everywhere was clean and neat around her.

Finally, there was time for some much-needed rest and relaxation. After four years of Kelty, anyone would need a vacation!

Slowly, she carried the bucket and rags back to the hall closet. As hard as it was to imagine Kelty cleaning his room, here was evidence of it: someone besides herself had definitely been in here, rearranging things. The box of rags was on a shelf farther down, the sponges farther up. And the whisk brooms were now bundled all together, though Barbara normally kept them separated according to size. Sighing with exasperation, she rearranged things the way they should be.

Then she sat down in her neat little den and switched on the television to the Shoppe-at-Home Network. They had been advertising a pretty set of patio furniture that she had been thinking of buying, but right now a nice, well-dressed man, rather bouncy for his advanced age, was getting very excited about a smokeless fryer. Despite his enthusiasm, Barbara remained skeptical. She found her mind wandering to Kelty, and whether he had found a place to sleep last night. Perhaps he had had to sleep in his car. Well, that wasn't her worry, thank goodness. He was free to wander; she didn't own him.

Many years had gone by since she and he were on anything more than business terms with each other. Yet, now, she found herself remembering when he first came to stay: how glad she had been to have a man in the house again. And, though he could never have measured up to her Frank, of course, there had been a time when she had found Kelty's bohemian ways attractive. Funny, how you forgot those things! His easygoing manner, his sense of humor were qualities she had once admired. How had things changed between them? Familiarity had bred contempt, she supposed, on her part as well as his.

And now he had left, thinking he'd find a better place – somewhere where people would appreciate him! Where, far from expecting any type of civilized behavior, they would see his slovenliness as an aspect of his artistic personality, and indulge his bad habits – for a time at least. That sort of thing got old very quickly! Kelty would find out soon enough that other women would be even less tolerant of his piggishness than she was. Let him find out for himself how good he had had it here.

Irritably, Barbara got up and started wiping the already spotless wainscoting.

"I do like a man who smokes cigars," said Garnet, regarding Kelty across the length of her very small and cluttered kitchen table. "Put the ashes anywhere. It makes no nevermind to me!"

She had offered him asylum for as long as he needed to stay. Kelty, who had been looking around for an ashtray, now knocked the ashes onto his breakfast plate, where they stuck to the yellow remains of his sunnyside-up egg.

"Don't let me interrupt your routine, Garnet," he said. "I don't want to be any more of an imposition – "

"You're no imposition! And I *have* no routine."

She continued to stare at him, chin cupped in hand. A bit unnerved, he asked, "But surely you have something planned for today."

"Oh, I have a few things up my sleeve, but nothing it would do to talk about."

He thought it better to leave that one alone. But after a time, she added, "If you talk about things, they don't work out. You shouldn't talk – you shouldn't even *think*."

"Is that the philosophy upon which your empire is based?" He was only half joking. Garnet was a much more accomplished practitioner of the Art than he, and perhaps that did have something to do with her attitude.

"Oh, yes," she replied.

"I don't know how well that would work for me," Kelty said. "It's important for a writer to be explicit, to have an outline."

"Yes, of course, but that's your trouble. You write about magick, but you're too intellectually engaged to perform it properly. That incantation you were talking about – for raising poltergeists?"

"Yes."

"Well, you said yourself that nothing happened."

"Nothing ever happens. Well, almost never. A few times I've been able to do simple spells. And once, when I was a kid, I started a fire."

"Now, that's not easy. That's very difficult. Tell me about that."

"There's not much to tell. I had this book with the fire lighting spell in it. A cousin and I made a pile of sticks and leaves. He was a real annoying kid – kept harassing me about how stupid this was, and how there was no such thing as magick. I didn't believe there was, either, at the time, but I really wanted to shut his mouth. And I did – the fire lit."

"How nice for you!"

Kelty breathed out cigar smoke thoughtfully. "Of course, it blew my mind, too, and I've spent the last thirty years trying to find out just what happened that day – though I've had very little luck since then, with fire-starting or anything else... My cousin finally decided I had nothing to do with it – that the bonfire had been lit by spontaneous combustion or something." Kelty mused. "Maybe he was right."

"Or maybe," said Garnet, "it was your resonant emotion."

Kelty looked questioning, and she continued: "People always think we witches get our powers from an alignment with bad or good forces. But the source of our success is really emotion – strong emotion. Some people find it in anger, some in pity, some in the desire to dominate. You might find it in annoyance."

Kelty laughed out loud. "In that case, the poltergeist incantation should have worked! My landlady was standing there, annoying the heck out of me while I was doing it."

"How do you know it didn't work?" asked Garnet with a slow smile.

Now it was Kelty's turn to stare.

The week went by, and Barbara thought she was going crazy.

Although there were other things in her life – the women's club, the bowling league, volunteering at the Red Cross – her primary occupation had always been that of housewife. She loved her home, loved decorating and cleaning it, entertaining in it. She was somewhat restless by nature, and whenever anything was bothering her, she found scrubbing or mopping or polishing helped ease her mind. It was a bit irrational, but she always felt that, if her house was neat and in order, everything else was bound to fall into place sooner or later.

Ever since Kelty left, the need to keep busy was especially strong. His going had left a gap in her schedule and, though it was hard to admit, in her affections, too.

And yet, no matter where she looked, she couldn't find anything to clean! Nothing needed cleaning. Certainly, since Kelty had moved out, there was less laundry and fewer dirty dishes. She had expected that! But there should have been other things – the settling of dust, the tarnishing of silver plate, the falling of leaves from the neighbors' tree onto her driveway. Every morning she searched, but could find no dust, no tarnish, no leaves.

And there were other things, like the laundry. The night that Kelty left, there had been three items in the downstairs linen hamper – Barbara remembered counting them quite clearly. Then, in the course of the day, she had thrown a few more things in – another dish towel and the two rags she had used on the wainscoting and on the chair rungs, though they weren't really dirty at all. That should have made six. But, when she looked in the hamper that evening, there were only three pieces of linen in it: the ones she had put in that day. Either she had miscounted the day before, or she had done the laundry herself and forgotten about it, or someone else had snuck in and taken them out during the night. All three alternatives seemed equally ridiculous. Still, it was hardly something she could call the police about.

At night, she always took a hot toddy now while she watched TV. Though it helped to knock her out a bit, she had rather unpleasant dreams, always about the house and vanishing messes. And there was always someone in the background, someone angry, who was blaming her for something, she didn't know what.

On Friday, it was her turn to hostess the garden club. She decided to have the girls out on the patio, and was depressed, upon looking things over beforehand, to find that even the grass seemed to have stopped growing.

"The place is gorgeous! As spotless as ever," Pat Ingersol said, inspecting Barbara's terra cotta pots, under which not a speck of mud or humus lay. "You could eat off of these bricks! I can't seem to keep my patio neat, no matter what. While I'm sweeping up under one plant, another is dropping its leaves. And my house is worse!"

"I could come over and help," said Barbara. "Really, I'd love to!" She had continued to protest until she realized they were all looking at her as if she had two heads.

The girls were cheerful and noisy, as usual. Afterwards, she had taken the dishes into the kitchen and then gone out to walk a few of them to their cars, light-hearted from the good company - and also because, to be strictly truthful, a few of the girls were quite pigs, and there would be a lot of crumbs and other mess to attend to. The whole patio would need scrubbing down!

But while she and Pat were chatting about roses, Marie and Carmen had gone back to use the little girls' room. Or so they said – they were gone quite a long time. And Barbara could have cried when she saw what they had really done: cleaned up! Washed the dishes, wiped the counters, even swept all the cheese and cracker crumbs off the patio. You would never know anyone had been there.

It was all too much. Alone in her shining home again, Barbara wept as if her heart would break.

Finally, as the sun set, she got up and mixed herself a screwdriver. She hadn't much appetite and the orange juice, at least, was nutritious. While she was making it, the phone rang, and so unnerved was she at the sudden trill in the middle of such silence that she dropped the glass on the floor and broke it.

She started to pick up the shards, but the phone kept ringing, so she dropped them again and ran to answer it.

It was old Mrs. Cantor, reminding her of the Red Cross meeting next Tuesday at ten, and asking if she could come early to help set up the coffee urn and the tray of cookies. "What's the matter, dear? You don't sound quite like your usual, chirpy self," asked Mrs. Cantor. "Are you taking good care of your health?"

Barbara, touched, assured the octogenarian that she was fine. She hung up, went back smiling to the kitchen – and found that the glass on the floor had been removed, the spilt orange juice mopped up, and a new glass with vodka and orange juice left sitting on the counter, centered neatly over a cocktail napkin.

Feeling faint, she looked down at her hand. There was a little cut, right on her finger, new, from the broken glass. It was proof that this was not a matter of forgetfulness on her part – a glass really had fallen on the floor. Nor could the garden club girls be the culprits this time, nor Kelty.

Either someone was in the house playing tricks on her or she was really going crazy.

She checked the kitchen garbage pail. Yes, there were the pieces of broken glass, and several crumpled paper towels.

She stood, sucking her cut finger and thinking...

Then she picked up the glass with the orange juice and vodka, held it over the floor, and slowly, deliberately loosened her grip. The glass slid from her fingers onto the floor, shattering on the hard tiles.

Without picking it up, she went into the cupboard and took out the tin of flour. She took off the lid, tossed it on the floor, then sprinkled the flour all over the counters and sink.

Next, she took all the eggs out of the refrigerator and threw them, splat! splat! splat! against the cabinets. She took out peanut butter, and grape jelly for good measure, smeared them both all over the kitchen table. Sprinkled a bag of dry spaghetti over that, and a box of corn flakes.

In the living room, she ripped open three pillows and swung them around until everything was covered with feathers and loose cotton batting. Took the dishes out of the china cabinet, rearranged them in complicated stacks on the dining room table. Sprinkled salt and pepper over them.

She burnt newspaper in the fireplace and smeared the ashes all over the mirror above.

In the den, she turned the TV around backwards, tore up a magazine and threw the pages all over, took from the cupboard a couple of board games and three packs of cards, and tossed them, each in turn, up into the air. They scattered over everything.

After similar sabotage in the bathroom and Kelty's room, Barbara went back to the kitchen, got the bottle of vodka and one more glass, and carried them up to bed.

"I don't know why you're so worried," said Garnet. "It's not like she'll be able to sue you or anything."

At the cluttered kitchen table (which, unlike Barbara's, was always in that sorry state), they sat now over a very strange seafood concoction that Garnet had whipped up, and that Kelty had secretly dubbed "Low Tide at Three Mile Island." The conversation continued on the subject of the poltergeist spell.

"It just seems like a dirty trick to play," he said. "If it did work, I mean."

"From the way you describe things, it would serve her right," replied Garnet, spooning up something gray and limp.

"You don't understand this woman and how she is about her house!" continued Kelty. "She would go mad if there were something loose there, throwing furniture around and breaking her little knick-knacks."

"Teach her to be less materialistic," said Garnet between chews.

Kelty pushed back his bowl. "I think I should go over there tonight and make sure everything's all right."

"Well, it's up to you," said Garnet slowly, putting down her spoon. "However, as you know, these polts are easy to call forth, but very difficult to send away."

Kelty thought about that. "Would it be invisible?" he asked.

"No, probably not. Just hard to see. But still, it's something that could go very bad, unless you do it just right."

Kelty had stood up, and now he paused, looking down upon Garnet's badly parted mop of hair.

She looked up at him coyly. "You might need my help."

"I suppose I would," admitted Kelty.

"And I don't feel up to it right now. I have to be in the right mood, you know."

Kelty considered this, then asked, "When do you think you'll be in the right mood?"

"I have no idea," said Garnet. "It's sort of like cooking for me – I have to feel *inspired* – my resonant emotion being the creative or gestative urge." She pushed her empty bowl away. "My, that hit the spot," she said cheerily. "And now, how about some oxblood cheesecake? It's really good, you'll be surprised."

Kelty sighed and sat back down again.

It had been only five-thirty when Barbara had gone up to her bedroom; now, it was past midnight. She had drunk quite a bit – enough to nod off a few times but not enough to forget about what she had done downstairs – and how she would have to, sooner or later, go back down again to see what, if anything, had happened in her absence.

Enough time had passed now, certainly.

She had left the bedside radio on for comfort and company. Now, she switched it off and sat listening. The house was quiet.

She got out of bed, put on her robe and tied it, and ran her hands through her hair a few times. She found her slippers and put them on. She opened the door to the bedroom, stood listening again, then proceeded noiselessly downstairs. She stopped three steps from the bottom and switched on the light.

It was dreadful to look at, but wonderfully heartening at the same time – the living room, in a complete mess, just as she had left it. Feathers and batting scattered over the oyster shell carpeting. Smeared mirror. And on the dining room table close by, the dishes stacked exactly the way she had left them.

In the kitchen, joyfully, she ran her eyes over the sticky table, the mucky counter, the floor littered with glass and clotted with goo.

Oh, what a relief! There was certainly nothing wrong with her, or the house, either. It was all some mix-up, or some weird confluence of circumstances that had misled her into thinking that something bizarre was going on. Oh, what joy, to be reassured that everything was back to normal – *had* been normal, in fact, the whole time!

And, most of all, to see that now she really did have a big cleaning job on her hands.

"I'll let it go until tomorrow," Barbara said aloud, cheerfully. It was close to one in the morning now. What kind of neat freak would be cleaning at this time of night?"

She turned to go back up the stairs – and realized that she just couldn't do it. She just couldn't leave the house in such a state! She wouldn't be able to sleep, knowing that such a mess was downstairs.

"No," Barbara said. "If it takes me all night, I'm going to get this house back into shape. Other people might be able to live in a pigpen, but not me! I'm just not made that way." She went to her cleaning cupboard, took out the bucket and the whole box of rags. She would start in the kitchen, and work from ceiling to floor.

She had filled the bucket with soapy water and was just dipping her rag in when she heard a noise in the TV room.

It frightened her more in regards to her sanity than it did as a physical threat. The sound itself was not in the least disturbing or unusual – it was only that of the carpet sweeper going back and forth, back and forth over the TV room rug. And now she heard a voice, too, like the voice she had been hearing in her dreams: annoyed and querulous.

The voice stopped, and so did the carpet sweeper. But now Barbara heard footsteps, and the sound of the hallway cabinet opening and closing. Barbara put down the rag and carefully climbed off the stepstool – her knees were shaking, but she held onto the counter tight. Slowly, she walked into the TV room and switched on the lamp.

There was no one there. But the TV room was perfectly clean.

No board games, no cards on the floor or over her easy chair. The TV was turned around the way it was supposed to be. The magazine pages, too, were neatly piled together on the table.

And, from farther back in the house, down the dark hallway: the sound of that voice again, petulant and jeering. Barbara followed it. It seemed to be coming from Kelty's room. But, as Barbara approached, it stopped.

At the doorway of Kelty's room, she felt for the wall switch and turned on the overhead light. Nothing but four bare walls met her eyes. She went in and stood in the middle of the empty room, under the light. No one was there.

But just then, the door, which she had thrown open, pushed to a little. And behind it, in the corner, she saw a figure – a figure smaller somewhat than herself, but very familiar nonetheless – wearing neat little clogs on its feet that looked just like her clogs, and a head scarf like hers, and the type of tailored blouse and slacks she favored. The figure had its back to her – it was bent over and using one of Barbara's whisk brooms to sweep up some of the pillow batting that must have blown back behind the door. And it was talking to itself in a piping, nagging voice:

"Look at this! What a mess. Certain people should live in a pigsty, they really should. And expecting me to clean up after them – "

Barbara stood and stared as the creature straightened up, turned around, and fastened its little eyes at her. The two of them stood, staring at each other under the shadowy glare of the over-head light, for a full minute. Barbara, with a swoony bafflement, realized she was looking into her own face. Except for scale, she and this trim but sour-looking little lady were mirror images.

"Finally!" the tiny woman said in a singularly unpleasant voice that Barbara would have preferred to think was nothing like her own. "Decided to drag yourself out of bed? After I've gotten most of it cleaned up, of course. Where do you get the idea that my pur-pose in life is to follow you around and clean up after you? Do I look like your servant? *Do I?* "

Barbara backed off as the little *doppelgänger* came at her, arms familiarly akimbo, pushing its mirror face into hers, and delivering a non-stop torrent of abuse. Finally, feeling she'd go crazy if she heard another word, Barbara dodged and ran out of the room, es-caping from the sight of that face – but not from the sound of the voice, which shrilled all the louder, and in such familiar accents, after her:

"You should have to live with yourself, that's what! You should have to live with yourself!"

A Cure for Hypochondria

At three, while Candace was out getting groceries to stock the kitchenette, Larry, on an impulse, picked up the phone and dialed his ex-wife's work number.

"Shipping and receiving, this is Pauline speaking," she said.

"Pauline?" he hesitated, embarrassed all of a sudden. Why in the world, at a time like this, was he calling his ex-wife? "Pauline, this is Larry. I just called to say hi."

"Well, hi," she said, a bit suspiciously. "Where are you calling from?"

"Actually, you won't believe this, but I'm calling from a cabin overlooking the ocean, with a lot of pine trees all around. I'm at this real ritzy medical institute. Kind of like a resort hospital. My room's got all the latest equipment, *plus* a stone fireplace, wet bar..."

Pauline, who had kept silent on the other end of the line until this point, broke in – "A *resort* hospital?"

"Yeah. In Northern California. Some kind of alternative medicine place."

"You flew to California? For another medical consultation?"

Larry could hear the disgust in her voice, but he had something to say that would stop her cold. "Yes – and this time, I've been diagnosed."

"You're kidding," Pauline said. "You mean they actually found something wrong with you?"

"Yes, they have," Larry continued. "And one of the first thoughts I had, after the doctor told me, was: poor Pauline. My poor, poor ex-wife. All those years we were together, I was as sick as a dog. And you never believed me." He tsk-tsked, shaking his head. "You couldn't even find it in your heart to be generous and give me the benefit of the doubt. You *left* me."

"I left you after you won all that money," Pauline corrected him angrily. "You won the lottery, and you quit working. Before that, you were just a bit of a hypochondriac. I could live with that. But staying home all day with nothing to do, you imagined yourself getting sicker and sicker. When you tried to force me into pretending you were sick too, into *enabling* you, *that's* when I left you. And I didn't take a penny of your money, either!"

"All right, all right," Larry put in. "I didn't call to argue. I called to tell you that you were wrong. I *am* sick, very sick. I have poisons in my system, really bad poisons – unusual ones that none of those other doctors could identify. Now, this doctor..."

"What doctor?" asked Pauline tensely.

"I don't remember his name… It ends with a 'man,' I think. 'Hoffman' or 'Fineman' or something. Anyway, he diagnosed me properly. And not only that, but he's developed a treatment for it, too. They give you this medicine through an IV tube. The doc says I'll start feeling better immediately."

"And I suppose going to this institute was the idea of that fast little blonde number you call wifey now?" Pauline asked.

"Hey, don't disparage Candace," Larry said. "She loves me selflessly."

"She treats you like an infant!" Pauline broke in. "She fusses over you like you were a houseplant! Larry, she's an *enabler*," she said slowly, as if spelling it out for him.

"Pauline, Pauline," sighed Larry. "You've been listening to too much talk radio again. You learn a new word like that and all of the sudden you think you're a Ph.D. in psychology. Anyway, selfless devotion, like what Candace gives me, is something you could never understand."

"I understand, all right," murmured Pauline. "You're gullible enough to fall for anybody's line. Larry – " she said, suddenly very earnest, "Larry, listen – I'm kind of worried about you..."

"*You,* worried about *me?* A little too late, don't you think?" Larry laughed. He knew it was a rotten thing to say, but he couldn't help himself. This call wasn't going the way he planned it. He had thought that telling her "I told you so" would feel a lot better than this.

Pauline ignored the jibe. "Why don't you give me your number, Larry?"

"Uh, actually, I don't know what it is," he replied. "It's not printed on the phone anywhere."

"Then give me your address."

"I'm not sure of that, either," he replied sheepishly.

"Don't you even know where you are?"

"Listen – Candace handled all the travel arrangements, and she drove us here. I wasn't paying attention. I wasn't feeling well."

Pauline bit her lip to stop herself from telling him what a dope he was. Something in the pit of her stomach told her this wasn't the time for reproach.

But he heard it anyway. "I know what you're gonna say," he said, "And I don't want to hear it. I gotta go. My first treatment starts at four."

"Larry, listen, I don't think you ought to –"

"Pauline, Pauline," Larry interrupted. "Why can't you just wish me good luck? Say you're happy for me. Admit that you were wrong. Because you *were* wrong, you know. The doctor says my condition is very serious. Says I came to him just in time. You never believed it, but I was on the verge of dying."

Even if Pauline had a reply to that, it was too late. Larry had hung up – he had heard Candace's key in the lock, and now she was hurrying in with some groceries.

"Sweetie, I'm so sorry!" she cried. "They're so slow at that little store. The line took forever. I was worried sick about you the whole time!" She dropped the groceries on the counter and ran to him, felt his forehead, touched his hands. "What were you doing while I was gone?" she asked, looking at him closely.

"Oh, nothing," he replied.

Just then, there was a knock on the door. "Come in," Candace called, not letting go of Larry's hand.

The doctor entered, tall and distinguished-looking, carrying his medical case in one hand, and pushing an IV pole on wheels with the other.

That's odd, Larry thought. I've never seen a doctor carrying his own stuff around before. They usually have nurses or orderlies to do that.

"I can see you're not feeling too well, Mr. Conti," said the doctor. "You're looking even worse than when I saw you earlier. We'd better start your treatment right away."

He tied a rubber ligature to Larry's arm below the elbow and started looking for a good vein.

"Doc, I've been thinking," Larry said. "Maybe we should put this off for a little while..."

The doctor didn't look up from Larry's forearm as he swabbed it with alcohol and, removing a needle from its plastic sheath, slowly inserted it. Larry jumped. "Nonsense," the doctor was saying. "It's much too late to back out now."

He held Larry's arm down flat. Candace was still holding onto his other arm. He hadn't realized before how strong she was. Of course, she had always been the one getting plenty of gym time in while he was home, resting.

The IV began dripping briskly. He could feel the cold fluid running into his vein.

"Candace!" He turned to her helplessly. "I don't think I want to go through with this." She smiled at him serenely, distantly, as if he were a million miles away.

He began to feel that way, too. He couldn't move a muscle anymore. He was getting dizzy...

Through fluttering eyelids he saw Candace let go of his arm and quietly put her hand into that of the doctor's.

Now it all makes sense, Larry thought, drifting into unconsciousness. How Candace and the "doctor" always seemed to work so well together – how they always seemed to back each other up –

And how he, Larry, was no longer on the verge of dying.

He *was* dying.

The Bride in Black

(written after a visit to Winchester Mystery House, San Jose, California)

My grandmother was no stranger to hard work, and she knew what it was like to do without. She had grown up on a farm and, after marrying at the age of eighteen, had raised five children – all by herself during the two years Grandpa was away fighting World War I. There was a short, happy respite in the 20's, and then came the Great Depression. Only with the greatest difficulty had she and Grandpa been able to keep a hold of their little house. All in all, Grandma had had to skimp and save to make ends meet pretty much every day of the first fifty years of her life. Later, she inherited a little money from a rich aunt and things got easier. But she still stuck to her frugal ways.

Her one indulgence was in indulging us, her grandchildren. She let us run wild in her house, rifling through her sewing kit for craft supplies, carrying away her good blankets to string up pup tents in the living room, and playing carpentry shop with Grandpa's tools in the garage.

She was often exasperated with us, but never really angry – except one time that I still remember vividly. She caught us and a few of the neighbor kids in the darkened hallway, with all the doors closed, sitting on the floor around a Ouija board. I was holding a flashlight over it so we could read the messages that the spirits were sending us, and my older brother and sister were acting as "mediums."

Grandma almost had a fit. She sent the neighbor kids with their Ouija board home and then scolded us for a half hour until we were all in tears. When she finally felt she had gotten through to us, she brought us all into the kitchen, distributed cookies and candy all round, and sent us outside to play in the sunshine.

Later on, when we were older, she told us a story which explained why she had been so upset with us that day.

She was only sixteen when her parents sent her away to stay with a rich old lady who wanted a young companion. The old lady's name was Miss Tufte, and she lived in an amazing mansion near the farming town of San Jose, in the Santa Clara Valley. It was a large estate, really, with pistachio and almond orchards all around. The lady lived a retired life, but with all the trappings of a modern and gentile existence: fine clothes and furnishings, indoor plumbing, and an electric motorcar as well as a coach and pair. There were plenty of servants. Unlike most old maiden ladies, however, Miss Tufte was not constantly demanding attention from the local parson: she had other interests.

She was, in fact, known for her eccentricities. People spoke of these tolerantly because of her wealth, her advanced age, and the many disappointments she had had in life, although I can't now remember what those disappointments were. But her oddness was well-established at the start of Grandma's story.

Grandma's parents worried about all this when making the decision to send her forty miles away to work among strangers. But her school teacher, who had recommended her for the post, knew the old lady's housekeeper very well and had visited the estate. She assured everyone that there was nothing to worry about – Miss Tufte was just whimsical and adamant about having things her own way, as rich old ladies often are.

The coachman who picked Grandma up at the train station was polite but not talkative, and Grandma – her name was Rita, actually – was too much in awe of him to ask many questions as they drove down a bumpy, dusty backroad, turned into a long, well-tended private lane that cut through a grove of pecan trees, and passed through enormous iron gates into an extensive front garden.

When Rita caught a glimpse of the mansion, she didn't know what to think. It was in the Queen Anne style, a very popular type of architecture among the wealthy in that era. But, rather than one big house, it looked more like a jumble of houses pushed together and piled up, one on top of the other. It was all in yellow clapboard with green trim; the roof was redwood shingle; and, mostly, it was three stories tall, but there were parts of the structure that were only a story or two, and parts that were four or even five stories tall. The windows, trimmed with ornate gingerbread and curlicues, were of all shapes and sizes; decorative spires bristled from every rooftop and gable; and chimneys stuck out all over, nonsensically: some were so short that their smoke would have blackened the windows above them, had they even been able to draw!

Altogether, the house reminded Rita of the "castles" that the grocer's children sometimes made out of cracker boxes, potted meat tins, and old bottles. The house was a fantastic mix of stately grace and irrational whimsy.

The coachman drove to a side door where the housekeeper, Mrs. Arden, came out to greet Rita kindly. Soon, she was enjoying a sandwich and cup of coffee in the large, well-appointed kitchen, and watching the cooks and servants bustle around, getting lunch ready: first, for Miss Tufte, who generally ate alone in her rooms upstairs, and then for the army of servants and workmen who ate at all different times and in different dining rooms.

Mrs. Arden sat with my grandmother, drinking coffee and asking her about her background and what she knew how to do. She was friendly enough, but every time Rita tried to ask about the house in general or Miss Tufte in particular, Mrs. Arden changed the subject. Finally, she said, "You'll be meeting her this afternoon and then I'm sure she'll tell you all you need to know."

Soon after, Mrs. Arden went off to see about something else, and Rita had time to look around her. She noted that the house's odd architecture did not end outside but continued indoors: the kitchen was large but oddly shaped, with plenty of jogs and outcroppings in the walls that had no apparent function, and four different doorways that took a step or two, up or down, to enter. There were plenty of cupboards, but the sizes were not at all uniform and many of them looked too small, too shallow, too high up, or too low down to be of much use.

As Rita's eyes ranged over all this, she noticed a round, putty-colored face, which at first she took to be a decorative wood carving, sticking out among the cupboards, high up in the wall opposite her. The eyes were looking downward, right at her. She studied it for a moment or two, then turned to see if any of the servants might be unoccupied and able to answer her question about the meaning of the carving. But they all seemed very busy. And, when she looked at the carving again, the face was gone – there was a closed cupboard door where it had been.

Rita exclaimed, and one of the *sous-chefs* turned to her and put a finger to his lips as if to warn her to say nothing.

The face did turn out to belong to Miss Tufte, whom Rita met an hour later, after being led by Mrs. Arden for what seemed like a mile through narrow hallways which, annoyingly, went only a few feet before turning right, then a few more feet before turning left, then turning right again, then turning left again; that went up stairs and then down and then up again in an entirely nonsensical way; and that passed through room after room, some filled with furniture, some bare, and some only half-built, with exposed wall studs and half-laid floors. None of the rooms were occupied, except for the occasional servant or carpenter.

They passed through these rooms and up a wide, carpeted stairway, where Rita was surprised to see, set upon every other stair, a small bowl of fresh milk.

"Does Miss Tufte have cats?" Rita asked.

"No," said Mrs. Arden.

"What are the bowls of milk for, then?" Rita persisted.

"Those are to keep away the small demons," Mrs. Arden said shortly.

And, of course, Rita didn't know what to say about that, so she said nothing.

At the top of the landing, they passed under a heavy garland of some kind of branches and small, green fruits which gave the whole hallway a pungent smell, and which, Mrs. Arden now offered, were there to "keep off the larger demons."

And, on either side of the double doors at which she now

knocked sat a China lion as tall as Rita herself, with a great vase between its paws in which were more fresh branches with red ribbons tied to them. Mrs. Arden whispered that these were to welcome the good spirits.

Mrs. Arden's knock was answered by a command to enter, and they came forward into a large and beautiful parlor, with deep carpets and flocked wallpaper, crowded with furniture and curiosities that looked to be from Egypt and other strange places. An old lady, dressed in black, who did indeed have a round, putty-colored face, sat in an armchair next to a hearth in which a small fire burned.

"So, here you are at last," Miss Tufte said in a genteel but noncommittal voice, barely looking at Rita. She closed up a paperbound book, which appeared to be some sort of almanac, and put out a small, plump hand as if to shake my grandmother's, but then motioned instead to a chair nearby. My grandmother sat down. "Rita – Rita Stul, isn't it?" Miss Tufte asked. "R-i-t-a, S-t-u-l, it is?"

"Yes, Ma'am," said my grandmother.

"And your age?" asked Miss Tufte, glancing at a man with unkempt hair, sitting in a corner, who was writing in a notebook.

"Sixteen, Ma'am," Rita said.

There was a pause while Miss Tufte looked at the man in the corner, who continued to write. Then he looked up and nodded.

"Fine, fine," said Miss Tufte, turning back to Rita. "I'm sure you'll do excellently. I'm sure she'll do, Mrs. Arden," she nodded to the housekeeper. "These are my good friends, Mr. Shepard and Mrs. Hainsley," Miss Tufte continued to Rita, gesturing towards the man in the corner, who nodded again curtly; and to another chair in a corner, in which sat a large woman with a white, somber-looking face. Mrs. Hainsley looked up absently, nodded at Rita, and went back to a sheaf of papers she was examining.

"There is just so much going on right now. Developments, Mrs. Arden," Miss Tufte said to the housekeeper, who was still standing at the door. "Developments of great portent. Signs, I'm afraid, of – of – developments."

"Oh, dear," said Mrs. Arden mildly.

"Mrs. Hainsley is double-checking," Miss Tufte rushed on, her voice rising. She was speaking to no one in particular, and she fixed her gaze upon some imaginary point in the distance, the way shy people do when making a public address. Miss Tufte had been, my grandmother told us, a beauty in her time. In her wedding photos, she looked plump and sweet and a little simple, like a fluffy, white kitten. Her manner in these latter days vacillated between timidity and imperiousness. "I am most careful about these things, it may be noted," she continued. "Someone once called me gullible. I am anything but! I have everything checked and double-checked most carefully. At the moment, Mrs. Hainsley is checking Mr. Shepard's results. He knows it, and doesn't mind. And I have him check Mrs. Hainsley's results. She doesn't mind. How is it looking, Mrs. Hainsley?"

"Not good," murmured Mrs. Hainsley grimly. "Can I get something to eat?"

"Certainly, certainly. Anything, if it helps you concentrate! Mrs. Arden?"

Mrs. Arden nodded and turned to leave.

"And take this young thing with you for now," cried Miss Tufte. "I'm quite happy with little – "

"Rita," my grandmother said.

"Little Rita, yes. But Developments..." Miss Tufte raised her hands helplessly. "Instruct her in the Precautions, Mrs. Arden. I will send for her later. I fear – I fear..."

Miss Tufte stopped abruptly as if she heard someone calling, though no one had – no one, at least, that Rita could hear, and she and Mrs. Arden went out of the room.

"She's very..." my grandmother began.

"Yes," agreed Mrs. Arden decidedly.

"And – perhaps I shouldn't mention it, but I saw Miss Tufte looking at me through a little window in the kitchen – "

Mrs. Arden leaned towards my grandmother and said in a low voice, "Yes, she does that. She likes to keep an eye on things. You have to be careful about what you say and do around here. But we know most of her little tricks, and they don't bother us much. You'll get used to them, too, in time."

"What are the Precautions?"

"I'll show you. You'll learn them," replied Mrs. Arden, walking ahead, "in time. There are quite a few of them."

They continued down the hall, away from the main staircase.

Mrs. Arden now opened the door of a little room at the far end, just before the servants' stairs. This room, on the same passageway as Miss Tufte's suite but two doors down, would be Rita's. Miss Tufte's personal maid, Bertha, and the other servants slept upstairs, on the third floor. Rita's room was a small chamber, plain and simple, but pleasant enough, with a window facing east, a single bed, a dresser, washstand, and fireplace – in which, once again, Rita was surprised to see a coal fire burning.

Mrs. Arden took from the dresser drawer a little bound notebook, in which was copied out a list of instructions.

"'Number one,'" read my grandmother, taking the notebook from Mrs. Arden, "fires in hearths must never be allowed to burn out."

"They ward off the bringers of evil, whose preferred mode of travel is up and down chimneys," explained Mrs. Arden, smiling apologetically. "It gets a bit hot around here in the summer, but she does insist."

"'Number two, bell must be rung at midnight and two o'clock *ante meridian.'"*

"The bell in the bell tower – McGraw handles that, but we must all know each other's duties in case anyone forgets or falls sick. The bell serves to call the spirits from their haunts. What with all the seances and all, they tend to accumulate during the day, and the bell recalls them to the netherworld."

"Oh, dear," said Rita. "I thought the fire and milk and everything kept the spirits away."

"Not the good spirits. Miss Tufte summons the good spirits to advise her and tell her the future. But, unfortunately, once you open the door, the undesirables sometimes slip through."

"Hmm, what an uncomfortable thought," continued Rita. "'Number three, no man in my employ shall grow a beard or mustache, and visitors with facial hair must enter the house backward...!'"

"The spirits don't like facial hair, it seems. It disturbs the ether or something. I'm not quite sure."

"May I ask you something, Mrs. Arden?"

"Yes?"

"Do you believe in the spirits, too?"

The housekeeper laughed and whispered, "Of course not, but don't ever ask me again. We must all be very serious about it, and at all times follow every item in this book to the letter. Believe me, the ruckus that's raised when she finds something not done, or done improperly...!"

"But keeping the fires going all day and all night, even when there's no one in the room – the whole house might burn down!"

"Well, now, we must remember it *is* her house, and if she wants to take the chance, who are we to say otherwise? Of course, we all do worry about fire, but it's one of those things you learn to live with, like the earthquakes. You were born here in California, I expect, but me, being from back East – it took me a while to get used to the ground shaking under my feet and pots and pans flying around, I can tell you! But I've learned to live with it, and the fires, and the spirits. It just takes time. I daresay we'd all get out in time if anything did happen. And most of the other Precautions are harmless. Taken as a whole, she's a good enough mistress, and we're paid very well."

Rita shook her head. "I just wonder what our pastor back home would say about all this."

"He'd say," Mrs. Arden whispered, "that she's a dotty old lady with more money than sense. And you need this job, I suppose. There's no harm done in indulging her, I'm sure."

Well, my grandmother tried to settle into the routine at that house, but there was no routine to be had. It came out that she had arrived at a bad time, Miss Tufte being completely unsettled by some shadowy upcoming event predicted unanimously by all the divines in her employ. The servants all agreed that they had never seen the old lady so nervous. At all odd hours, she held meetings with seers and prognosticators, seeking various means of discourse with the spirits, whom, she claimed, she could feel hovering around her, trying urgently to speak.

It had been her habit for many years to base all her decisions on advice from the spirits. The odd architecture of the house was due to influence from that quarter, for whenever the spirits became restless, they demanded additions or changes to the structure, based on their own otherworldly sense of esthetics and the ethereal patterns in which they traveled. My grandmother, as it turned out, even had the spirits to thank for her employment: they were the ones who had demanded that Miss Tufte's new companion be exactly sixteen years of age and hail from "the North."

At first, Miss Tufte used Rita mainly for double-checking columns of numbers, the results of some complicated formula that translated people's names, the weather, and other factors into mathematical quantities. When Miss Tufte saw my grandmother had a knack for such things and worked quickly and quietly, she began to rely on her more, having her take notes on important meetings with spiritual advisors and read to her from books on predicting the future and warding off bad luck.

My grandmother soon came to regard Miss Tufte, as the housekeeper had suggested, as merely a dotty old lady whose beliefs did no harm except to her own pocketbook: the constant building and renovating, the housing and feeding of the mediums, not to mention the crossing of palms with silver, must have added up to a hefty sum. But, though Rita felt at times a dangerous inclination to laugh out loud at some of the messages that came through from the other world, the thought of what Miss Tufte would do if she so much as smiled made her feel appropriately solemn once more. Just to watch the old lady as she sat greedily taking in each and every word, grunt, and gesture from the mediums was enough to remind her how deep and absolute was Miss Tufte's belief that the spirits were indeed present and struggling to communicate with her.

The dire predictions of upcoming disaster didn't worry the household staff. The gardener's boy, who was actually a student of engineering taking a break from classes at Stanford, said that it was a matter of group hysteria; that the mediums all fed off each other; and that, after the first had predicted a small mishap, the second, not to be upstaged, predicted a larger one; the third an even larger one, etc., etc.

"But what if they're right?" asked one of the maids, a nervous girl.

"They've never been right before," snorted McGraw, the gardener. "Why should they be right now?"

The rest of the servants laughingly agreed.

On the other hand, sometimes the situation did make Rita uneasy. It was one thing to stand outside in the garden, laughing at the jibes of the irreverent Mr. McGraw and his assistant, and quite another to sit listening above-stairs, in the gloom of the stuffy, muffled, overheated parlor. And when, at times, my grandmother felt a creepy sensation that she and Miss Tufte were *not* alone, she couldn't laugh it off as well as she would have liked.

One afternoon, my grandmother had a bad scare. Mrs. Hainsley, who had been the scheduled fourth for that afternoon's seance, had a migraine, and Rita was ordered to take her place. Well, she had already assisted a few times before and, though at first she had found the experience disconcerting, she now had little interest in it either way. There was no reason to expect anything other than the usual cryptic warnings.

Miss Tufte had Rita draw the heavy drapes in the sitting room, making it dark except for the light from the fire. And then Rita helped Mr. Shepard rearrange the furniture. Mr. Shepard was today's facilitator, and very picky about these things, and insistent that everything be in synch with the spirits' afore-stated preferences.

Then they sat down together around the seance table: Miss Tufte at the east end; Mr. Shepard at the south; Mrs. Chen, a specialist in Eastern astrology, to the north; and Rita to the west. There was nothing on the table, the cloth of which had been removed, leaving the bare mahogany exposed. At Mr. Shepard's direction, they joined hands and closed their eyes.

Several minutes passed uncomfortably for my grandmother, during which the only sensations were the touch of Mr. Shepard's and Mrs. Chen's hands on either side of her and the sound of Mr. Shepard's loud breathing. She didn't dare open her eyes, but felt unutterably sleepy in the warm darkness. Then, she began to feel annoying little prickles against her skin, sensations as if something were almost but not quite touching her. The sensations were quite maddening, but she couldn't pull her hands away to scratch herself. At last, Mr. Shepard spoke:

"Is anyone there?... Is anyone there?... Is anyone there?"

He chanted the call over and over, to no avail.

"We wish to speak to the Spirits..." he finally added. "We gather in good will... Is anyone there? Is anyone there? Is anyone – "

Suddenly, there was a loud knock on the table, which gave Rita a start and made her heart pound unpleasantly.

"Ah, welcome!" said Mr. Shepard with businesslike joviality. "And to whom are we speaking?"

A series of knocks ensued, which were either a code worked out in previous sessions or maybe the *lingua franca* between the two worlds – my grandmother had never been interested enough to ascertain.

"Sriman Singh, very good," Mr. Shepard said finally. "You remember Mr. Singh, Miss Tufte?"

"Yes," came the reply from the Eastern side of the table.

"Mr. Singh," continued Mr. Shepard, "Will you be so good as to answer some of the questions Miss Tufte has for you?"

The knocking reply came, which Mr. Shepard translated: "'Be... brief!' Yes, we certainly will. To come to the point: We have been receiving reports from the spirits of some impending unpleasantness. Can you tell us, what do you see for the inhabitants of this house?"

More knocks. "'*Disorder... catastrophe... chaos!*' – Oh, dear," continued Mr. Shepard, with somewhat complacent concern. "Should we – should we all leave this place?"

The reply came: "'*Devastation... cannot be escaped.*'"

"And what about the mistress of the house? What aura do you see surrounding Miss Tufte?..."

More knocks. "'*Black!*'" Mr. Shepard exclaimed, as if genuinely surprised at what must have been his own answer – for my grandmother never doubted that he or his accomplice was making the sounds. Still, whatever the cause, the effect was evident and troublesome: Miss Tufte began to breathe in loud, quick gasps. It was really too bad, thought Rita – they went too far.

"You mean, Miss Tufte will –" continued Mr. Shepard reluctantly, "– will soon be entering the realm of the spirits, which you now inhabit?"

And a single, violent thump averred, "'*Yes!*'"

Miss Tufte was rocking back and forth now and murmuring to herself in a whining but unintelligible voice. Frightened for her, my grandmother opened her eyes. The old lady's face was alarmingly white, her mouth twisted in fear, but her eyes were still shut tight. There was really nothing to be done about it – interruption would be considered unforgiveable until the ghost had had its say. And Rita was sure Mr. Shepard – or was it Mrs. Chen who was responsible for this latest plot twist? – one or the other of them, certainly, would soon come up with some recipe to forestall disaster. Neither of them would want to kill the goose that laid the golden egg.

"Is there anything Miss Tufte can do," Mr. Shepard now asked, "to avoid this turn of events?"

The knocking replied, "'*Nothing!*'"

Mr. Shepard paused, nonplussed, and then continued, "Come, come, Mr. Singh! I am sure you are playing with us. There must be *some* hope – "

The knocking came violently again: "'*No hope!... unless she... become another!*'"

"You are facetious, Mr. Singh!" Mr. Shepard retorted.

Beneath their arms, which rested on the table, a tremor now began, which grew in magnitude until finally the table was rocking violently, side to side at first, and then reeling on its pedestal. Rita cried out and tried to move away, but Mr. Shepard and Mrs. Chen held both her hands tight. The table continued to rock violently for perhaps a minute; then it fell back into place as if someone had finally let it go. Then there was another single, loud rap upon the table.

Mr. Shepard started and cried out, "Who's there?!"

"*I am the demon Bis,*" came the reply, not knocked out in code this time, but audible. Rita actually heard a harsh voice which seemed to come from the throat of Mrs. Chen, to the right of her, though Mrs. Chen's eyes were half-closed and her mouth hung open, slack. Rita knew it must be an illusion, some sort of ventriloquism; nevertheless, it was horrible to see and hear. The voice was deep and mocking, and it panted between its replies as if with a barely restrained violence. It frightened my grandmother badly, and she began to cry. Despite her trance, Mrs. Chen held her hand in a vice-like grip, much stronger than before.

Mr. Shepard seemed to be fighting to maintain his composure. He muttered something to himself, perhaps some incantation against evil, and then asked, "What do you have to do with us, Demon?"

"I await my time," came the gloating, guttural reply from the petite Asian mouth.

"I ask again," Mr. Shepard said, "what have you to do with anyone here? Begone!"

The voice laughed awfully. *"I await my time,"* it repeated. *"When the heavens fall and the fire is quenched, I will come to fetch my bride."*

"What? Who?" asked Mr. Shepard.

"The white-headed virgin – the bride in black!"

Once again came the laugh, gloating and cruel, and the table gave one last, malicious jerk. A crystal vase holding lilies seemed to jump up of its own accord from the mantlepiece and shatter itself on the hearth near Miss Tufte's feet. Then all was silent, except for the sound of my grandmother's loud sobbing, for she couldn't free her hands to cover her mouth until Mr. Shepard, exhausted and perplexed, announced, "It's over. We're alone."

He sat at the table, wiping his face with his handkerchief, oblivious to everything, and Mrs. Chen woke up from her trance as if from a healthful nap. She and my grandmother helped Miss Tufte, who seemed barely alive, away from the table and into her armchair. Servants were called, and after they arrived, Rita was finally allowed to leave.

She ran back to her room and had a good cry. She couldn't understand anyone subjecting themselves to such proceedings, even the crazy Miss Tufte. Surely the old lady had been as frightened as Rita was herself? Perhaps it had all started out innocently, but now it was definitely out of hand. The old woman might have died of fright.

After a time, my grandmother calmed herself by resolving never to take part in another seance or to have anything to do with Miss Tufte's spirits, ever again. Feeling better, she went downstairs to the kitchen.

Mrs. Arden took Rita into her private parlor that evening and, after sending out one of the girls to make sure Miss Tufte was still too ill to spy on them, listened to the whole story. She agreed that it was a shameful scene, and she approved of Rita's plan to refuse to co-operate in any further such goings-on. But then, she reiterated her opinion that there was nothing really to be alarmed about.

"You see it all the time in the newspapers, how these fortune tellers and mediums and such are just charlatans," she said. "They have a big bag of tricks. They make spirits appear and shake hands with you, or play the trumpet even! It's all done with mirrors and wires and things. That's why they insist on turning all the lights off."

Rita knew all this was true, but still, she went up to her bed that night reluctantly, regretting that, on the second floor, she was so far away from the rest of the household staff. Even though being dormered so close to Miss Tufte was considered a great social and career advantage, Rita would have gladly sacrificed this honor for the sake of some cheerful company. But there didn't seem to be any recourse.

That house was never silent at night. Besides the rustling of the fire in the grate, the house creaked and groaned continuously. Its unusual architecture often reminded Rita of an old Gaelic drawing she had once seen in a book. It had featured men and animals with fantastically long arms and legs that twisted and tangled together, stretching all around the edges of the page. In just the same way, Rita thought, the house seemed twisted and tangled and stretched. At night, there was such a parade of thumps, thwacks, and twangs that she fancied the parts of the house trying to free themselves from each other. These noises had not bothered her much before, but now she lay awake and listened to the boards shiver and moan up the hallway, down the stairway, down in the parlor, and then suddenly – crack! – on her own bedroom floor. All this, as well as her thoughts, kept her up for some time that night. Finally, exhausted, she fell asleep.

But then she was bothered by strange dreams. As she lay flat on her little bed, she felt as if it were slowly spinning. When she sat up, the bed jolted to a sudden stop. Or so it seemed. This happened two or three times.

She thought the problem might be related to the glass of wine that Mrs. Arden had given her and, turning on her side, fixed her eyes on the window of her room. This looked out on the usual jumbled assortment of walls, gables, and chimneys, a scene which was hardly restful, but which at least provided a view of a fixed distance. But then, dropping off again, Rita dreamt of an ugly little face, pressed up against the window glass, looking at her. Soon, there was another, and then another, each stranger and uglier than the last, crowding up with their noses, cheeks, and lips flat against the windowpane – some solemn, some smirking, all staring at her with large eyes popping out of their oddly shaped little heads. Their hands, too, with long, crooked fingers, pushed against the glass and grasped at the window frame, as if to tug it sideways. And, as they pushed, the room itself began to spin, turning away from the first faces outside the glass, toward a multitude of faces surrounding the whole house; all taking turns keeping it spinning, and all craning their necks for a peep at her inside her little room.

Needless to say, Rita slept poorly that night.

Later, she learned that, after the seance, Mr. Shepard and Mrs. Chen had stayed in consultation with the barely conscious Miss Tufte. They refused all food – a thing unprecedented in all the time since the first otherworldly consultant had descended upon the house – but had frequent recourse to the liquor cabinet. Bertha was called to fetch smelling salts and cold compresses. She reported to the others that Miss Tufte looked near death already, and that the prediction was close to making itself come true.

But finally, towards midnight, the mood in the sitting room changed. Some conclusion seemed to have been reached, and a plan of action settled upon. A hearty cold supper was ordered up and made short work of. When the serving man came back from delivering the dessert tray, he reported that Miss Tufte seemed to have regained her equilibrium and was even smiling at some small jest Mr. Shepard had made.

The next morning, Miss Tufte called Rita in to write some letters for her. The content of the letters was no different than usual, and Miss Tufte, if anything, was more friendly and encouraging than she had been on previous days, but my grandmother was a bit worried by the odd, appraising way Miss Tufte kept looking at her.

"You are about my size," the old lady finally said in a musing voice. "And your pretty blonde hair –" (my grandmother had very fair hair, almost tow-colored) "– would be set off well by black. I have a few nice silk dresses that I no longer want. I will make a present of them to you."

"Thank you, ma'am," said my grandmother, though she really didn't like the idea of wearing such heavy, old-fashioned costumes.

Later that afternoon, Bertha brought an armful of Miss Tufte's clothing and dumped them on my grandmother's bed. "You're to wear these tonight, lucky girl," the maid said. "Express orders."

At supper, Miss Tufte nodded her approval of my grandmother's new look and told her that she wished her to continue wearing the dresses.

"From now on?" my grandmother asked, surprised.

Miss Tufte exchanged glances with Mr. Shepard, who was having supper with them, then turned back to Rita and said, "Yes, from now on. And your hair – ah, Mr. Shepard, weren't you saying something about Miss Stul's hair?"

"Ahem – yes," said the mystic, after swallowing the remains of a mouthful of roast pork. "I was commenting that her hair would look very well if it were worn up – something like yours, Miss Tufte."

"I think so, too," said Miss Tufte. "Tomorrow morning, I'll send Bertha to show you how." And the old lady closed her mouth tightly, in a way which suggested that the matter was settled.

Well, this was an era, my grandmother explained, in which an employee did not argue with her employer, no matter how eccentric or personal the demand. And so Rita had no choice but to accede to Miss Tufte's wishes, and to let Bertha dress her hair in an ugly bun, nearly on the top of her head, and so severe that it made her ears (or so she imagined) stick straight out sideways. It was humiliating, and my grandmother cried about it, and worried about what the gardener's boy might say.

But that wasn't the end of the strange changes. That evening, Miss Tufte called Mrs. Arden to her bedroom, and later, while Mrs. Arden and a couple of the maids were busy pulling up bed linen and transferring clothing and boxes, Miss Tufte told Rita that she had decided that her bedroom was too cold at night, and that the two of them should exchange rooms.

And at the breakfast table the next morning, they exchanged places.

Well, of course, my grandmother realized what Miss Tufte was up to: that she was using her as some kind of substitute or decoy to confuse the spirits. She was angry, but her pride wouldn't allow her to show it, and she acted as if she didn't suspect a thing. Mrs. Arden agreed with this course of action, and said that Rita should simply ignore the whole thing.

It wasn't so easy, though. Maybe it was the summer heat, made worse by the fires and the heavy clothing she now had to wear; or maybe it was spending so much time, as she did now, with Miss Tufte in her parlor, adding up more columns of numbers, or copying out long passages of books on spiritualism, or just sitting, waiting for Miss Tufte to think up some other type of busy work – because it did seem that the whole point was simply to keep her in the room. Whatever it was, my grandmother began to feel very ill, and melancholy, and uneasy. At night, in Miss Tufte's pretty bedroom, with eucalyptus logs crackling in the wide fireplace, she would have the dizzy spells again, even without the wine; and she would feel that the room was moving around her, and that she could see faces and hear whispers outside the windows, which had to be left open all night because of the oppressive summer heat.

All in all, she was very miserable, and despite the good salary, and how much her family needed it, she didn't know how much more she could stand.

But the days did pass, as they always do. That last seance which my grandmother attended, the one in which the Demon Bis had supposedly spoken, had been in the last week of July. Now it was the middle of a hot August night. Rita had fallen asleep quickly, worn out by another day's abundant tedium and strain. She was still asleep and, as she tells us, lying on her stomach in Miss Tufte's huge mahogany bed, dreaming of her aunt's farm, and of trotting along on her cousin's pony, Nick. Then the dream shifted and Nick turned into a table, and suddenly she was back at the seance again, with the table shaking – except now she herself was on the table, lying on her stomach, and being tossed around on it while Mr. Shepard, Miss Tufte, and Mrs. Chen watched with clinical interest.

She woke up from this nightmare to find that the bed beneath her really was shaking violently. There was a terrible roaring sound, and the sound of breaking glass as Miss Tufte's perfume bottles and *objets d'arts* fell, one-by-one, onto the parquet floor. The lamp stand fell over, and the heavy mirror on the wall came down and shattered glass all over the dresser, which went on hopping and dancing as if in celebration. Added to this, the irregular tolling of the bell in the tower, sometimes loud, sometimes barely heard, announced without the aid of human hands that this was an earthquake, and a severe one. She sat up in bed, not knowing what else to do besides stay put: she was more likely to be crushed by falling objects if she ran, or at the least to cut her feet on broken glass.

Meanwhile, innumerable splintering and cracking sounds signaled the damage that was being done to the structure of the house itself. In the stables, frightened horses neighed, and from above came the voices of the servants calling to each other, some frantic, some in control and advising calm. And from her own floor, down the hall, in the direction of Miss Tufte's room, Rita heard terrible shrieks.

After a while, the shaking turned into an unpleasant swinging, which made Rita nauseated again. Soon after, however, the swinging died down, and the movements stopped altogether.

Later on, from outside the house, Rita was able to see the results of this mighty event: walls separated, chimneys broken, and turrets pulled away from their bracings and leaning into thin air.

But there was no time for looking around now. Outside, the dawn was just breaking, and there was just enough light to see by. Rita got carefully out of bed, put on her dressing gown and a pair of walking shoes, and then hurried down the hall to Miss Tufte's little room, inside of which the old lady was having noisy hysterics.

Rita grasped the doorknob, turned it, and tried to push the door open, but she couldn't. The door was not locked, but neither would it budge.

"Miss Tufte, Miss Tufte!" my grandmother called. "Come and open the door!"

The old lady didn't reply, though she stopped screaming. Instead, she was babbling to herself, some sort of prayer or incantation.

Meanwhile, one of the manservants came up behind my grandmother and tried the door. It wouldn't open for him, either, though he put his whole weight against it. He stood back, looked at the door frame, and pointed out that it was no longer at right angles with the door. The door was jammed into the frame – it could no longer swing free.

While Miss Tufte alternately babbled, howled, and moaned, other men came and speculated on what could be done: would a jack help? or would it make more sense to cut through the door? or even the wall? There was no lack of carpenters and workmen in the house, thank goodness, but this turned out to be a double-edged sword since, between them, the men couldn't seem to come to an agreement as to the best course of action. And the noise Miss Tufte was making on the other side of the door made it hard to debate the issue calmly.

Meanwhile, the rest of the house had to be attended to as well, whether its mistress was in a state to care about it or not. The cook and the plumber bustled down to see about the stove and gas pipes, and the butler called to the maids to fetch buckets of water and go around to all the rooms, putting out the fires in all the hearths lest scattered coals or a broken chimney cause the whole house go up in flames.

Someone went outside to see if Miss Tufte could be reached through her window, but this was found to be too risky, since the bell tower nearby had toppled and was now leaning precariously against a roofline; and besides, the whole ground below the window was littered and piled with broken glass and fallen bricks.

But this talk of windows reminded Rita of another opening she had noticed in the little room when she had slept there herself. It was yet another one of the eccentricities of the house, just a framed hole with a shutter, really, set in the wall between the room and the servants' stairs behind it. Rita ran to the stairwell and pushed its little door open, but the hole was so high above the level of the stairs that, even standing on tip-toe, she could just see the top half of the room: and only a part of the room at that, because the wall with the little window in it was set back behind a jog in the bedroom wall, making it easy to see out from the room but difficult to see in.

My grandmother called to Miss Tufte through the little hole, but Miss Tufte did not answer. She seemed busy doing something on the floor next to the fireplace. Suddenly, Rita understood – the fire in the hearth had burned low, and Miss Tufte was trying to relight it!

"Miss Tufte, don't light a fire!" Rita cried, remembering what the men had said about the fallen bricks. "The chimney might be broken!"

Miss Tufte would not reply, and kept busily at what she was doing. By her moans and ejaculations, it was clear that the fire would not catch, and that the old lady was in despair about it. My grandmother couldn't make sense of this until she remembered the seance, and the prediction that "the fire would go out," and that this event would be a precursor to the appearance of the Demon Bis.

Rita redoubled her efforts to get through to the old woman, who continued to ignore her and to cry over her fire. She had had just enough success in lighting it to fill the room with smoke. Miss Tufte began coughing violently and Rita herself had to move away from the window to get a breath of air.

Suddenly, Miss Tufte gave a loud shriek. Rita still couldn't see what was happening but assumed she had gone into hysterics again, or maybe had caught her dress on fire. She kept calling to her to keep calm, and to take what water was left in the carafe and use it to put out the fire, but to no avail; and soon Rita covered her ears, because the things Miss Tufte was now crying out between her screams were horrible: blasphemous prayers, dreadful promises – frenzied words of supplication to the Demon Bis.

Hearing Miss Tufte's screams, much more horrible than anything that had gone before, one of the men had finally taken an axe to the door. The other men joined in, and soon they had made a break big enough to fit through. They got through the opening only a minute or two after the last sounds from the room had ceased.

They were relieved to find the fire that Miss Tufte had tried to light had never taken and was now out. It was clear the chimney had sustained a lot of damage: several bricks had fallen down from the fireplace into the hearth. They opened the window, which the earthquake, in its idiosyncrasy, had left intact, and cleared the room of smoke.

But Miss Tufte herself was nowhere in sight. Mrs. Arden checked in the wardrobe and my grandmother knelt down to look under the bed, but they found nothing.

It was the men examining the chimney who found her: she had somehow climbed up into it and been caught, quite high up, in the part of the flue where it was narrowed by the shifting of the bricks.

They had quite a time pulling her out. It seemed she had wriggled up there with such determination that she was "tight as a cork," as they put it. At first, it was necessary to be careful; but when they felt the body going cold, they knew there was no point in worrying any longer. They tugged Miss Tufte out and laid her on the bed.

The doctor came some hours later. My grandmother was called upon to give testimony to what she had seen through the little window, and to affirm that, as far as she could make out, there had been no one else in the room with Miss Tufte at the time of her death.

The doctor was busy with more important things and had no time to unravel mysteries. He declared the cause of death to be myocardial infarction complicated by dementia praecox – which meant that, in his opinion, Miss Tufte, already feeble of mind, had lost her wits completely in the earthquake and attempted to escape out of the room through the chimney. The exertion involved in this had overtaxed her heart and killed her.

He had no explanation for the questions the men asked him, about how she had managed to climb up the chimney with both hands raised so high above her head; and of how, in that posture, she had managed to climb up so far, to where her clean, bare feet dangled nearly four feet above the hearth.

My grandmother scoffed at modern psychology, which denies the existence of demons and devils, and which prefers to believe that the most monstrous acts – of disgruntled loners shooting into crowds of strangers, of men murdering their sleeping families or, for that matter, of old ladies stuffing themselves up chimneys – are committed by the mere individual. To her, it made more sense that a sort of teamwork is involved, and that a perennial Evil hovers over all of us, especially the most vulnerable, ready and waiting to be of use. According to my grandmother's version of events, Miss Tufte, in her desire to avoid suffering and arrange her own destiny, welcomed a power into her house that she couldn't control. And, in the end, that power came and claimed her as its own.

Old-fashioned ideas, yes; but ones born of experience. And so, we were never allowed to play with Ouija boards.

La Llorona

Yolie sat on the stone bench in the cemetery, waiting for her boyfriend.

Since last June, this had been their secret meeting place. During the summer it had been a pleasure to feel the coolness of this corner spot, of the stone seat tucked deep and low under the canopy of a low-branching olive. But now, Yolie shivered and remembered that Autumn was coming.

She began to look around for a warmer place to sit. But suddenly it occurred to her: Jimmy might not see her in the accustomed place, might not realize she was waiting for him, and go back home. Better to stay where she was, after all.

She had been waiting for a long time now, maybe two hours. Soon, it would be completely dark. Impossible to go back for a sweater now, even if she had been willing to take the risk of missing Jimmy: the iron gate was closed. The Mission custodian had made his rounds long ago and had pulled the heavy, wrought-iron wings of the gate together, chaining and locking them, as he did every night. And, as usual, he had pulled down the iron ring that fit over the two front spikes of the gate, so that no one could squeeze in between, where the chain was slack. But he never gave more than a quick glance into the grounds to make sure there was no one inside, and never came back to this part of the church property until the next morning.

It was not very often that Yolie came here alone, hiding by herself behind the Italian cypresses until the custodian passed. Usually, she met Jimmy outside, and they entered together, either through the gate or else over the top, Jimmy helping her climb. Coming in by herself meant taking a risk, because she couldn't get out by herself. The walls surrounding her were six feet high, made of crumbly adobe and old lime plaster, impossible to scramble up – your shoes scraped off the sandy sides without finding a toehold. And as for the top, pieces of broken bottle had many years ago been embedded into it, all around. The only way she could get out now was by climbing the gate, and she wasn't very good at that. You had to stand on the narrow rails, sideways, only the edges of your shoes to balance on, then step carefully over the spiked top, one leg at a time, and jump down on the other side. With Jimmy's help, she could do it without hurting herself much. She had never tried it alone.

The eastern sky was dark and the red light was fading from the west over the Pacific, an hour's drive away. Yolie daydreamed about Jimmy and herself watching the sun go down at the beach – better yet, alone together on Catalina Island. He said he would take her there one of these days. They would ride down to San Pedro on his motorcycle and take the ferry. You could swim on Catalina, fish, hike, or ride bikes, Jimmy told her. Secretly, Yolie had thought she'd like to eat at one of those nice restaurants with an ocean view and go through the shops for souvenirs to bring home to her little sisters – combs and other things made out of shells.

She tried to pretend they were there now, lying out on the hot sand, but it was too cold and dark to imagine it properly.

He must be working late at the shop, she thought. His boss said he was a good worker. That counted for something, although not much to her mother and father. They didn't want their daughter spending time with an auto mechanic. They wanted her to get her bachelor's degree and marry a professional man with an even higher educational level – a doctor or lawyer, or an engineer. At their prompting, Yolie had asked the counselor for information about college, but her heart wasn't in it. She might be young, but she knew that her parents, who had never had much schooling themselves, were naïve to think a college degree would bring happiness.

Yolie sighed. Twenty years ago, a girl who just wanted to stay home and take care of her husband and babies would have been a source of pride to the family. Her grandmother, if she were alive, would have taken Yolie's part. It was her grandmother who had taught her about cooking and cleaning and how to take care of good linens, and those hours at Nana's little house had been some of the happiest times of Yolie's childhood. Her grandmother, though, would certainly have told her it was wrong to sneak in here at night with Jimmy. But Nana, she argued silently, I just didn't have the courage to come out in the open, to tell them I'm not interested in the kind of life they want for me.

Not until today, anyway – not until she had had to. There had been a terrible scene at home when she told them about the baby coming. Her father had said many hurtful things. Her mother had just cried...

She remembered that she mustn't think unpleasant thoughts now that she was carrying the baby. Nana had always said that. If she wanted the baby to prosper, she had to think happy thoughts. And, really, everything *would* be all right. Jimmy loved her and wanted to marry her. She would just have to persuade him to do it a little earlier than they had planned.

The last light was fading from the west and the cemetery would soon be left in darkness. She had never been afraid here before. Her memories of this place were good ones. Her family had come here every Sunday after Mass to lay flowers on her grandmother's grave. She remembered racing her sisters to this very bench, to get the best part of the shade before settling down to enjoy the donuts and chocolate milk their father would buy for them at the parish hall, *if* they had been good in church.

And this summer – the evenings she had spent here with Jimmy – they had pretended they were in a lovely private garden, their own, and that they themselves had chosen which trees to grow and what color rose bushes to plant.

But now, she was beginning to feel uneasy. It was very quiet. Outside the cemetery walls, she could hear the cars going by with a hollow sound, like rolling waves. It was a lonely sound. She tried to concentrate instead on listening for the purr of Jimmy's bike.

If she had not been so upset after the argument with her parents, she would never have come in first.

But, really, she was sure, everything would turn out fine.

She looked behind her, scanning the cemetery grounds. They were not very big – about the size of a grocery store parking lot. But the cemetery was very old. The oldest graves, those of the early priests from Spain, were in the Mission gardens on the other side of the church. Here, most of the markers dated from the first part of this century. Many of them held old black-and-white photographs of the deceased, encased in glass and embedded in the stone: smiling people dressed in their best clothes for studio shots. At the time the photos were taken, had any of the subjects been able to see into the future, to see the people standing at their grave, looking back at them? Yolie used to wonder. Her mother said they could see them now, from Heaven, or from Purgatory. It was good to say a prayer for them, wherever they were. She and her sisters had once tried to find which gravestone was the oldest, but they had never managed to reach a decision. She would have been glad to occupy herself with the task now, but it was too dark to read the markers, especially the old ones, which were mostly fashioned out of wood that was now disintegrating with age.

Yolie peered through the gloom. The wooden crosses were hardly visible but the later ones, made of white marble, almost glowed in the dark. Some of these had larger structures, miniature temples with pillars and statues of angels. And at the back wall, Yolie could see the old fountain which never really ran, though the pipes had leaked continuously for years. It seemed to refuse to be fixed – every time one leak was stopped up, another sprouted, leaving at least enough of a trickle for the birds to bathe in.

But now, as Yolie strained her eyes towards the fountain, she thought she could see a white plume of water spraying up from the middle of the bowl. There must be a patch of weeds or something growing there, she thought, that looked like a fountain spray. The sound of the traffic outside, too, seemed to have become more akin to the sound of rushing water. Or maybe the fountain really was working?

Just as the last light faded and darkness became complete, something moving near the fountain caught Yolie's eye. It was a young girl, stepping carefully between the grave markers, hopping over the flat ones embedded in the grass, and coming Yolie's way. She was wearing a frilly dress of yellow, with white polka dots and puffed-up sleeves that made her look like a child; although, as she came nearer, Yolie saw she was almost as tall as herself.

"Good evening," the girl said in Spanish. "It's kind of scary here in the dark like this, isn't it?"

"Where did you come from?" Yolie asked, surprised out of her manners.

"I was over there behind that tree near the fountain. I saw you a while ago and wanted to come talk to you, but didn't know if I should, until I saw you looking at me."

"But what are you doing here?" Yolie asked.

The girl hesitated, then said, "I'm waiting for someone. What are you doing here?"

"I'm waiting for someone, too."

"A boy?" the girl asked, smiling wisely.

"Yes. My boyfriend," Yolie replied with dignity.

"Me, too. I've been waiting a long time..."

Yolie didn't say anything. She had been waiting a long time, too, but didn't want to talk about it to a stranger. She wished the girl would go away, even if it meant being here alone. It would be very awkward if she were still here when Jimmy came.

"Don't worry," the girl said, as if reading Yolie's thoughts. "When your boyfriend shows up, I'll disappear."

Yolie didn't reply.

"...*if* he shows up," the girl continued, watching her.

"What do you know about it?" Yolie asked sharply.

"Well," the girl said in the same worldly-wise tone, "Men are men, you know. You can't rely on them for any length of time. They play their games with you until they become bored, then run off to find another game somewhere else."

"What do you know?" Yolie said again. "You're too young to be talking like that. If I were your mother, I'd wash your mouth out with soap."

"I'm not as young as I look," replied the girl. "I've had a lot of experience with men and, believe me, they're all alike. Even your boyfriend," she sneered. "You think he's different because he has blond hair? They're even worse."

"How do you know my boyfriend has blond hair?" Yolie demanded.

"I've seen you here before."

"You've been spying on us?!" Yolie raised her voice in anger and surprise.

"Oh, of course not. I'm not interested in what you do here. I have my own worries. I've just seen you around, that's all. And I can tell you: watch out for that one. He'll make you sorry."

Tears of anger and shame were rising in Yolie's eyes but, just then, she heard the sound of Jimmy's motorcycle pulling into the parking lot outside. She got up and ran to the gate.

There he was, tall and handsome in his motorcycle jacket and work boots. She reached her hand out to him through the railing and he kissed her fingers, then climbed easily over the gate.

"Came in without me, huh?" he asked. "Been waiting a long time?"

She nodded, waiting for her throat to loosen. She didn't want him to know she had been crying.

"Man, am I glad to see you," he said, hugging her to him as they walked toward their usual spot on the bench. Jimmy noticed Yolie rubbing her arms with the cold and helped her into his jacket. Then, putting his hands inside the jacket and pulling her to him, he kissed her again. "Let me warm you up," he whispered.

Then Yolie remembered the girl. "Jimmy," she said in a low voice, "There's someone else here."

"What?"

"A girl. She's in the cemetery. I was just talking to her."

Jimmy looked around. "Where is she now?"

"I don't know," said Yolie, looking around, too. The girl was not in sight. They got up and searched behind each tree and even between the rows of gravestones, but couldn't find her.

"Well, Babe," Jimmy said with mock gravity, "I think you've seen a ghost."

Yolie clutched her stomach in genuine fright. What would her grandmother have said about seeing a ghost when you're carrying a baby?

"Don't worry," Jimmy continued. "I'll protect you."

He sat her back down on the bench and started kissing her again, but she pushed him away.

"What's wrong now?" he asked, exasperated.

Yolie didn't say anything. How could she begin to explain? She was too upset, and she was sure that girl was somewhere near, watching them.

"Yolanda, darling," said Jimmy in his warm, persuasive voice. "I've been thinking about you all day, looking forward to spending this time with you. You don't know what it means to me." He put his arms around her again. "Sometimes I get scared, thinking you might not feel the same way."

"Oh, Jimmy, of course I do."

"Do you love me?" he asked.

"Yes," she replied breathlessly.

But after a while, she pushed him away again.

"Are you going to tell me what's wrong with you tonight?" he demanded, angry now.

"I just don't feel like it, is all," she said stubbornly, fighting back the tears.

Jimmy breathed in heavily, and Yolie could tell he was trying to keep his temper. "Do you want to go home?" he asked.

"No."

"Listen, Yolie, I've been up since real early. I don't have the patience for this... Are you going to tell me what's wrong with you or not?"

She couldn't answer.

They sat for awhile in silence. He tried to kiss her again, but she didn't respond.

"I don't need this," Jimmy muttered under his breath. "Do you want to go home?" he demanded again.

"No." He must be able to see how upset I am, Yolie thought. If he cares about me, he'll put my feelings ahead of his own selfish needs. Unless the girl with the yellow dress was right about men – and about Jimmy.

"I don't like little girls who play games," Jimmy said. "And I'm not going to waste any more time waiting for you to decide whether you're in the mood or not." He got up. "For the last time, are you coming or not?"

"No."

"So that's the only word you know now," Jimmy threw back at her as he strode off. "I guess I should be glad that I found out this early."

She was just about to burst into sobs when he turned and walked back to her. She lifted her face, wet with tears, hopeful. But all he had to say was, "Can I have my jacket back?"

Silently she slid out of it and handed it to him. "Thank you," he said coldly, and walked off. She watched him climb over the gate and drop down to the other side. A few seconds later, she heard his motorcycle revving up. The sound moved across the parking lot and down into the street, then slowly faded into the distance.

She could hardly breathe for crying now, her stomach muscles contracting painfully with each long sob, and all the while she was thinking, this is not good for the baby. But she couldn't help it. What could she do now? Where could she go? Not with Jimmy, and not back to her parents. She had told them she didn't need their help.

And she couldn't get out of the cemetery. Even if she had somewhere to go, it would be dangerous for the baby if she tried to climb over the gate by herself. She had refused Jimmy's help out of pride, but she should have thought about the baby first. Her father was right, she was completely irresponsible. She had nothing to give this baby: not a father, not a real mother. And the sin was her own, but the baby would have to pay.

Anxiety swept over her as she looked into tomorrow, the next week, the coming year. And tonight – how would she get through tonight?

"So, I was right about him," a voice at her side said. Yolie started up, frightened out of her tears. She stared at the girl in the yellow dress, and all the worries of the moment before were extinguished by a supernatural dread.

The girl grinned, pointing over their heads. "I was in this tree all the time," she said. "You never even looked up there." Her smile faded. "I'm sorry, but I couldn't help overhearing the whole thing."

Yolie was too frightened to argue with the girl, too frightened to think of what to do.

But the girl did not seem menacing now. Rather, she seemed touched by Yolie's tears. "I know I seemed harsh earlier," she said in a motherly tone. "It's just that I knew what would happen. I felt so bad for you! Come, sit down here and rest. Calm yourself. This is not good for the baby. Yes, I know all about the baby. I can tell by looking at a woman that she is with child."

She used the old-fashioned phrases of a Mexican midwife, the phrases Yolie's grandmother used to use.

"Please forgive me for being so unkind to you before," the girl continued. "It's just that I've been through all this myself, and I felt frustrated, watching the whole thing and knowing I couldn't help."

"You've been through this before?" Yolie asked.

"Oh, I know the joys and pangs of motherhood as much as any woman," the girl smiled with sad wisdom. Her face looked much older now. "And let me tell you a secret: men and children, they're both the same. They take and take from you, and they leave you with nothing in the end."

"No, it's not his fault! It's not the baby's fault," said Yolie. "I'm the one who made everything wrong."

"That's not true, Yolie," the girl continued with gentle sadness. "You did nothing but give of yourself. You made no mistake but being born a woman. It is the fate God made for us: to be mistreated, to be used up and discarded. When your baby doesn't need you anymore, he, too, will leave you and never look back. You will be old and sick, with nothing to live on, just able to scratch up enough to keep yourself alive, watching the world go by from some dark corner. And so the years will stretch on. This is all you have to look forward to."

Yolie sobbed noiselessly, her head buried in her hands.

"There is only one way out, Yolie, and you know what that is."

Yolie looked up in horror. "It's a sin to despair! It's a sin to – to – "

"The omnipotent Creator has not given you much of a choice," the girl replied calmly.

"How do you know all this?" Yolie whispered, staring. The darkness seemed to gather below the girl's eyes like black tears; the abdomen under the frilly yellow sash seemed scooped out, emptied.

The girl turned those empty eyes away from Yolie. "I am much older than I look. I have had dozens of men – been abandoned, the same as you, dozens of times. And," she added, waving her arm in a wide arc across the shadowy cemetery, "I have many children."

Suddenly the shadows lightened, and before them, in a vision, Yolie saw a room, lit up with pink and golden light. It was a play room, with toys, picture books, all manner of playthings strewn around the floor. On the floor and all over the room, children played – mere babes and older ones, some building with blocks, some playing tag or leapfrog, some feeding dolls with tiny bottles. When one would bump into another, or fall off its rocking horse, or get into some other trouble, kind, gentle arms reached down and lifted the child back to its feet tenderly, and a blue-veiled head would bend down to receive a kiss of loving gratitude in return.

For a while, the two girls watched together. Then Yolie's companion in the yellow dress called out to the children: "Babies! My babies! Here is your mother. I just want a kiss from you. That's all. Please."

But the children did not or would not recognize her voice. The girl moved forward, trying to walk into the vision. But, with each step she took, it moved farther away from her. And as she made an attempt to throw herself into the golden room, the vision shrank and disappeared, as if a window had been shut.

The girl, having fallen, lay on the grass for some moments, motionless; but then she turned back to Yolie, tears in her eyes. "They'll never let me come to them. They're too cruel! They don't love me! No one deserves to be treated the way I am. No one!"

With horror, Yolie stared at the girl. Stories that her grandmother had told her many years ago came vividly back to her – stories of a ghost who could be heard crying near running water – a woman ghost who cried perpetually because she had drowned all her children – *la Llorona*, the crying one.

The girl had gotten up and was coming closer to her now. She had seen the terror in Yolie's face. Now she would never let her get away. Slowly she approached the tree against which Yolie had backed herself. Yolie knew she could not run. She covered her face with her hands.

"Look at me," the girl commanded. And slowly, Yolie uncovered her eyes – she could not help it.

The shadow of vengeful anger had passed away from *la Llorona's* face. Once again, as she came closer to Yolie, she seemed merely to be a young and harmless girl. "I show you all this for a reason, darling," she said poignantly. "Not to scare you, but to show you that, just as I was right about your boyfriend, I know about babies, too. My babies had no father, like yours will have none. I had nothing to support them with, nothing to offer but shame and do-ing-without. I took their lives back because I didn't want them to suffer. I suffered more than they ever did. And now, look what they give me in return. They've had the angels bar the gates of Heaven against me, I'm sure of it."

"No – no," murmured Yolie. "You must ask for forgiveness –"

But she could say no more, because *la Llorona's* face was close to Yolie's own face now. It was like a yellow mask, and the eyes were like mirrors, and Yolie was overwhelmed by the darkness and the cold in them.

"I don't need forgiveness. I have found my own happiness," she said in a cunning voice. "Here, in this world. I am free to roam wherever I please, wherever water runs. And I have many friends. There are many other spirits like me – many right here in this cemetery, our given home. Come on! I'll show them to you!" She laughed, taking Yolie's arm. "They are not all as pleasant as I am to look at – some are quite horrible even – but I know you'll be polite. You are strong enough to stand it. Your baby, however..."

La Llorona began to tug Yolie away from the tree and farther into the cemetery grounds. But just as Yolie, unable to stop herself, took the first few steps with her awful companion, she heard a cry from outside the cemetery gate. Someone was calling her name.

It was Jimmy! She could see his figure standing at the gate. "Yolanda! Yolie!" he called again. "Where are you?"

The spell was broken. Yolie jerked away just as *la Llorona* tried to grab her by the hair. "Here I am!" Yolie screamed, run-ning terrified through the maze of gravestones to him. She heard a cry to fury behind her and realized that the demon was coming quickly behind her. "Help me up, Jimmy! Help me – !" she cried as she reached the gate and began to scramble up. Jimmy climbed up his side of the gate and, grabbing hold of her, tried to tug her up and over.

"Something's got you stuck!" he muttered as he pulled. Yolie kicked her legs in wild panic, clinging desperately to Jimmy with one arm, guarding her stomach with the other. "I'm so sorry, Yolie," Jimmy murmured in her ear, shocked by her terror, unable to pull her over or to see what was holding her down. "I love you, Baby, you know that. I'm so sorry."

Just as he said this, they heard a bitter cry, an animal howl, from the ground below Yolie's feet. Yolie, now free, clambered up and over the gate without regard to her footing, and would have fallen straight down onto the bricks below if Jimmy had not kept his hold of her. She slipped out of his arm, but slowly enough to break her fall and land her safely down onto the pavement.

It was not until several months later that Jimmy could get Yolie to tell him what had happened that night in the cemetery. She would not discuss it with anyone until after the baby was born, for fear of it being harmed by even talking about such things. Then, when she had delivered a perfectly healthy little boy, Yolie still didn't want to talk about it. She immersed herself in the affairs of a happy young housewife and new mother.

It wasn't until the proud grandparents' request to babysit over the weekend was granted, and Jimmy finally took Yolie to Catalina Island, that she told him the whole story. As they sat in the sun overlooking the round bay and its little blue and white boats, she told him the tale of *la Llorona* as her grandmother had told it to her, and of how she, Yolie, had found herself caught in the cemetery with this same evil spirit.

"You probably think I dreamt the whole thing," she said, glancing sideways at his face after she finished her story. He was a practical young man, and she expected him to laugh or to explain her experiences away somehow.

He had been looking out to sea, but now he turned to her, his face thoughtful and serious. "No," he said. "I don't think you dreamt it. Something unusual happened to me that night, too."

His story was brief. He had been too angry with Yolie at first to remember that she had trouble climbing the gate and getting out of the cemetery herself. Halfway home he had remembered, turned around, and ridden back into the parking lot. He had killed his motor, though, because he was still irritated and didn't want her to hear him if she had managed to get out herself. He looked through the gate and saw that Yolie was no longer sitting on the bench – in fact, was nowhere in sight. This must have been when Yolie was behind the olive tree.

He was just about to go back home when he saw a soft light

moving in the far right corner of the cemetery. It seemed to back up into the adobe wall nearby to him and fade away. He rubbed his eyes and tried to get a better look, but could see nothing else.

Suddenly, he was startled by an old lady standing at his elbow, dressed in black lace, with a lace mantilla over her head. The old lady said something to him in Spanish which, of course, he couldn't understand. But she was adamant that he do something: she kept gesturing at the gate, pointing to something inside, and crossing herself. Not knowing what else to do, and becoming infected by the old lady's anxiety, he had called out to Yolanda.

With all that happened immediately after, he forgot about the old lady. But if she had still been there, they would have noticed her, wouldn't they have?

"Did the lady have a cameo locket around her neck?" Yolie asked quietly.

"Heck, Yolie, I don't know! You know I don't notice those things," Jimmy replied. "I think she had something round and old-fashioned-looking hanging from her neck, yes."

"And she came from the northwest side of the cemetery?"

"Yes."

"Jimmy, don't you remember? I took you there once to see it. That's the part of the cemetery where my grandmother is buried."

Jimmy and Yolanda still visit the cemetery every Sunday and leave flowers on her grandmother's grave. But they make sure to come early, and they never linger after dark.

Three Candles

"I have here three candles," Ruben, reaching into his duffel bag, announced in the voice of a stage magician.

"So what?" chuckled Alfie, dragging his fishing gear in through the front door of the cabin. "Where should I put this stuff, Dave?"

"That's fine, just dump it all there," David replied. He was our host for this fishing trip: the cabin was his.

"You sure?" I asked. "I thought fishing gear was *verboten* in the house. I was going to stow mine in the barn, like your wife wants, but – "

"Beth's currently not in residence," David said. "She went off to some female relative's or other."

We all breathed a sigh of relief at that, though of course not out loud. Alfie was the only one with lack of tact enough to say, "All right! Let the good times roll!"

"Shut up, Alfie," I said, trying to make up for his indiscretion. "That's what *your* wife said when she saw you heading out the door."

Ruben, a bachelor, laughed. "Every time I get serious with a lady, I talk to you guys and get an anti-marriage booster shot. Is it really that bad?"

We all groaned loudly. Alfie stuck out his neck and pulled his sweatshirt back. "See these marks, man? She just took the choke chain off this morning."

Personally, I was already missing my wife, and I knew Alfie and Patty were crazy about each other. But of course, we couldn't admit that. And David's wife was another matter – a real nag, fussy about her surroundings, vindictive when you accidentally

123

said the wrong thing – none of us could ever understand what Dave saw in her.

Ruben was still standing there, holding up his candles with a mysterious smile on his face.

"Whatcha got there, boy?" Alfie asked after making himself comfortable on the sofa.

"I have here three candles," Ruben repeated.

"You already said that."

"They are no ordinary candles."

"Oh, yeah? They look ordinary."

"They are magic candles."

We all laughed. Ruben held a finger to his lips.

"You may well laugh," he continued. "But I met a weird old man down in the village coffee shop who seemed to know a lot about me."

"I bet he did," snorted Alfie. "Did he say you were a lying bum?"

"He told me a lot of things," replied Ruben thoughtfully. "I was impressed. So, when he told me to buy these candles off of him, I said, what the heck."

"Oh, magic candles!" cried Alfie. "I see! Uh huh. How much did you pay for them?"

"That, I was instructed not to divulge."

"Three for a dollar would have been about right," I put in. They looked like ordinary candles, the kind women put in candlesticks for dinner parties.

"You know," said Ruben, "my grandfather was a *curandero,* which is to say, a witch, or healer, in Mexico. The old man knew that. He also said I was an honest man who would try to bring the truth to light. Even though I feel that last part is true, it's vague enough that you could say he just made it up on the spot. But how did he know about my grandfather?"

"There are a lot of strange people living around the mountain here," said David. "There's some kind of New Age cult. They think the mountain is sacred, or has some mystical influence, I don't know. Beth's father is into that stuff, actually."

"Then, if these don't work," said Ruben, "I'll know who to get my money back from. The sins of the father-in-law..."

"If they don't work?" asked Alfie. "What are they supposed

to do?"

"Allow us to call up the spirits of the dead," replied Ruben, matter-of-factly.

David, Alfie, and I guffawed.

"If I were dead," David said, "I don't think I'd want anyone calling me up. I hate answering the phone even in this life."

"Hey!" said Alfie, grabbing Dave's shoulder. "That reminds me of a story, about this workaholic businessman who was accidentally buried with his beeper..."

"The idle prattle of unbelievers," Ruben said in an aside to me.

"...And so at the funeral, this thing starts going off, and everyone in the church is checking their beepers. And finally they figure out it's coming from the casket! And the dead guy's wife stands up and says, real exasperated, 'Will somebody please call his boss back and tell him Bob finally found time to die?!' "

"How do they work?" I asked, ignoring Alfie. "Do they all do the same thing?"

"No. This one," Ruben held up the yellow candle, "allows us to see the spirits. This one," he held up the dark green candle, "allows us to hear them. And this," he held up a deep russet one, almost the color of dried blood, "allows the spirits to materialize."

"Well, then, let's light up one of those babies and see it work!" encouraged Alfie. "Do you have any choice of who you get? Could you materialize some friendly chicks?"

"Yeah, we'll get you the Bride of Frankenstein. Where are the matches, David?"

David handed him a package of matches from above the fireplace. "Don't you have to say some magic words?" he asked.

"No, just light 'em up and watch 'em work," said Ruben, scratching a match to flame and touching it to the first candle, the yellow one.

"Get a candleholder or something," I said. "Dave's wife's gonna kill him if she finds candle wax on her coffee table."

"Oh, that's all right," said David. He said it kind of strangely and I was sorry I had said that in front of him – after all, no guy likes to admit he's afraid of his wife. So I found a candlestick myself on the mantle and handed it to Ruben. He turned the candle downwards, letting the wax drip into the bowl of the candlestick, then planted it firmly in. "Now," he said.

We were all four silent, watching the flame. "Obviously there's some draft somewhere," said David.

"Do we look into the flame, Ruben?" I asked.

"Come to think of it, I don't know," Ruben replied. And after a while, he added, "I don't see anything. Do you see anything?"

He glanced up at the rest of us. David and I grinned back at him, but Alfie, his eyes growing wide, said in a trance-like voice, "Oh my gosh!"

"What?" we all asked.

"Dead spirits – hundreds of them – all around us! The spirits of all the fish who've been murdered in this house!"

"Oh, just can it, Alfie!" I said.

"Their flesh seared, squirted with lemon, then consumed in an awful rite of gluttony –"

"Be quiet, Alfie," said Ruben, gazing at the candle flame intently. "I want to see if this works."

"Hey, he really believes in this stuff!" Alfie exclaimed.

"You would too if you had talked to that old man," Ruben replied.

"Maybe there's some psychotropic drug in the candle that's released when you burn it," I suggested. "Something that makes you see things."

"Oh, great, we'll be busted for possession of hallucinogenic candles!" cried Alfie. "My teenagers will love that!"

"Shut up and concentrate," Ruben said.

"On what?"

"Just concentrate!"

We sat, Ruben and Alfie on the couch, me in an armchair, David sitting on the edge of the coffee table with an amused smile on his face. The room seemed to grow darker as we stared at the yellow flame, and I realized for the first time that night had fallen. Sitting there in the dusk, our eyes had gotten used to the dark. The candle flame formed a little glob of hot light that danced, then grew still, then danced again. A minute or two passed and nothing happened, but no one liked to say anything because Ruben was still sitting staring, concentrating I guess, and we were all sort of in the habit of following his lead on things.

Finally, after about five minutes, he made a gesture of disgust and stood up. We all smiled to each other. "Looks like you got taken, pal," Alfie said.

"I don't know what I was expecting," Ruben replied.

"Hey, it's five-thirty," David said, getting up and switching on the lamps. "I'll heat up the vittles. Let's have a game of cards."

"We want to get to bed early," Alfie put in. "Everybody up at four for the fishies. Agreed?"

We moved over to the little dining table that sat between the living room and the kitchen. David went into the kitchen and started getting the food ready.

"Tomorrow, I'm going looking for that old man," Ruben muttered, opening a pack of cards.

"Just report him to the Better Business Bureau," said Alfie, "Magic Candle Division."

"They'll ask you if you've traded in a cow for any beans recently," I added. "Hey, Dave, do you need any help in there?"

"No, thanks," David said, coming out of the kitchen. "I think I can handle unwrapping a frozen pizza. Damn pilot light is out in the oven, though."

"Maybe that's the ghost!" cried Alfie. "The ghost of the pilot light. Pretty exciting, huh?"

We were dealing out the cards and David was in the living room, hunting up the box of matches, when there came a loud shattering sound that made us all jump. We looked up to see David, standing over the mirror that had been balanced above the fireplace, but that now lay broken on the floor. In his hand he held the box of matches, and his face was white and sick-looking. "Beth," he said quietly to himself.

"What?" said Ruben. We had all jumped up and were over near the fireplace now. "What happened?"

David had been staring at the wall where the mirror had been. He now turned slowly to look at us, and then to look down at the broken pieces of glass on the hearth bricks. "I don't know. I must've knocked into it," he said.

"Seven years of bad luck," Alfie started saying, but Ruben told him to shut up and go get a trash can. He knelt down and started picking up the larger shards of glass. "What did you say about Beth, David?"

"I thought I saw her in the mirror," David said. "I could have sworn I saw – I mean – but she's with her cousin –"

No one said anything. Ruben and I were cleaning up the glass; Alfie carried in a plastic garbage bin from the kitchen. "The candle's out," he said.

For some reason, we all turned to look at it. The flame had indeed died. The yellow candle remained there on the table like a man wrapped in a shroud, buried standing up.

We all remembered, then, what the candle was supposed to have shown us. Ruben, Alfie, and I all looked at each other, and I knew we all were thinking: this must be a coincidence, the lighting of the candle and David seeing Beth. Anyway, Beth was no spirit – she was alive.

"Maybe somebody came in," Alfie said.

He strode over to the front door and opened it. There was only darkness beyond the cabin now. None of us could see much beyond the first few yards of the clearing where our cars were parked and, beyond that, the dim outline of the barn where David kept a goat and a few chickens, more as pets than as a food source.

"No extra car out here," Alfie reported.

"Maybe it's too dark to see," I said.

"No," Alfie replied. "I would be able to see the reflection of the metal, at least. I can get a flashlight..."

Ruben went back to the bedroom and came out again with a look on his face that told me he'd found nothing and no one.

Meanwhile, Alfie went out and got the flashlight from his car. He beamed it around the clearing and down the road. "Nobody out here, and the barn's padlocked," he said when he came back in.

"What did you see?" I asked David.

"Nothing, I guess," he replied, kind of shaking his head like he was trying to clear it. "It must have been my imagination. I thought I saw someone standing right behind me."

"And it looked like Beth?" asked Ruben, who had come back down.

"I thought so," David admitted. "It must've been the lamp." He glanced back at the big beige ceramic lamp in the corner. "Yeah, that's what it was," he concluded.

But his face was still white and the rest of us were feeling a little shaken up, too.

I figured somebody had to say it, and it might as well be me. "Why don't you call Beth, Dave? Just to make sure she's all right?"

David made a kind of sickly laugh. "Yeah, I guess I should."

He went into the back bedroom, where there was a phone. Ruben, Alfie, and I finished picking up the rest of the glass.

Five minutes later, David came back, looking a little better. "She's fine," he smiled. "She's just back from shopping, and they're going out to dinner and a movie." He went over to the liquor cabinet and got out some whiskey and a shot glass. "I just caught her, luckily. Anybody want some?"

The rest of us opted for beer. I got the pilot lit and the pizza going. We started a round of Texas Hold'em.

"Well, that was pretty exciting," said Ruben, looking at his cards. "I wonder what it was you saw, David."

"I told you," David replied. "It must have been the lamp."

"Some Halloween," said Alfie. "My kids are going to freak when I tell them about this. Not to mention Patty. She'll be cuddling up to me for weeks after I tell her this one. Nothing she likes better than a good ghost story. 'Course, I'll have to tell her Beth died in a car accident or something."

"You jerk, Alfie," I said.

"Otherwise, there's no ghost," he went on. "Hey, aren't we gonna use that other candle?"

We all looked at him.

"Well, heck, why not?" Alfie continued. "Maybe somebody else will see a ghost this time."

"The second candle was for hearing," Ruben put in quietly, his eyes on his cards again.

"Hearing a ghost? That's fine with me."

"Cut it out, Alfie," I said. David was sitting with us, looking now, if anything, a little too calm. He had downed two shots of whiskey that I had seen. He was smiling at Alfie with an amused expression, but I didn't see any reason to take chances.

"Listen to Mrs. Worrywart," said Alfie. "You can stuff cotton in your ears. They're Ruben's candles, anyway, and he paid good money for them, and I want to see what happens with the second one."

129

Ruben smiled. "Just as you wish, Master Alfred."

"Well, great," Alfie said after a pause, as if he were a little surprised. He got up and went into the living room. "Anybody want to watch?" he called out.

"No, we think you're old enough to use matches yourself," Ruben replied. David laughed like that was the best joke he had heard all year.

"The green one?" Alfie asked from the living room.

"The green one," Ruben confirmed.

Alfie came back a few seconds later. "Well, it's lit," he said, rubbing his hands together. "Get ready to hear the Voice of the Dead."

"This is so dumb," David said.

"Wait! Wait!" cried Alfie. "What's that? I hear a moaning sound."

"That's Jefferson Airplane," David snorted, "on the radio in the kitchen."

"Well, maybe they're all dead by now. Are they all dead by now? Then we would be hearing spirits."

"You're an idiot, Alfie," Ruben said, his eyes on his cards.

The game continued, the four of us playing in silence. Every once in a while someone would start a topic of conversation up, but it would kind of fall flat after a while. I catalogued the sounds as they came, and I knew everyone else was, too: the radio playing Billy Joel now, the toilet tank gurgling behind the adjoining wall, a hot rod vrooming down the highway half a mile away. Ten minutes passed, then twenty, and there was no unusual sound. The candle continued to burn brightly in the living room, but we stopped being aware of it, and stopped listening. Alfie started telling us some ridiculously involved story, which none of us believed for a minute, about his wife's brother's wig shop, and a motorcycle cop with a toupee.

We didn't notice at first when David, having gone into the kitchen to check on the pizza, didn't come back out.

"And so this cop has funeral detail the next day, you know, to escort the cars," Alfie was saying, snickering in anticipation of the punch line. "And it was this ex-mayor's funeral, and it was gonna be on TV and everything... Hey, Dave," Alfie interrupted himself. "It's your turn, and you're missing a great story!"

David didn't answer.

"And my brother-in-law still hadn't realized that his kid had laced the adhesive with itching powder... Hey, David, whatcha doing in there, still puzzling out the pizza box instructions?"

I got up, then, to see what David was doing. He was standing in the middle of the kitchen, leaning forward and gripping the counter like a man on a pitching deck, listening to the voice on the radio.

It was a woman's voice, pleasant enough, saying "It's so dark, and something's weighing me down," or something like that. Then there was a pause, unusual in radio – usually they keep the chatter going, or the music, or whatever – but there was only silence for the space of maybe five seconds, and then the voice again, "I'm trying to come back to you, but I can't see you. Darling, help me..."

"David," I said. "What are you doing?"

He just turned and looked at me with a face so sickened with horror that I was paralyzed myself. We just stood there, him and me, listening. "It's so dark, so heavy," the voice continued. "Help me find the way..."

"What's going on in here?" asked Ruben, coming into the kitchen. He paused, listening to the voice, with Alfie behind him.

"It's just a coincidence," Alfie said after listening for a minute. "It's one of those old programs. Drama programs. You know – "

He went over to the radio and started fooling with the dial before anyone could stop him. There was the screech of static and suddenly the kitchen was filled with mariachi music. *"Te amo sinceramente,"* a deep-voiced guy was sobbing, *"pero tú no me quieres..."*

David looked like hell. He didn't have to tell us that the voice we had heard was Beth's. Alfie and I got him into the living room and sat him in the armchair.

"This is really weird," Alfie kept saying to me in a low voice, or as low a voice as he could muster. Alfie's low voice is anybody else's normal one. But David didn't appear to be processing. He sat rigid in the armchair, staring at the carpet.

The two of us left him there and went back into the kitchen on the pretext of checking on the pizza. Ruben was still there, trying to get the voice back again. But he couldn't. The connection, whatever it was, from wherever, had been broken.

"Maybe someone's playing a trick on him," I said to Ruben

and Alfie.

"Maybe," said Ruben, "But, either way, he sure is taking it oddly."

"What do you mean?" I asked.

"Look at him. He's scared to death. Seems to have his own reasons for believing that voice was Beth's."

"Well, anybody'd be scared – "

"But if you, Gary, saw your wife – or Alfie, if you saw Patty – even if you thought it was a ghost, or ESP, or whatever – things like that do happen, I believe it – but, would you be in shock like that? You'd be scared, yeah, but your main concern would be to get in contact with her asap, to make sure she was all right."

"He did call Beth," Alfie put in.

"Did he?" asked Ruben.

We all looked at each other, remembering that we only saw him go into his room and come back five minutes later. And the walls partitioning the cabin were so thin, you normally could have heard a phone conversation pretty clearly from where we had been.

I put my head around the corner to check on Dave. He was still sitting there, but he was no longer staring at the carpet. He was staring at the dark green candle – which, I now noticed, was out.

"So what's your point, Ruben?" asked Alfie, suddenly angry, whether out of fear or loyalty to David, I wasn't sure.

"This is incredibly stupid," I said, fighting off a horrible case of the creeps. "Someone's playing a joke on us."

"Sure, fine. It's a joke," said Ruben. "But the question still stands: *where's Beth?*"

"Maybe we should ask him," I said angrily.

"Go ahead," Ruben replied with maddening calm.

I went over and sat on the couch next to David's chair. "Dave," I said, feeling like a complete jerk, "It looks like someone's playing some sort of joke on you – "

"Yeah, yeah. That's it," David murmured.

"But we can't help wondering if Beth really is all right."

He didn't say anything – just kept staring at the three candles on the table.

"I mean, are you sure you talked to her?"

He didn't reply.

"Because Ruben has this theory that, if you were seeing Beth, maybe something is wrong with her, maybe –"

"What are you saying?" asked David, snapping to.

"Where's Beth, David?" It was Ruben now asking. He stood at the hearth, his arms folded, and his voice had that edge it gets when he feels someone's pulling something over on him.

"I told you," said David, acting amazed. "She's at her cousin's house. I just talked to her."

"Are you sure?" Ruben asked.

"What is this?" asked David. "Hey, who the hell do you think you are, coming into my house and talking to me about my wife?" He was standing now, his face flushed, with an exaggerated stance of anger like he found some kind of relief in it. Alfie and I just looked at each other helplessly: Dave's temper was something you didn't want to deal with.

But Ruben was implacable. "I'm your friend, Dave," he said with his familiar attitude of calm insistence. "And whatever's going on between you and your wife, we're in it now."

"What are you saying? Just – *just what exactly are you saying?*"

"I'm asking you to tell us the truth."

"Go to hell," said David, sitting down again, burying his head in his hands. "My wife's in Texas."

"Then why were you so upset hearing a voice that sounded like hers on the radio? Or thinking you saw her in a mirror?"

"You don't believe me," David said, wagging his head with exaggerated sarcasm. "You think I killed my wife. Great friends you are. I buried her in the basement or something..."

"That's a funny conclusion for you to reach," said Ruben.

"Oh, come on, this is ridiculous!" Alfie boomed.

"You think if you light that candle, she'll come back to get me!" David said in a mock-ghoulish voice, making his hands claw at the air like a melodrama phantom.

"He's nuts! You're nuts!" Alfie said to Ruben.

"Light the candle!" David cried. "You want proof? I love my wife and she loves me! You're the ones with the problem! Light the third candle! Here, I'll do it."

I can promise you, no one in the room really wanted to see that third candle lit. Honestly, we were all badly scared. But no one could afford to back down, either. It was just one of those situations, like a narrow road out in the middle of the mountains somewhere, where you just keep going because backing up is impossible.

Dave took the matches that lay on the table and tried to light the third, brick-red candle. I had to take the matches from him, his hands were shaking so badly. So it was I who lit the third candle and put it in the candlestick.

Whether there was any cause and effect involved, I don't know. But at that point we became aware of a cacophony of noise coming from outside, in the barn. The goat was bleating piteously, the hens were up and squawking hysterically. Nothing else, no sound of a coyote or any other predator knocking around.

"Those chickens sure sound upset," Alfie said, or rather croaked – he couldn't seem to clear his throat. "They won't be giving any eggs tomorrow. No good for chickens to be..." he trailed off.

But none of us had the nerve to go out to the porch and see what was scaring the livestock. We just stood where we were, where we had been when I lit the third candle. David sat in the armchair, looking like death, with this crazy little smile on his face that made us all turn away from him. For the next several minutes we continued to stand, straining every muscle to hear what came next, anything that might give us some idea of what was out there.

But there was only silence.

And here we come to the climax of the story, or rather, the anticlimax. Because, not to be misleading, I have to admit that nothing happened that night. After that noise from the barn, which could have been caused by anything, which might even have begun earlier without our having noticed, we heard little else. The goat and the chickens settled down; the candle burned steadily, as we all sat or stood looking at it, going through our own private agonies of suspense. Occasionally there'd be a rustle or a creak outside, and I'd feel like someone had snapped my spinal cord like a rubber band. But after this had happened a half-dozen times, it began to get a little old, and we started telling ourselves that the noises outside were nothing that we wouldn't have heard on any normal night, and that a coyote indeed had been responsible for the livestock scare.

Well, it was an awkward situation, to say the least, and we were all dead tired by that time – we had all driven down after work. Past midnight, we started to get a little goofy. Alfie began telling some of his worst jokes, and I can tell you I was never so happy to hear Alfie's worst jokes in my life. We all laughed, you know, the way people do after a big emotional strain.

There was no point in thinking about fishing the next day; dawn was only a few hours away and we were in no shape for the Great Outdoors. We stayed up, playing cards, talking about old times in high school, and getting good and drunk, until a ways past 2 a.m. Dave had crashed long before that. He had gotten maudlin, crying about Beth, talking about how much she loved him, saying she was too good for him, and getting angry at us for disparaging her, though none of us had. We were all just as happy when he finally passed out on the sofa.

As for Beth and her whereabouts, Alfie, Ruben, and I didn't talk about it. For my part, I was sure that tomorrow we would all be saying an embarrassed "Hi!" to her on the phone. Alfie and I would find a way to patch it up between David and Ruben; after all, the accusation had been a spur-of-the-moment thing. We could put it down to too much beer, glossing over the fact that Ruben hadn't been drunk at all: Dave wouldn't remember that. And even if he did, he'd be as predisposed to make it up as the rest of us. Old friendships aren't something to break up over something stupid like this.

But there was no point talking about it tonight. Besides, Ruben could be very stubborn at times about admitting he was wrong.

Sometime in the dark, I felt the floorboards hefting with the weight of someone walking quietly across the room, and of the front door being pulled open and then shut again. But I didn't open my eyes. I just thought, "That's Dave, gone out to feed the animals." That was his habit in the very early morning, to feed the animals in the barn, first thing. I wondered if he was going to try to get us all up for fishing and hoped fervently that he'd leave us alone.

Then, suddenly, I remembered the candles. I lifted my head to look at the mantle, where Ruben had left it. Yes, the last candle was still burning, though there was only a gutter of wax left to feed it. It would soon be out. I put my head down and fell back to sleep.

I woke up uncomfortably a couple of hours later with Ruben and the sun in my face.

He was standing above my sleeping bag, between me and the living room window, the shade of which he had pulled up, letting in the painfully bright morning light.

"Pull that thing down again, man!" Alfie cried from the floor a few feet away. He was lifting his head out of his sleeping bag and waving it around like a fish caught in a net.

Ruben smiled grimly at us and said, "You two had better get up. There's something I need to show you."

Ruben loved his drama, and that's all he would say. Alfie, casting around pathetically for something to grab and pitch at Ruben, finally gave up and hunkered back down into his sleeping bag. But I got up and pulled on my jeans and boots. "Where's David?" I asked.

Ruben still didn't say anything – just gave Alfie a good kick and told him, "Unless you want to be questioned by the sheriff in that prone position, I'd advise you to get up and get dressed."

Then he walked out to the front porch, with me following, glancing over my shoulder at Alfie, who was sitting up now, staring open-mouthed at us.

Ruben, comporting himself that morning with a grim sense of vindication, was at least kind enough to warn me before we went into the barn; which, he explained, he had found unlocked and open when he first came out looking for David, a few minutes before.

Still, it was a shock: on the cement floor of the barn, only a few feet inside – I might have stumbled over it if Ruben hadn't pulled me back – lay the dead body of our friend Dave. His skin was gray. He had been dead for some hours – that was obvious, if for no other reason than the look in his eyes: no one could have lived long with a look like that in their eyes. They were wide open, staring down at what lay across his legs and in his lap. The face – Beth's face – was turned away from us, thank God. But what skin could be seen was liver-colored and bloated; the hair was matted, and the dark blouse she wore was stained darker with old blood. All over – stuck to her blouse and pants, in her hair, and on her bare feet and hands – were bits of straw, as if the body had been covered over in hay. The arms were lifted above the head and lay on either side of Dave's waist, as if he had been carrying her by the arms, or as if she...

Dave was found to have died of natural causes. Beth's head had been bashed in. She had been dead for at least three days. That left us in the clear.

We were questioned closely, though, and had to admit that we had been playing a sort of truth-or-dare game that night, and that Dave had gotten defensive when we asked him where Beth was.

The authorities figured that Dave, afraid that one of us might go snooping and find his wife's body, had gotten up early to hide it better. He had managed to lift it out of the storage bin, but then had collapsed, either from the physical exertion, or from anxiety, or both.

The story about the candles they dismissed as nonsense – just as we would have done if we hadn't been there ourselves that night.

I wish I could dismiss it all as nonsense. Especially when I wake up at night and think of how Dave's wife might have greeted him that last time, when he came to remove her – to rescue her? – from that storage bin.

Free to Good Home

"Does anyone have a story to tell?" the chairman of the Give Up Gambling Association called out again.

It was a rainy Wednesday night and the hall, though containing only a third of the number of ex-gamblers that it might in better weather, still sheltered some thirty souls. The chairman, who had already stretched out his introductory remarks as long as possible, stood now in silence, praying that someone would come forward to speak.

True, he could without blame adjourn to the social portion of the meeting now, but he knew that these thirty in the audience were no mere punch-and-cookie moochers, here for free food and entertainment. These thirty, who had braved the inclement weather outside and now sat dripping in their folding chairs, were the most desperate cases, those most in need of the strength and inspiration that GUGA had been instituted to provide.

Unfortunately, they were also unprecedentedly taciturn.

Usually there were two or three persons willing to come forward and tell their story, to testify to the evils of gambling and how they found the strength to give it up. But tonight, if it weren't for the monotonous beat of rain against the roof, you could have heard a card drop on a baccarat table and know what suit it was from the sound.

"Will no one come forward?" asked the chairman again, desperately.

Just then, there was a self-deprecating cough and someone stood up in the back. He was a small man, wizened, though of

138

middle age, dressed in a drab suit and wearing over his head one of those plastic rain hats that are designed to fold up and go in your pocket.

"If no one else wants to speak..." be began hesitantly.

"Good, good, come up to the podium!" the chairman cried jovially, waving his arms in a rolling-up motion and encouraging the audience by pantomime to clap. The drab man came shuffling forward, almost tripping on his folding chair, and then on a purse someone had left in the aisle. But, finally, he got to the front of the stage, where he fumbled to light a cigar, as the chairman attempted to introduce him. "This is Mister –"

"Just call me Harry."

"Of course. As everyone knows, we don't use last names at our meetings."

"My last name is Quigley, if anyone wants to know. I'm not a gambler myself, and for those taking notes, well, there it is, if you can spell it."

"You're not a gambler?" asked the chairman, wondering in this case what the man was doing here.

"No, I'm not a gambler," replied Harry, puffing on his cigar contentedly, "I just came in to get out of the rain."

There was an awkward pause. Maybe this wasn't such a good idea after all, the chairman was thinking.

"But," continued Harry after another puff, "I like to talk. I sure do – I could talk all night. Not often I get an audience this big, either, outside of funerals."

"Oh," the chairman replied.

"And I have a brother who used to gamble," continued Harry quickly, as if suddenly remembering. "That's right, my brother Johnny used to be a gambler, but he gave it up, cold turkey, one fine day. He told me the story... Kind of an odd story... It involves cats."

"Cats?" asked the chairman weakly, sinking down in his chair.

"I like cats," called out a woman from the audience who looked like she had had a drink or two to keep off the cold before coming in tonight. "I'd like to hear a story about cats."

"I bet you would," replied Harry, eyeing her with vague disapproval. "But that's all the more reason you should give up gambling immediately and forever. Gambling and cats," he continued,

139

his voice sinking low and ominous, "don't mix."

The woman looked nervous, and the rest of the audience, puzzled. "I see I have captured your attention," said Harry, and began his story:

In the early years of his manhood, my younger brother Johnny was pretty worthless. Chief among his many bad habits was a passion for gambling. He was spectacularly unlucky, but this only encouraged him to gamble more. We all know that a little knowledge is a dangerous thing. Encouraged by the rest of us to continue his education, Johnny had taken a class in statistics at the community college, which he flunked, of course. But one idea had pounced upon his brain like a hand-vac upon a dust bunny. And this was the concept of statistical equality: that a coin, flipped multiple times, will sooner or later come up with an equal number of heads and tails. Applying this to his favorite hobby, he reasoned that the more money he lost in gambling now, the more he was bound to win later on, when things evened up.

We all tried to point out the error in his logic – that a coin toss is not affected by the result of the tosses that came before it – but he was, I'm afraid, a very stubborn kid, and persisted in his belief that, somewhere above, there was a piggy bank filling up with all the money he had ever lost, and that someday, the bank would burst and rain down money on his idiotic head.

So he lost money with complacency, even eagerness.

At the time of our story, he was doing reasonably well, for Johnny. He was employed driving a bus – the L.A. to Las Vegas line for Autumn Tours, a senior citizens' travel group. With his flighty temperament and impermanent style of living, jobs were hard to keep, but he had been working this one for an unprecedented three months when the fateful day arrived and he met up with his nemesis, the Old Man with the Umbrella.

This part of Johnny's story always serves to remind me that we shouldn't judge him too harshly. Obviously, there is a hidden episode somewhere in Johnny's life, some point in his infancy where, perhaps, he was dropped on his head, or left out in the sun, or tossed up into a revolving fan. My parents don't remember any such occurrence, but it's possible they have blocked it out. At any rate, something must have happened to have made him so singularly stupid. He certainly didn't take after the rest of us.

Because anyone else, seeing an Old Man with an Umbrella on a trip from Los Angeles to Las Vegas in the ides of August would say to himself, "What in the world is this Old Man with an Umbrella, on a trip from Los Angeles to Las Vegas, in the ides of August, doing?" Not a parasol, mind you, but a big, black, heavy, rain umbrella.

My theory of early brain damage is pretty much proven, I think, by the fact that Johnny didn't ask himself this question – until it was too late, that is.

His first encounter with the Old Man with the Umbrella began when the latter came up behind him while he was driving through the deserts of Nevada, and, grabbing him by the shoulders, shrieked: "Driver! Toorn dis bus aroun!!"

The Old Man was very old and frail, but emotion had turned him into a titan, and Johnny had to grip the steering wheel to stop from being swiveled around to a backwards-facing position, which, even he realized, would have made driving difficult.

He tried to get the old man to loosen his grip, but couldn't, so he pulled over to the shoulder of the road and asked him what the trouble was.

"I los my umbella!" cried the Old Man in some kind of heavy ethnic accent, the origin of which is better left unexplored. He exhibited the emotion of someone who had just discovered that the swizzle stick in his complementary orange juice was in reality a bar of plastic explosive. "Toorn dis bus aroun, ah? I tink I mighta lef it back in dat ressroom, rounabou Needoo."

Now, Needles was a good hour's drive away at this point and Johnny had no intention of going back there for an umbrella. But he's a kind boy, whatever else his failings, and he didn't like to disappoint the old man. "Did you look under your seat?" he asked, putting on the parking brake and getting up at the same time to look himself.

The old man turned pink with indignation. "What do you tink I am, ah? Kinda idiot?" he sneered. "O course I look under da sea!"

"No, he didn't," said another old man, his seatmate.

"I didn't see him look there," agreed a lady behind them.

"I did, too!" cried our Old Man. "I look dere a coupla dozen time, I..." And his mouth hung open as Johnny pulled the umbrella out from under the seat. Then, suddenly, he grabbed the umbrella, kissed it, kissed Johnny, and settled back down in his seat, looking straight ahead with a sweet smile of complete customer satisfaction.

Later, when they had reached Las Vegas and the hotel parking lot, and everyone was filing out of the door, the Old Man drew Johnny aside and told him, "I wanna to give you little giff, for fining my umbrella."

"Oh, no, I couldn't, well, if you insist," said Johnny, loathe to deny the old man the pleasure of giving.

"Ah ha, I see you are a man of honor," cried the Oldster. "You do not like to take presen."

"No, really, I don't mind –"

"But perhap you take a little loan?" the old man continued briskly. "I loan to you money, lessay, two hunna dolla? You pay me back after you win at da table. I know!" he continued, pointing at Johnny's chest and winking his eye. "I can see, you win big today! Ah? Ahhh!"

And so it was arranged that the two hundred dollars would be, nominally, a loan. Johnny signed his name in the Old Man's spiral notebook, and the Old Man handed over the money with his best wishes for "Break da bank!"

Johnny admits that, at this point, he had gotten the impression that the Old Man, being a bit confused, was bound to forget about the loan, or forget who he was, or lose the notebook. This was an especially comforting assumption after Johnny lost, as who but he could expect otherwise, the entire $200 in his first fifteen minutes at Twenty-one.

So it was with genuine surprise that he greeted the appearance upon his doorstep, three days later, of two large men of virile and bloodthirsty aspect. They introduced themselves as "Grampa's boys," and intimated that they were there to collect the debt Johnny owed.

It was a while before Johnny could take in the situation, but he was helped along the road to understanding by Grampa's Boys, who obligingly rapped their knuckles on his head to help knock any loose wires back into connection. Whatever his other emotions might have been at this juncture, it must at least have warmed Johnny's heart to see two fellows enjoying their work so much. "Knock, knock, who's there?" they cried merrily while working Johnny over.

But all in all it was a painful interview; nor did Johnny receive any real comfort in the realization that he had been right: the old man was confused. Because his confusion had not, as Johnny had hoped, made him forget the debt, or forget Johnny, but rather it had caused him to forget the amount, and to tell his grandsons that Johnny owed him, not two hundred dollars, but two thousand.

Parenthetically, it was reported several months later, in the *Times,* I believe, that an old man had been arrested for running a particularly heinous scam in which he gained the confidence of innocent young bus drivers by pretending to lose his umbrella, then lending them money, and demanding it back at exorbitant rates. But that was much later, too late to help Johnny out. The thought of calling the police at this juncture never entered his battered brain.

No, after Grampa's Boys left with what little money he could give them, and he had rested up from the mild concussion *they* had given *him*, with the promise of more to come if he didn't pay up in full, Johnny realized that what he needed at this point was a little help from his friends.

He spent the next few days in a feverish assay of everyone in his acquaintance, in an effort to raise the requisite $1,993.75 still owed. Nearly everyone turned him down: he was a notorious moocher and no one took his stories of desperate circumstances seriously anymore. He tried to contact me, also, but I was at a Tai Chi Ch'uan convention in Beijing at the time, and so never received the message. To be honest, I can't say that I would have lent him anything, anyway. He had not paid off a debt since Watergate. I think his teacher from second grade, now in the P.E.O. home, gave him a dollar, but that was about all he was able to raise.

A friend of his from high school, a successful urologist now, refused to give him any money. But, quoting the old "Give a man a fish" excuse, gave him a tip that he himself had used while short on cash during medical school.

If there is anyone in the audience with too strong sensibilities, they might consider leaving the room now, or at least covering their ears for a moment while humming a low tune. For my narrative must now treat of the seamier side of life, as the introduction of a urologist to the scene may have already implied, although the ugly facts I must present to you have nothing, *per se*, to do with that specialty, but rather with the realm of biomedical research. For the urologist had, in fact, suggested that my brother collect and sell stray cats to the county hospital research institute, where they would be used to test pacemakers, heart valve implants, etc., before these were put into humans. The urologist assured my brother that the animals were very well treated and that many of them went on to lead long, happy lives, albeit on a low salt diet and with the admonition to never go near microwave ovens.

The Institute paid $20 per cat, and, since every newspaper every day carried multiple listings of cats being given away for nothing, it was a simple matter of pick-up and delivery. Of course, you couldn't tell the gentle souls who were giving the cats away that Fluffy's final destination would be a cozy cage in a physiology lab, but then, as the urologist, who, like so many of his brethren, was a bit of a sophist, assured my brother, "What they don't know won't hurt them." And deception was imperative, for those cat lovers, he warned, like any other type of fanatic, could be dangerous when riled.

Now, the fact is that my brother Johnny dislikes cats. More than dislikes, he loathes and fears them with a fervor unparalleled. If he were walking along Interstate 10, say, from Santa Monica, heading for Jacksonville, Florida, and if, halfway there, he met up with a cat in the road, he would turn around and go back to the coast and take Highway 40 instead. Which is to say, *he doesn't like cats.*

The source of this fear was an experience he suffered at the age of seven, when a cousin of ours, somewhat of a bully, tricked him into going into the closet during a game of hide-and-go-seek, and then lobbed into the dark with him a stray tom he had caught in the backyard and worried into a state of active despair. When we finally got Johnny out several minutes later, he was more dead than alive. My mother gave him hot coffee with a little whiskey and he revived, but for weeks after he couldn't bear a cat even in a picture. My sisters had to take down all their kitten posters and we had to be very careful to intercept the mail and check all the greeting cards, especially the ones from old spinster aunts. And he has never fully recovered: to this day, he cannot pass a Hello Kitty shop without averting his eyes and crossing to the other side of the street.

We got revenge on the bullying cousin, all right, but that is another story, and I am sure all of you are as anxious to hear the rest of this one as I am to tell you.

It serves to illustrate the very depths of despair that poor Johnny had reached to say that he now stooped to consider the venture that the urologist advised. And let me say, parenthetically, that urology and financial speculation don't mix anymore than gambling and cats do.

But, after racking his brains for twenty-four hours more, trying to think of another way to earn the money fast, Johnny came up with nothing beyond dredging all the city's fountains for change. And he almost got arrested when he tried that.

So, like the martyrs of old, he saw that he must face the lions. In reality, he would have preferred lions to cats, but the Research Institute didn't want lions, and he saw with bitterness that it would have to be cats.

Thus it was that he found himself pulling up that fateful morning in front of 301 North Oak Street. He had found the address in an ad in the newspaper which ran:

> "*FREE TO GOOD HOME* -- *Kittens & Cats, all ages & breeds. Inquire at 301 S. Oak betw. 2 and 6 pm. Donation apprec. but not req. KITTEN RES-Q MISSION.*"

Picture in your mind, ladies and gentlemen of the jury, the kind of house where you'd find a spinster lady with lots of cats living, and I'm sure your mental picture would be accurate. There's one in every neighborhood. Old, run down, surrounded by big shady trees. A lazy house, with a wide front porch, and three cats visible even from the opposite side of the street, where Johnny had parked his old Monte Carlo. Two of them, black and white, lay on either side of an iron swing near the door, on a cushion with the stuffing falling out. Another, a huge, orange monster, lay on the porch steps, sprawled right across them, licking its paws in a way that suggested to Johnny a tiger of the Bengal jungles, casually grooming the explorer's blood off its coat. Just thinking of walking up to that twenty pound bundle of golden-eyed, inscrutable malice made Johnny's heart pound and his palms sweat.

Not to mention the thought of stepping over it. The way it had positioned itself on the stairs, he'd *have* to step over it, when, with one swipe, it could latch onto his pant leg and refuse to let go, thus in an instant reducing him to a screaming bean baby.

And that would have ruined everything. For, as the great minds among my listeners will have already grasped, it was imperative that my brother not show the slightest sign of discomfort. On the contrary, he absolutely had to con this Kitten Res-Q person, who-ever he or she might be, into thinking that he actually *liked* cats.

Think of a man about to go under the dentist's drill, having to look that drill in the eye and smile at it. Think of a child, about to receive a paddling from its father, telling him, "Thank you, Dad, I know this builds character." Think of a victim of the Salem Witch Trials, nodding affably and winking a cheery eye at the grim co-lonial magistrate who holds the match that will soon light up the faggots piled round her stake. And you will realize something of the situation my brother was in.

Despite a year of acting classes, back when he thought he might make his fortune doing commercials – before, that is, he re-alized there was actually some effort involved – Johnny thought the odds of his being able to convince this cat lady to give up a half-dozen box of assorted kittens to him were pretty dismal.

And he couldn't help feeling sorry for the cats themselves, the-oretically at least. But what kind of choice did he have? No, it was the law of the jungle at this point. He'd have to go through with it, and then promise himself never to get into this sort of jam again.

Resolutely, Johnny punched his cigarette out in the Monte Car-lo's rusty ashtray and left the car, keeping his eye on the tiger upon the stairs. He strode across the street with a look akin, I imagine, to that which portrait artists always give George Washington at the crossing of the Delaware.

He got over the curb, onto the front lawn, and then stopped. His nerves had failed him. He could go no farther.

And then a miracle occurred. The orange monster suddenly jumped up and ran into some hibiscus bushes at the side of the house. Johnny felt a swell of manly pride and with difficulty restrained himself from pumping his arm up and shouting that he was the king o' the world, until he heard the screen door slam and realized that it was not he who had chased the cat away. Someone was coming out of the house.

A little girl was walking slowly and carefully down the steps now, cradling and cooing to a dainty white kitten in her arms. As Johnny watched in disgust, the kitten made a friendly swipe with one pink paw at the girl's pigtail, and she giggled delightedly. Behind her, a woman who was undoubtedly the mother unit chattered away to a third female standing in the doorway.

Johnny approached cautiously, giving wide berth to the kitten of course. He was surprised to see that the doorway female was not a little old lady but a young woman, in her twenties maybe, with long, brown hair and beautiful brown eyes. She was dressed a little eccentrically, in kimono, shawl, clogs, and striped stockings, and her conversation ran all to cats, so he knew this had to be Mrs. Kitten Res-Q. Or was it Miss?

"I really can't thank you enough," the other woman was saying. "Really, Jennifer's been begging me so long for a kitten, but being a single parent – we don't have health insurance for ourselves even, there's no way I could have afforded vet bills and all that. When I heard about your Mission, I was so happy. I don't know how you manage to get free health care, but we couldn't have had a pet otherwise."

"Well, the vets all know me," the cat girl replied in a peculiarly sweet, soft voice. "And we have lots of bargaining power because of our sheer numbers. And we do have a few very generous donors who are as concerned about the health and welfare of our kitty waif population as I am. Just give him lots of love, that's all we ask."

"Oh, we will, we will," the woman gushed, hugging the kid, who was hugging the cat. Johnny felt as if he had stumbled into a melodrama: "Dr. Quinn, Cat Vet," or something equally appalling.

The cat girl was standing at the doorway still, wiping a tear from her eye with one knuckle, and waving goodbye – not to the people, it appeared, but to the kitten – when Johnny approached her and, mustering his most charming smile, asked if this was the Kitten Res-Q Mission.

"Well, what do you think it is, the hardware store?" retorted the girl. "Didn't you hear what I was saying?"

Johnny admits to being a trifle taken aback at the roughness of the rejoinder. The girl had such a sweet face. But anybody who loves cats, he figured, must have plenty of character flaws.

He smiled again nervously. "I'm sorry. I guess that was a dumb question."

"Yes, it was," she replied.

"It's obvious who you are."

"And it's obvious who you are."

This had Johnny thrown for a loop. Had someone tipped the girl off? "I beg your pardon?" he asked.

"Aren't you from the collection agency?"

"Why, no, of course not!"

"Oh, well then!" cried the girl. "Come on in!" And she led him into the house, which was as run-down as the outside had been. They entered the living room and she asked him to sit down. Looking around, Johnny noticed a cat lying on an armchair. Another cat sat on the window seat. Another one crouched strategically on the top of a bookcase. Another one was perched upon the mantlepiece, licking a candlestick. Several cats were sprawled upon the hearthrug, and more were coming in and out of the kitchen door, which was apparently a sort of commuter artery in what Johnny was beginning to realize was not really a house so much as a cat metropolis. The whole place bristled with them. Even in his worst nightmares, he had never imagined such a thing.

As he stood regarding a threadbare ottoman, checking carefully in case a cat was concealed somewhere in the ticking, he felt a smart tap at his ankle and almost jumped sky-high when he saw that it had been administered by a paw underneath the coffee table.

Luckily, the cat girl didn't seem to notice his alarm. "Hey, I'm sorry about how I was acting – watch out for the litter box there – but they've been hounding me, and if you've ever been in that situation – don't sit there! That's where Susie had her accident – you can't be subtle with those guys, you know. They're after your blood."

"I know the feeling," admitted Johnny, after he had found a

place on a rickety, hard-backed chair, incredibly uncomfortable but with the saving grace at least of no hiding places.

"And you don't look like a cat person," said the girl, plopping down on the sofa, taking one of a cloud of cats upon it into her arms and staring at him as intently, though not as unkindly as before.

"Oh, yes! Yes, I am. I love cats." Johnny forced what he hoped was a sappy, love-struck look onto his face.

"So you're here to adopt one?"

"Yes. You see, Miss – "

"Call me Franny."

"What a pretty name. My grandmother's name was Fanny."

"*Franny,* not Fanny. With an *r.*"

"Oh, sorry."

"And don't tell me your other grandmother was named Franny with an *r.*"

Johnny laughed to cover up his consternation. This girl showed unusual intelligence for a cat lover. And she was watching him like a hawk. The next cat that came by, he'd have to force himself to pet. He shivered at the prospect and wondered if a person could see another person's skin crawling.

The girl was waiting for him to speak.

"My name," he began gravely, "is John Quigley, and I work for Cherryvale Academy – a home for troubled youth."

He handed her the photo ID that he had been given during his short term of employ at Cherryvale. It was a sort of rich kid's lock-up, a place where captains of industry sent their miscreant offspring so they would not be forced to mix with the rabble at juvenile hall.

There was no date on the ID card and, of course, Johnny didn't mention he no longer worked there. He had enjoyed his work, and been very popular with the boys – his all-night card parties and delivery service to and from Small's ("We're Always Open") Liquor Barn were a big hit with them. But the administration didn't like it one bit and had insisted on a parting of the ways.

Franny took the card, studied it, and gave it back.

"We do our best at Cherryvale," Johnny continued, "to give our children the love and attention they need, and as much of a home atmosphere as possible. But one thing they haven't had is pets. Too much trouble, the administration thought. I personally have led a campaign over the last year to have the policy changed. And, I'm very happy to say, I've succeeded. I hope you will allow me to take some of your darling little charges back with me today. If you could have just seen the looks on our boys' faces, Miss Franny, when I told them where I was going, and what I would be bringing home!"

"Well, I don't know," said Franny. "I don't feel so comfortable with the idea of one of my cats going to live in some sort of teenage commune. What if they forgot to feed them or something?"

"Oh, I can vouch for the treatment your cats would receive. I personally will oversee their care and do daily checks to make sure the cats are treated like royalty."

"I suppose you came to me, as opposed to the Pound, because I don't charge anything," commented the cynical female.

"Well, you see, Miss Franny," Johnny explained regretfully, "I could just barely get the Board to agree to changing the no-pet policy. It would have been impossible to persuade them to allocate funds. And, besides, who can really pay for the love of a pet?"

Just then, a unusually large and lissome Siamese got up from its pasha-like indolence on the sofa, jumped down, ambled easily across the room to where Johnny sat, and, to his extreme terror, hopped onto his lap. Johnny had to bite his tongue to stop from crying "Aiieeee!" like the characters in comic books, his principal form of reading, did when confronted with a similar situation: when being thrown out of a flying helicopter or torn limb from limb by a giant squid, for instance. Between the way the cat was looking at him and the pain in his tongue, which he had clamped down on a little too hard, he almost swooned. He came back into focus to realize that Franny, as well as the Siamese, was watching him carefully, and that she expected to see, horror of horrors, a little pet, a scratch behind the ears, or somesuch other obscene gesture of affection from him to the thing on his lap.

Straining every muscle of his face, Johnny smiled. And in an act of will to be understood only by those who have fought their way back from paralytic seizure, he raised a cringing hand. Placing it on the cat's flat skull, he curled one finger and began to scratch.

"There, Kitty, Kitty," he said weakly. "There, Kitty."

And he really wished the cat would have listened to him and stayed There. Unfortunately, perhaps misconstruing his gesture as a genuine overture to friendship, the cat stood up on his lap and, putting its forepaws on his chest, raised its face to his and began to lick his jaw. Too late, Johnny remembered the barbecue beef sandwich he had wolfed down in his car before coming here, and realized that maybe he had wiped his mouth a little too cursorily at the conclusion of that meal.

"Oh, he likes you," cried Franny. "Look at that! Fred likes you! And he's normally so picky."

"Ah ha ha," wheezed Johnny mirthlessly. He knew that wasn't sufficiently enthusiastic but it was all he could manage, seeing as he was expecting any moment that the cat, his appetite aroused, would sink its teeth into his throat and tear out his windpipe. That was a really upsetting thought. He needed his windpipe. Though he had never appreciated it before, it struck him now that a windpipe was a really good thing to have. Girls went for guys with windpipes.

"Freddy, come on, what bad manners!" came the voice of his mistress, from very far away, it seemed to Johnny. He noted with what annoyance he could muster under the circumstances that she was not bothering to get up. "Anyone would think you weren't fed enough! Just push him off, Mr. Quigley."

"Oh, I don't mind," Johnny breathed out of the side of his mouth, the side opposite to the one that the kitty was now licking. The idea of touching the cat was unthinkable to him. The only tenable policy at this point, he knew instinctively, was to sit stock still and wait for the cat to finish having its way with him. This was bound to happen sooner or later, he told himself, fending off panic. And anyway, if the cat had any decency, any sense of sportsmanship at all, he would soon abandon such defenseless prey in pity and disgust. A mouse could have put up a better fight than Johnny at that moment.

Through a haze, he heard Franny the cat girl's echoing laughter...

Finally, Fred was sated. Jumping down from Johnny's lap, he found a spot of sunshine on the carpet and settled in the middle of it, licking his chops.

"I have to admit I'm a little jealous," Franny was saying. "Fred seems to have taken a real liking to you. But, gee, it would be hard for me to give him up."

"Oh, no no no!" cried Johnny, reanimated from a state of waxy catatonia by the suggestion.

"But you seem to get along so well..."

"I could never take him away from you," Johnny insisted, feeling his face all over to make sure there were no chunks missing. "That is, if you're so attached to him. Heavens to Betsy, no. I'll just take some small cats, some – what do you call them? Kittens. I'm sure the boys would prefer kittens, anyway. It's getting late. I hope you don't mind. If you'll just scoop up a few and put them in some sort of box or bag or something..."

"Are you sure you know how to take care of them?" Franny asked suspiciously.

"Oh, of course, of course. We always had cats at home. My first word was meow, they tell me."

"Well, I do have three litters right now, and I do need to move them out. I suppose I can let you take some on a contingency basis, and do a home check tomorrow. How many did you want?"

"How many can you give me?" Johnny asked, standing up and eyeing the door. But the look on Franny's face made him realize this was not the right response. He laughed as if he had merely been making a pleasantry, then quickly calculated: Cats, like dogs, had five or six babies at a time, didn't they? Three litters would mean, at the most...

"We have eighteen residency bungalows, and each one has asked for a cat," he smiled.

"Gee, that's just the number of kittens I have available right now," said Franny wonderingly. "What a coincidence."

"Yeah, I guess it was meant to be," replied Johnny brightly.

"It'll cost quite a bit to feed all of them," Franny warned.

"Oh, we'll scrape by."

"I spoil my cats a little, you know. They're used to fresh meat, straight from the butcher's block."

"Of course, of course! That's the way I feel about it. I'd rather give up my dinner than see the poor little darlings try to choke down that awful canned stuff."

"I think it's better that way. A natural diet. Good for their coats."

Johnny realized just in time that the girl was talking about the coats that Nature had given the cats already, and caught himself before expressing an impetuous intention to rush out and buy them little windbreakers.

"Of course, of course," he murmured merely.

"Well, come into the pantry and I'll show you the first litter." She stood up and led the way out toward the back of the house, Johnny following, light-hearted in the belief that his ordeal was about to come to a successful conclusion, the poor sap.

"The pantry is a favorite birthing place for our queens. It's so quiet and dark," Franny was saying.

"Quiet and dark?"

"Yes, and tiny. Only one person can fit in there at a time, so I'll go in to reassure the queen, and then step out and let you see them."

"Is Queen a nervous sort of cat?" asked Johnny.

"No, no. 'Queen' is the term we use to refer to the mother cat." She turned and gave him an odd look. "I'm surprised that you, as a cat lover, don't know that. Here we are. Are you feeling all right, Mr. Quigley?"

Perhaps my brother was looking a little green at this point. Who could blame him? As he stood staring at the narrow doorway within the little hall, Johnny was experiencing a flashback to the time, so many years ago, of his original cat-trauma. And now he was being asked to enter through this narrow portal and expose himself to the same horror again? Could his soul survive? Would his sanity remain unbroken?

"I'm fine," he smiled weakly at Franny. "I just forgot to take my iron pill."

She insisted he sit down at the kitchen table for a moment. She poured him a cup of tea and set a buttermilk scone in front of him. Her hand touched his shoulder sympathetically.

What a sweet girl, he said to himself. *I could have loved you,* he thought. *You could have saved me from myself, brought out my better nature... if only, at an earlier age, you had had the self-discipline to say 'no' to cats.*

Meanwhile, she had slipped into the pantry. She would be out any minute, Johnny realized. And the thought occurred to him, also, that this was his last chance to call the whole thing off – to walk away, catless, from this house. Or better yet, to stay, to talk to the sweet cat girl, to tell her his troubles, confess the shameful crime he had been contemplating, paint for her a picture of the awful retribution which awaited him in the hands of Grampa's Boys (or rather in their fists and boot toes), and beg her to help him.

Johnny awoke from this reverie to see Franny looking at him quizzically. "Anything the matter, Mr. Quigley?"

"No, everything's great," Johnny replied heartily.

"You don't look great. I hope you're not ill – no bacterial infections, no blood diseases or anything?"

"Of course not, I'm just a little tired from staying up late last night, wrapping Christmas presents for our Bangladeshi relief project."

"But it's July, Mr. Quigley. And Bangladesh is a Muslim country."

"Oh, good! Then I guess it doesn't matter when they get there."

"You know, Mr. Quigley," said Franny with a sly little smile that it would have been well for Johnny if he had read properly, "I hope you're being honest with me. I hope you're not a – " the girl's pretty face transformed suddenly into a mask of hostility, and she spat out the word – "*vivisectionist.*"

"No, I assure you," replied Johnny innocently. "We're non-denominational."

"I mean, you're not one of those people who sells cats to the medical researchers."

"Me?" Johnny looked at her, wide-eyed. "Me?" he said again, shaking his head in disbelief, shuffling his feet, and gasping in exasperation. "You mean, me?"

Franny looked at him appraisingly but said nothing.

"How can you think such a thing?" Johnny asked in a hurt tone. "I love cats. Here, let me see those little cuties – "

And he got up before he could lose his nerve and marched into the pantry closet.

Johnny remembers it as being cold in there, and dark – awfully dark. This was partly because there were no windows, and partly because, as he realized when he turned around, Franny had closed the door noiselessly behind him. He grasped the doorknob to open it again, then twisted and tugged at it desperately, but it wouldn't

154

turn. The cat girl had locked him in!

"Hey! Open the door!" he cried.

"Not on your life, you vivisectionist!" cried the girl.

Johnny gasped in horror. He realized now the desperate situation he was in: trapped, helpless, and at the mercy of a cat lover!

Breathlessly, he heard Franny's maniacal laughter echo through the kitchen. And then she began talking, apparently to the cat, Fred. "I know you liked him, Sweetie, but I could tell right away he was one of those –" (here followed a string of unrepeatable expletives). "Imagine, handing our kittens over to him! Gassing is too good for him – I'd like to torture him to death! But maybe we can work something out. At any rate," she said with a cheerful lilt to her voice, "There'll be plenty of fresh meat for the next few days!"

Fred didn't say anything, but Johnny could imagine him nodding in agreement with the girl. Yes, he had liked Johnny, though not so much in friendship as in the more culinary sense of the term.

But what, Johnny wondered, had the girl said about gassing being too good for him? Backed up against the door, a strange hissing met his ears, and there was a funny smell...

He could dimly see, by the light of the crack under the door, just before the cat girl stuffed a rag into it, the gas pipe that led to the kitchen stove. It had apparently been modified somehow, and was now spewing carbon monoxide into the sealed enclosure. Feeling around, he located the stem of the valve which she must have opened when she came into the closet. But she had removed the handle, and there was no way to turn it off!

Johnny fell to his knees and tried to find the opening in the pipe, to plug it up, but the cat girl had been too clever, and he couldn't find the hole. Perhaps it was somewhere in the wall. He started scrabbling wildly at the lath and plaster, trying to pull it open with his fingers.

It was impossible, of course. Johnny collapsed to the floor, woozy with the gas. "At least," he comforted himself, in what might have been his last words, "there aren't any Queens in here after all."

Drowsily, he heard the cat girl humming to herself in the kitchen, knocking around among the pots and pans, and asking Fred where her recipe box was. Far away, he heard the doorbell ring.

He blacked out....

Suddenly, a booming voice in the kitchen shouted, "Where the hell is he?"

"You're mistaken, Mr. Simms," the cat girl was saying in a placating voice. "That young man might have come up to my house, but he's gone now. I sent him away."

"Well, somebody better find him quick or I'm gonna ram that ugly car of his out of my driveway. Can't even pull my car out to go to work. Guys like that should be shot!"

"Oh, I agree, Mr. Simms," the cat girl replied. "Shot, or gassed, or whatever. But maybe it's a better idea to call a tow truck. If you'll come back to the front room, where the telephone is – "

"Help!" cried Johnny weakly. "Help! HELP!"

"What's that?" asked Mr. Simms.

"Oh, just the TV," replied the cat girl sweetly. "I guess I left it on upstairs."

"It's not the TV!" Johnny rasped. "I'm here, in the closet! She's trying to poison me! Let me out!"

There was a pause while Mr. Simms apparently zeroed in on him. Finally Johnny heard his voice again, close to the door. "Are you the owner of a '76 Monte Carlo?"

"Yes! Yes!" cried Johnny. He realized now he must have parked badly out of nervous preoccupation over the looming cat ordeal. It was the luckiest mistake of his life. "Let me out and I'll move it!" he cried.

Mr. Simms shot open the deadbolt and pulled him out. Johnny vaguely remembers the look of baffled fury on the cat girl's face, and the more urbane and philosophical disappointment on that of Fred, as Mr. Simms dragged him out of the kitchen, through the house, and back to his car.

"That girl tried to murder me!" Johnny gasped. "She wanted to feed me to her cats!"

"Write Dear Abby about your love problems," said Mr. Simms. "Your car's blocking my driveway, and I gotta get to work."

And so it was that, by the meerest of happenstance, Johnny escaped out of the Kitten Res-Q Mission alive. He got into his car, pulled away from Mr. Simms' driveway, and left North Oak Street, and his former way of life, for good.

Perhaps it was the close call he had had. Perhaps it was some salubrious effect of the carbon monoxide upon a brain for which any change must have been an improvement. But Johnny that day made the first intelligent decision in his life: he made an oath before God never to place another bet again.

He got another job in Los Angeles, about as far away from Las Vegas as you can get without falling into the Pacific Ocean. And he stopped gambling – well, with his own money, at least. You see, he now works as a broker on the Pacific Stock Exchange.

The chairman took a deep breath. "Thank you, Harry. What an interesting and informative testimony this has been. Don't you agree?" he asked, turning to the audience, or what was left of them. There was a scattered clapping, intermingled with sobs and mutters of "Gassing was too good for him!" from the inebriated cat fancier woman.

Harry had gone over to the refreshment table and was surveying the spread. But for the late arrival of the Number 34 bus, he would have done so before the meeting began, as was his rigid custom. Fate, however, likes to throw its heroes this kind of curve ball every once-in-a-while, and as he eyed the paper plates of burnt cookies, the soggy bundt cake, and the urn of bitter-smelling coffee, he sighed with the type of stoic acceptance that he might have learned at the feet of the cat, Fred.

"It seems to have stopped raining," he commented. "I think I'll just run over to the Knights of Columbus hall. It's the last Wednesday in the month and, if I'm not mistaken, that's spaghetti night. I'm sure," he mused as he slipped out the side door, "they'd like to hear about my nephew Alonzo's religious conversion."

And that's the last they saw of him for quite some time.

A Tomato, Ripe from Her Garden

Certainly, I could not have found her so distasteful from the beginning, or the thing would have never been done. No: as I recollect, we got along tolerably well for some time. Slowly, however, and through no fault of mine or her own, this changed, until her mere presence in the room was noxious to me – while she herself, to the very end, felt no less hunger for my proximity than she had on that unlucky day when I first took her hot, pink hand in mine and, kissing it, asked her to be my wife.

I question my sagacity when I think of that fatal error. She and I, united in matrimony – forever. How could I have failed to calculate the result? How could I not have realized that, for my rather finely-tuned spirit to be tied for life to such a heavy, unperceptive, cloddish, farmwife of a woman would not fail to become, in time, continual torment – could not fail to lead, in short and inevitably, to some specie of violent conclusion?

My only apology is that I was young, ambitious; my goals thwarted in the most maddening way by lack of money and connections. Perhaps I did act without thinking the thing through. Rashness has, after all, been the fault of many a talented youth, and I was a young Hemingway with no war to run away to; a young Conrad without the sea. Yes! this is apt: in hindsight, I could have borne the rigors of war or the privations of shipwreck better than those cozy evenings on the sofa, those intimate, cloying morning hours at the breakfast table. I will admit that I overestimated my moral strength – a grievous tactical error... But is it fair to allow me to suffer so now – to suffer so – when it would take so little to render me happy again?

I was teaching at a college in the rural heartland of central California, a true hick town. Having worked my way through graduate school, much to the detriment of my research and writing, I had not been able to do as well as I had hoped when locating a first position, and I landed here, amongst the pumpkins and the bumpkins. I needed to get along; my ambition goaded me; I knew I was meant to construct great works for which the span of a lifetime would be pitifully short, and yet I was tethered to class after class of bleating sophomores and frosh, teaching the rudiments of English grammar: the elusive constituents of the complete sentence; "Verbs: They Make Things Go"; matters which these precious scholars would have known in grade school if they had been capable of learning them at all.

Her father was Chair of English, a jovial yet erudite man whom I truly liked – do like – very much, though I find some of his views a bit antiquated, as he knows. We have had many a lively dispute over Joyce and Steinbeck, during which I am not too proud to say I learned something.

I met her at his house, she being his only daughter, and was immediately struck by the differences between parent and child – differences both physical and mental. Where the father was slight of build, dark, and a bit sere, the daughter was large, buxom and blonde. Where the face of the father was quick and malleable, that of the daughter gave an impression of placidity, a dreamy dullness, if I must come out and say it. I found her best attribute to be her habit, throughout the meal, of sitting quietly and saying nothing; for, clearly, she had nothing to contribute to the conversation, and it is a kind of sense – a very rare kind of sense – to know when one has nothing to say. She sat and enjoyed her food.

Periodically, however, she would ask a question – a very simple one – to show she was listening, I suppose. Her father would smile and, glancing at me as if to beg my patience, would explain the little sticking point or smooth away the difficulty as simply as possible. At this, she would nod several times quickly, but would make no reply nor ask further questions. Thus, it was never clear whether she now understood or was simply too embarrassed to admit that she still did not.

The old gentleman was always kind to me – had, in fact, taken my side in a faculty dispute in which I had found myself otherwise undefended against the childish wrath of envious colleagues. I sympathized with his embarrassment now, and when his daughter would interject a question, more and more often it was I who would gently explain the point of discussion to her. The old man seemed grateful.

Of course, it occurred to me that there might be some personal profit to be made here: that being son-in-law of the Department Chair might lead to faster advancement; and, when the time came for me at last to move on to a better school, I would be ensured an excellent recommendation. The old man had many friends; he was well-liked within the many professional societies to which he belonged; he had connections of the type which I would be in a unique position to make use of – if I were, as I have said, to render him the not inconsiderable service of taking this poor little, heavy-headed calf of a daughter off his hands.

The prospect of marriage with such a young lady, as I have said, did not appall me at the time. She was not an ugly girl, though too thick-featured to be termed pretty. I do not wish to wrong her: some might have found her attractive. But she was not my type. During the time we spent together at her father's table, she was, as I have said, quiet and docile. She never wasted our time with prattle about the latest soap opera or sitcom drivel, or with brave tales of battle over the half-price counter at the local shopping mall, like most of the young ladies in town would have. Rather, she displayed a certain lack of emotion, a Germanic stoicism (her mother had been Pennsylvania Dutch) which made me think that, once we were married, she would keep to herself and disturb my quiet routine but little. An added bonus was that I would no longer have to keep house with her about. She cooked her father's meals and served them efficiently: plain fare, a little fatty, but quite good.

And so began my tentative forays. I leant a little closer to her at the dinner table, emphasizing in low, sonorous tones the differences between the Spanish Romantic Movement and the German. Later on, as we walked out into the moonlight, I would expound upon the supper table theme. She gave no outer sign of anything but intellectual stimulation, except for the coloring of her face, which began as I paid her my little attentions to resemble one of the prize-winning tomatoes I had seen at the local agricultural fair: "Butter Boy" or "Chubby Girl." Her father, who normally spent the summer evenings in his glider chair near the front screen door, would be conspicuously absent by the time we came back in. One evening, as I bade her *au revoir,* I proposed marriage. It quite took me back when she threw her arms around me and smothered me in kisses. She had, indeed, been ripe for the picking.

After a quiet wedding – she had wanted a large, blowzy affair, but reason prevailed – we went to live in the house in which her poor mother had grown up, left empty after the death of her grandparents. It had always been my bride's dream to inhabit this humble little wood-frame cottage, with its picket fence and *faux* wishing well, off the highway on the outskirts of town. I was willing to indulge her. With the rent money I had been paying, we set up our frugal household.

It was with great amazement that I watched the overnight transformation of my bride from girl to wife. What other event in the animal or vegetable kingdom can compare? The burgeoning of the rose bud, the swelling up of the blowfish to many times its size, the rearing up upon its hind legs of the great brown bear as she totters forth in search of honey, all lend something of an analogy. Not that my wife grew in the physical sense. No, thank heavens; she was already large enough. But her confidence, her presence seemed to expand. She was everywhere in the house at once. She hung about me, kissed me, caressed me, bothered me continually. And now, she began to talk – to talk incessantly, prattling about every little thing she saw, or heard, or thought, in the most annoying manner imaginable.

At first I was patient. We were still on our honeymoon, as she herself kept reminding me. And so I had hopes that this feverish cavorting would, like the springtime, pass on to a more sober season. But as days passed, and it showed no signs of doing anything of the sort, I became silent. I looked away when she smiled at me; I replied sternly when questioned and walked away to my study. She would follow me, jump into my lap, pat my cheeks between her hot red hands as if my head were a lump of dough and, making what

I'm sure she thought were endearing faces, her round blue eyes brimming with tears, would beg me to tell her what was wrong. But to no avail: I simply said that I had work to do.

Finally, she understood, and bothered me no more.

I had managed to secure a better teaching schedule that year – whether through the kindness of my father-in-law or otherwise, I don't know – and had time, finally, to pursue several projects that I had great hopes for. But the woman had not brought me good luck. Perhaps it was her starchy, soporific cooking. Perhaps it was the drone every blessed evening of the television in the other room, though I made her turn it down very low and shut the door between the living room and my study. I am inclined to simply blame it on her presence. Submissions to several journals were rejected, though I could have sworn by any oath my work was *far* superior to that which was already being published. Collaboration with a colleague broke down when he and I disagreed on a minor point; and, though I finally gave in, he decided the whole premise of the book was badly thought out, and the project was abandoned altogether. And my novel, my little pearl of great price from whose contemplation I had before derived such satisfaction, stumbled awkwardly from my fingers upon the keyboard and fell flat and lifeless upon the screen. For the first time, I feared that it would never walk, much less dance, as I had envisioned.

This was a dark age – a dark, wicked age. The man who derives vital sustenance from his dreams suffers in a way unimagined, unimaginable to others when those dreams fail, though his outward life be as secure as before. People thought I was happy. Though their opinions were not of serious consideration to me, they added to the torment, like being tickled with a feather upon the rack.

And she – she, who in a momentary lapse I had wed – she was a source of constant irritation to me now. She did not work. She stayed at home, kept house, cooked, and tended her garden. The house was set upon an acre of cleared flat land, upon which it was her main occupation to grow fruits and vegetables. Though this did save us a bit on the grocery bills, it would have been of much greater help if she found some formal employment. I told her so many times. But she made few inquiries, found excuses to reject whatever opportunities arose, and so stayed at home. She was always there when I came in. Though she rarely attempted to engage me in conversation now, her silence was fully as maddening as her chatter. Perhaps I found it even more so. Those great cow eyes regarded me always – mournfully, reproachfully, yet with great affection and hunger. I was bedeviled by her in a way impossible to describe, and I could not get away. In this small town, there was nowhere else to go. Even if some sanctuary were available, if an oasis had sprung up in the middle of the desert, any lapse on my part would have been noted and reported immediately to my father-in-law, who thought us happily married! Oh! The situation was intolerable. And I saw, in all my future, no way out.

I became a bit testy with my wife. I nagged and berated, though never in the presence of others, of course. And I swear I never struck her – physical violence has always been abhorrent to me. When she saw that I was in a black mood, she would avoid me. There was no question of her answering my jibes, slow-witted as she was. I could not drive her to leave me, I knew. She would not tell her father; she was still devoted to me – still loved me: I knew this by the way she responded on the occasions in which I pretended to regret my treatment of her. She would put up with anything from me, I realized.

And with this realization, we entered into a new phase of our relationship. No more did I wish to avoid her company. I watched her carefully, studying her behavior and habits, for the first time, with pleasure. At first, most of my actions took the form of little pranks, causing annoyance and wasting time perhaps, but doing no real harm.

She was knitting a sweater of a particularly difficult and intricate pattern. I would extricate pieces from inside the ball and cut them. When she took up her work again, I would from the other room hear her periodic exclamations of distress, as she stopped and re-knotted the yarn. Chuckling to myself, I would count the times this would happen before she would finally arise in great dudgeon to go back to the store and get a replacement skein. Of course, I cut this one in several places, too. It was wondrous how she never caught on.

I hid the toothpaste.

I untied her laundry line and let it fall into the dust.

I put a drop of tabasco sauce in the cat's food, causing the tom to behave in such an erratic manner that my wife, badly worried, took him to the vet, only to be told there was nothing wrong with the stupid beast. She had to take the vet's bills out of her grocery budget because she dared not ask me for the money – I had threatened to drown the cat many times before.

As our married life proceeded, I experienced the delight of an epicure in manufacturing more and more subtle and rare devices with which to torment my wife. One Saturday morning, after telling her we would drive to the city for dinner and a movie, I detached a couple of spark plug wires. That evening, what a puzzlement – I could not get the car started! Her face, which she had carefully though not subtly decorated with pink lipstick and blue eye shadow in honor of the occasion, went from happy clown to sad clown and back again each time the engine would catch and then die. Finally, wiping the disappointment from her eyes, she rubbed mascara all over the sleeve of her good white coat, and I told her I could not take her anywhere looking like *that.*

I had a pack of marked cards, a souvenir of an old college prank. In the evening, we played gin. I won from her the money she had saved to buy herself a Christmas dress, and told her I would not give it back to her, for this would serve as a much-needed lesson upon the evils of gambling – though I was the one who had goaded her into betting in the first place!

This was the manner in which we lived for many months. Whether my wife ever suspected me of being the cause of her more than usual burden of misfortunes, I can't say. She never once made an open accusation, or even questioned me obliquely. Apparently, it was beyond her mental powers to imagine such a thing.

But the day finally came when I was caught *in flagrante delicto,* in the commission of a particularly heinous crime, at least to my wife's way of thinking. .

As I have mentioned, she kept a vegetable garden. She had been gardening since childhood and, with little else to do now, spent the better part of each day out in the field, hoeing and planting, staking and watering, the simple arts of which she was expert in. Hers was the organic method: she would suffer no pesticides or chemical fertilizers to fall upon her tender seedlings. Her compost bins she constructed after great study and thought; they were unique in design, and soon, unbelievably, market gardeners from surroundings counties began arriving to study their architecture, and to hear from my wife's own lips the rationale behind her daring innovations, which were, from what I could understand, of revolutionary portent comparable to that of the flying buttress of cathedral fame.

My wife grew all kinds of fruits and vegetables, but the thrust of her efforts were in the growing of tomatoes. She cultivated several kinds, both sandwich and paste varieties, devoting about a quarter of the acre to them in all. I enjoyed very much the fruits of her agricultural labors, and for this reason I had never gone so far as to commit mayhem upon her plants, except for the Brussels sprouts, which I detest.

But this year, a friend had suggested she enter a few of her best tomatoes in the county agricultural fair competition. This was, as my wife communicated to me one evening when I was pretending to be kindly disposed towards her, a daring proposition, because all winners of the competition for the past thirty years had, without exception, employed pesticides and chemical fertilizers as the means of obtaining their huge and unblemished fruit. In fact, a major sponsor of the exhibition was the chemical mega-moghul, QuikkiGro. For vegetables grown organically to take any prize at all would be quite an upset.

At first, my wife demurred, not wishing to be goaded by ambition to get into something beyond her humble lot in life. Pride goeth before a fall, she said sagely. But her fellow organic gardeners continued to urge her to battle. It was true that, this spring, her tomatoes were thriving as they never had before.

She began to cherish great hopes. Before her eyes, it seemed a vision of Destiny hung. In the evening, after all her chores were finished, she would go out to the garden and walk back and forth between the plant beds, mulling with furrowed brow over the question of which varieties to submit under the four categories: best tasting paste, best tasting sandwich, largest, and most exotic. "Super Supper" or "Mr. Hardy"? I heard her muse. "Black Princess" or "Belgian Delight"? Never since we first married had I seen her so happy.

A few days before the competition, I made a little trip to the local nursery, where I paused before a bright display of rather bad-smelling bottles of QuikkiGro products. I chose a large brown one marked "Death to Aphids," whose label claimed it to be "the garden pest's worst nightmare." The active ingredient was a man-made chemical. The clerk at the counter, who knew my wife, looked at me with mute shock and disapproval as I wrote a check from our joint account. I got the impression that, as soon as I drove off, he would be on the phone, lickety-split, to the local vegetable law enforcement authorities, whoever they might be, as well as to the nearest QuikkiGro *apparatchik*. I winced, imagining the scandal that would ensue.

That evening, she went shopping. I went to the shed and got out the garden spray equipment. Attaching the watering hose to one end, I poured the proper dosage of "Death to Aphids" into the bottle. Turning the stopcock to open, I began spraying down the tomato rows, carefully soaking each fruit, one at a time, with the insecticide.

Parenthetically, I imagine my audience might wonder if, at this time, I felt any shame regarding my actions. I suspect I did, at some level – I am a deeply feeling man, and not an amoral lout, as some might think, judging by my present condition. Yet other emotions, which I cannot tell the origins of, had long ago taken hold of me, and I was principally filled with a sort of wicked glee. I remember feeling justified at so expressing my outrage at the tricks life had played upon me. Perhaps I had no such right. Perhaps I went too far. But then, whose fault was it that I suffered, that I suffer now? Surely I cannot be asked to accept responsibility for an outcome which I never sought?

Unfortunately, my wife came home early. Not finding me in the house, she came out to the back porch, where she saw the bottle of pesticide I had left there, and me, out among her darlings, spraying poison one by one into each of their little red or green faces.

Before this, as I have said, if she had any suspicions about my playing tricks upon her, she had kept them to herself and said nothing. Now, presented with evidence so striking, she could deny them no longer.

Seeing I was in a bit of an awkward position, but confident that I could still think up some explanation which would convince my simple wife of the innocence of my actions, I said nothing, but stood there, smiling with what I hoped was calm confidence. Perhaps the smile was what did it – perhaps it was more what one might call a smirk. At any rate, she took up a pitchfork that leaned within convenient reach against a compost bin nearby and started towards me, prongs pointing forward.

I saw it was no longer time for parley. As she thrust the pitchfork at my abdomen – and she was a strong woman – I dodged and ran for the house. She followed quickly behind. Reaching the porch, I took up a shovel that lay there and, whirling around – meaning only, I swear, to parry her next thrust – I struck her heavily alongside the head with the shovel's sharp edge.

She fell sideways upon the stepping stones.

I hesitated, not knowing what to do. I began to drag her into the house – but within a few minutes she was dead.

No one had seen us; no one could have heard anything: we had not even exchanged words. I sat upon the steps in the dusk, considering the consequences of calling the police and pleading self-defense. Even if, ultimately, I was found not guilty, I would be in for a very bad time. I was not popular in the community. My only supporter had been the old man, her father – who, despite the fact that it was all clearly an accident, conceivably might not view me with the same favor as before.

I had no money for high-priced lawyers. Who knew what a jury of farmers and insurance salesmen, with the decidedly anti-intellectual leanings I knew existed in this county, were liable to think of my plea? Given half a chance, they would speedily find me guilty of willful murder.

I panicked. By the light of the moon, I dug a hole between the tomato rows, very deep. It took me several hours. Finally, very late at night, I placed her body in the hole and covered it up again. It solaced me to think that she would probably have been perfectly happy to be buried here, in her own vegetable garden. She had given her heart and soul to her garden; now, she had given it her all.

While digging, I had roughed out the idea of remaining in town for a few days and covering up for my wife's absence, if anyone asked, by saying she had a cold. It was not likely that they would ask right away: she didn't work, nor had she a rigorous social schedule. The county fair was still a few weeks off. After withdrawing money from the bank and collecting any disposable assets, I would leave the country. I had a friend from long ago who lived among the expatriates in Mexico; I could rent a car under another name, drive down, and disappear. Better yet, there was an old Ford in the garage which was still registered in the name of some family member, now long gone. The license plates were still on, but no one would connect the car with me. It needed a new battery and some other minor work, but would, I was sure, make it well beyond the border. As long as I drove carefully, the chances of being stopped and questioned were small.

I spent a rather dreadful sleepless night, but the next morning went to the college as if nothing had happened. That evening, I began my preparations, stopping by the auto parts store and purchasing a new battery. Carrying it into the garage, I realized I was very hungry: I had eaten no dinner the night before and had had nothing all day. I went inside to fry a steak and, stopping in the garden, picked a few tomatoes and a handful of greens with which to make a salad. The steak was good; the salad, delicious.

Going back to the garage, I installed the new battery and turned the engine over; a little rough, of course. The spark plugs would need to be cleaned and checked, though hopefully I could get by without new ones: the clerk at the auto parts store might take note if I went in too often. Luckily, I had remembered at the last moment to pay for the battery with cash.

I worked for a few hours more. Then, exhausted, I went up to bed – though, as soon as I lay down, I began to feel hungry again. What I craved was more salad. Finding nothing left in the bowl I had tossed for dinner, I ran out to the garden in my pajamas and picked some more salad greens and tomatoes, along with a few ears of baby corn and some tender, new green beans. They were marvelous, and I slept the rest of the night like a top.

The next morning, I felt much better – time having lent, I

think, a bit of perspective. Things could have been much worse. My plans were going smoothly; no one had had occasion to ask me about my wife, and my behavior was just as normal. If anything, I felt better than I had in years. Before, I had struggled to conceal my impatience with colleagues, my disgust with the imbecility of my students. Now, my heart was light as I savored the knowledge that, in a few days, I would be gone from this seat of lower-middle-class learning forever. I looked forward to a new life in foreign climes. Giving up teaching, even for a life of wandering poverty, would give me the opportunity of concentrate more fully on my writing. My friend in Mexico, I knew, respected my talents and would help me in any way he could. And might not the events of the last few days serve as subject for a semi-autobiographical novel, in which I could explain fully what had happened, and perhaps not only receive pardon, but see my name, finally, on the New York Times Best-Seller List, to boot? Busy with bright plans, I had, if anything, trouble containing my cheerfulness.

There was one incident that morning, however, which helped me mimic more truthfully my usual surly behavior. I had carried a lunch bag with me to work, a rather large shopping bag actually, which is why, I suppose, one of the professors reached in and tried to carry away a few tomatoes from it – he *said* he thought they had been left in the refrigerator to be shared. I disembarrassed him of the notion rather emphatically. He apologized, but I was dreadfully irked. After all, a man's bag of tomatoes is a man's bag of tomatoes.

My equilibrium soon returned, however, and I struck up conversation with a very pleasant young woman, a graduate student in psychology, whom I met in the cafeteria, where I had carried myself and my tomatoes after the brouhaha in the English lounge. I went so far as to invite her over that evening to continue our discussion on Truth as it is defined in our separate fields. It quite surprised me when she said yes, but I was not in the least worried. What had I to worry about?

That evening, I fried up another couple of steaks and brought in some succulent zucchini from the garden, as well as more salad greens and tomatoes, all the while thinking of the young lady, and of the evening ahead. A few days ago, I had imagined never again to possess the freedom of pursuing companionship such as she might afford me. She was tall, slender, dark, with deep sloe eyes and a floating cloud of raven hair. In my mind's eye I saw her as one of Poe's fair intellectual maidens. I smiled tenderly, envisioning a magical night, made all the more poignant by the necessity of my fleeing on the morrow.

But somehow the thing did not go as I had imagined. The steak that I served her was large and the young lady could not finish it or the zucchini and salad, so I finished them for her – meaning the gesture to be one of intimacy, of course... though, thinking back, perhaps she thought it a little odd. Afterwards, I lit a fire in the living room and we sat on the rug, where I offered her wine, fresh vegetables, and dip. She nibbled on a carrot and watched me intently as I finished up the rest of the plate. Perhaps it was rude for me to talk with my mouth full – she asked if I had a vitamin deficiency, and left soon after, saying that, unfortunately, she had to get up early the next day. I kissed her hand and bade my lady Ligeia farewell! I could not tell her that our paths would never cross again.

I watched her from the porch as she drove away, and then I went to the garden for solace. I carried a bagful of fresh basil, oregano, and tomatoes to bed, with a little olive oil and sea salt. Oh – and a few sprigs of green onion. I had never tasted anything so good. I thought sentimentally of my wife, of how she was now free from the cares and petty resentments of the world, and blessed her for my full stomach.

The people at school the next day seemed to look at me oddly. Though no one touched my lunch bag, I noticed all eyes were upon me every time I went to the refrigerator. It was true, my appetite certainly was keen. Perhaps I did have a vitamin deficiency; perhaps the stress that I had been under in the last few days had depleted my metabolic stores. But was that any reason to stare at a man? On the other hand, perhaps I was exaggerating their interest in my movements. It would be quite natural for a person in my position to think he was being watched! Really, though, I was bearing up remarkably well, considering. And what was the use in trying to act the old sourpuss now, on my last day? I decided to give it up. I told jokes and greeted everyone I saw in the halls with an almost Christmas spirit, all the while thinking, wouldn't they be surprised when, after I was long gone, they realized what I had gotten away with?

I left school and went back home for a brief rest. I had one more class that evening: farmhands puzzling over the intricacies of poetic meter. And, though another thirty years of yammering away upon the subject would still not have cleared it up to everyone's satisfaction, I was compelled to attend. There must be no change in my schedule, nothing to pique curiosity or cause comment. Tomorrow, I had no classes. Late tonight, I would drive away from this flat rural crossroads forever – forever.

There was barely time to eat before class, which began at seven. I ran out to the garden and, moving from plant to plant, fed my way quite round the acre. A little from here, a little from there – it was all delicious. The paste tomatoes in particular were of an amazing succulence that night. I can taste them even now. (Oh! Did ever Tantalus suffer as I?) Sitting between the rows in the light of the full moon, I picnicked as a satyr might.

I came to class that night, they later told me, with the knees and seat of my pants stained with loam, my hair disheveled, and my mouth sticky with juice. I myself remember nothing of the sort, though I do remember the panicky feeling of realizing, in the middle of lecturing, that I had forgotten to bring a snack. I dismissed the class soon after and ran home as quickly as I could, incapable of denying my desires any longer.

Yes, perhaps these actions were a bit eccentric. But are they any reason to invade a man's privacy? The bohunks around here think so. Before I left school that night, after going back to my office to fetch my keys, passing quickly by my father-in-law's office, I saw several of my hayseed pupils in there with him. Apparently they had come immediately from class to tell on me.

I had finished packing the car with my wife's jewelry, our other valuables, and as much food as I had room for. It was the height of the season; my wife had farmed intensively, wasting no space, and there was still much more than I could carry away with me. What a shame it would be to leave the rest behind, I thought miserably, to wither away without ever having been tasted! I stood for several moments in an agony of indecision.

The report they made to the judge when they first brought

me in contained no mention of the little accident with the shovel. They had simply come to check on me at the request of my father-in-law. After searching the house, the deputy reported, and finding it empty, he heard a rustling outside. He called, but no one answered. The sheriff was summoned, and he with his man searched the grounds. They found the car loaded up for a long trip. Directing their flashlights towards the low noises among the vegetable rows, they finally found me, moving slowly from the eggplants to the bell peppers. I said nothing in reply to their inquiries: my mouth was too full, and, knowing they had come to take me away, I kept stuffing it, and stuffing the pockets of my jacket. They had to pick me up and carry me away.

The judge, being of an inquisitive turn, wondered what it was about the vegetables that had made me behave so strangely. He ordered an examination of the plot. The disturbed soil above the place where my wife lay was noticed; they dug her up and charged me with her murder.

And so I pace here in this concrete room, staring through a small window in my door at a clock in a wire cage, telling me it is close to seven. I cannot hear the clock ticking or any other noise from outside: they tell me I have been too noisy, and that is why I must be kept in a sound-proof cell. Can it be that I have been giving voice to my longings?

I pace and check the clock, and wonder if it is working right: it seems to have been verging on seven for the last hour now. I would ask the warden for the correct time, but I would not like to appear ridiculous. It's not as if I have a need for the correct time. My days, which used to be full with classes and meetings, with comings and goings, are now empty.

It is gray outside, and I can't remember if this is dusk or cloudy dawn. The lights, the temperature are always the same here. The seasons, as they are in love, as they were in her garden, have been taken away from me. There is left to me only longing.

Still, I pace. Sometime – sometime, a psychologist is to come and interview me. I am eager and perhaps a little nervous about this. So much depends on the first impression, and I am not currently feeling at the height of my logical powers. Hopefully, my credentials will stand me in good stead. Thank heavens, I will be talking to an educated man!

They cannot just let me go. No, there is a *corpus*, a literal *corpus*, and it is no use hoping they will release me today. But, perhaps, if I get along well enough during this interview, the psychologist (I must remember to call him "Doctor" frequently) will accompany me back for a little while. I must be careful – I must use my co-operation, my recollections as leverage.

But I am afraid – afraid I will say too much, will say anything, will squander my thoughts, will bind and tie myself for execution with my words. For the truth is – the truth is that I would give anything, say anything, do anything they want me to – just to go back there, to pluck and to feast! Or, if they will not let me feast – but I must not let them know this! – if they will not let me feast, I will barter my life willingly for one glorious mouthful – for only one taste... of a tomato, ripe from her garden!

Honey

"I see you."

Roger stared at the computer screen and the message that had just come through. Whoever it is, they can't be writing to me, he thought. No one knows I'm here.

He was listening in on electronic mail communications from various random sites. In the old days, he would have had some fun, wreaked a little havoc to indicate his presence. But he was no longer a kid and had no intention of doing any harm. On the other hand, neither would he bother to leave a message, showing these sad people where they were vulnerable. That was their problem; he had no desire to get involved. He would remain undetectable, above it all.

Truth to tell, it was pretty boring; but so was everything else. He was tired – tired of watching TV, tired of driving around in his Jaguar, tired of going out and eating at the same old cruddy cafes and fast food joints down in the village. It wasn't much fun doing these things alone, and he couldn't think of anyone who wouldn't soon become a drag to have around.

He lived on a mountainside near Mammoth Lakes, California, in a pseudo-rustic, split-level, eight-room "cabin" – well, what else could you call it? It was made out of logs. The cabin had been built for luxury by the original owners, and it included all that would be expected: expanses of picture window looking out onto forest and valley, a huge river rock fireplace, a party-sized deck with Jacuzzi spa from which you could practically reach out and touch the pines that surrounded it. After he had bought the place, Roger had had every gismo he could think of loaded in on top: a receiver dish, an in-home theater – there was even a helicopter pad outside in the back, though no one had ever used it. The cabin now resembled no known architectural structure so much as a boy's Lego dream house of mixed theme, a sort of resort/fort/pirate lair.

The only thing missing being the little action figures. The nearest neighbors were half a mile away and, except for the morose cleaning lady who came in twice a week, mainly to boil tea and use the restroom, Roger hung out alone and communed with his electronics – at loose ends, hovering above (and eavesdropping on) the busy human world, detached but curious, and with a resentment he refused to analyze or even admit to.

This morning, he was fooling around, hacking into systems that were easy prey but would, he hoped, provide access to something better. They hadn't, so far. He had been reading prosaic messages regarding medical coding and auto shipments. For a while, he had been amused by a conversation between two school secretaries who were using their e-mail accounts, probably installed at local taxpayers' expense and greatly touted as an educational necessity, to piece together rumors about a romantic encounter between a board member and the president of the P.T.A. Another guy in some sort of business Roger couldn't identify (business was never once mentioned during the interchange) was complaining to his pal about the laziness and incompetence of the people at headquarters, wherever that was. Dummies. Just because they weren't making any noise, these people thought they couldn't be overheard.

He had been fooling around with passwords again, trying to penetrate a site, by reputation impregnable, of an obscure techie organization on the U.S.-Canadian border. After several suspenseful minutes, during which time he thought he was in, then out, then in again, he had picked up from somewhere those three odd little words:

"I see you."

What could this be? Had the systems operator detected him? If so, he had a strange way of expressing himself. Leaving the computer, Roger went into the kitchen to start up some microwave popcorn. He wasn't about to reply without getting some better idea of what he was dealing with.

The microwave dinged and he got his popcorn out, bringing the bag back to his desk. Still nothing new.

Just as he was about to get out of the server, the message reprinted itself: *"I see you,"* it said again, adding this time, *"Do you see me?"*

Well, if that didn't beat all. Had he met up with another hacker? Instead of some sort of macho warning, these words were friendly, even playful. Roger was intrigued. He wiped his hands on his pants and typed out the message, "OK, you got me. I surrender with my hands up."

"No hands up," the reply came. *"Talk to me."*

Whoever it is must be just as bored as I am, Roger thought to himself. Or was this some kind of trick? Well, there was only one way to find out. "OK," he typed back gamely. "My name is Roj. What's yours?"

It took awhile. Roger had gotten down to the unpopped kernels at the bottom of the bag by the time a reply came through: *"Call me honey."*

So, it was a she! Getting better all the time, Roger thought. He would play it cool, though there was no use hiding from himself that he was a little excited. How long had it been since he had met a nice girl? And a girl with computer skills!

Honey. Of course, that wasn't her real name; that was why it had taken her so long to answer back. She had been thinking of what she wanted to be called. It's telling, Roger thought to himself, that she chose something so sweet and old-fashioned. None of this warrior princess stuff. Just a sweet, feminine, homey kind of name, the kind of name dads called moms. Honey. He was oddly pleased.

"I like that," he typed back. He wanted to know what she looked like, of course, but it wouldn't be polite to ask, and he didn't want to blow it. "Are you at work?" he typed.

"No."

"Are you on your own machine?"

"I dont speak english very good," came the reply after several seconds.

Ooh, la la, thought Roger, maybe she's a French girl from Quebec. He thought for a moment, then sent back, "Your computer is very good, eh?"

"Yes thank you" came the reply. *"How are you?"*

They talked all that afternoon – or rather, Roger talked. The girl, Honey, mostly listened. It wasn't clear whether she understood much of what Roger sent her. (Maybe she was using him to learn English.) But the few comments she did make were overtly admiring. He bragged a bit about himself, maybe, but she didn't seem to be turned off – on the contrary, she seemed to like him and to be eager that he should like her.

As the afternoon sun traveled down towards the horizon, shooting its rays more and more directly into the west windows of the den, Roger stayed hunched at his desk, hammering away at the keyboard, chattering really, about anything and everything, not believing his luck. His eyes ached, dazzled by the strain of picking out the typed images from the glare coming in through the windows opposite, but he didn't think to get up and draw the shades. Dark reverse images of the objects in the room stood out upon the screen. Typing away still, Roger was distracted during the construction of some particularly delicate autobiographical passages by a figure, head and shoulders, black against black – someone standing in the room behind him? He turned around once or twice, startled to think that maybe in his absorption he had failed to hear someone come in. But no one was there, of course.

Finally, realizing Honey might have other things to do and feeling awfully hungry himself, Roger suggested they hang it up, adding that he wanted to talk to her again soon. She said she kept late hours, too, and so they agreed to meet again that night, around eleven.

All that evening, driving down to the village, eating at the pizza place, driving back up again, wandering from wall to wall at home, Roger savored his excitement. He suffered pleasurably from butterflies in the stomach: down at the pizza place he had almost not finished his spaghetti platter. Then, back home, after making himself some coffee, he forgot about drinking it until it was too cold and had to be dumped. What's going on here? he admonished himself, grinning goofily, striding around the living room and waving his arms in solitary exuberance. Come on, get a hold of yourself – keep cool. Gotta keep cool.

He knew she was beautiful. He could just sense it. And besides, he had met lots of ugly girls in chat rooms: they were always ready to talk dirty and to go on about their face and bodies, but when you suggested meeting, they got cagey, because it had all been lies. Honey hadn't been cagey. She had said it would be "very good" to meet him. He had already decided he would ask her to come up, offering to pay her plane fare. No – he would insist upon paying it. She seemed to be some kind of foreign exchange student, probably poor. Thanksgiving break was coming up soon....

He took a shower, put on clean clothes, and vacuumed the rug. Laughing at himself, he even got out some long candles that the previous owners had left in a dining room cabinet, and lit them in the den, where the computer was. The flickering light upon the rough-paneled walls created just the romantic effect he had hoped for. When all was ready, he switched the machine on, feeling weak with excitement.

She was already there, waiting for him. Roger was moved. Honey wasn't a girl to put on airs or to arrive fashionably late.

"I have wait a long time for you," she said.

His heart melted. "Not as long as I have, Honey," he typed, and echoed mentally, not as long as I have.

He had planned to be nonchalant and darkly witty but her few words were so warm and accepting that he found himself expressing himself without reserve or hesitation. It was like climbing into the Jacuzzi outside on a cool autumn day. He felt enveloped by her affection, stroked and petted. He told her everything about his past – about his dog, Cammie, and how he had cried when she died; about how his parents had moved around so much that he never had time to make many friends; about the start-up of his company, and his role therein as hero-entrepreneur. How it had all fallen apart – though he was paid off well. About his loneliness, his regrets. Everything he typed seemed to enthrall her.

In the small hours, he began to lose track of what he was saying. But it didn't matter – the connection between them was so strong that he could have been entering random alphanumeric strings, and still they would have grown closer.

"What color is your hair, Honey?" he asked, craving to know

her better.

"Black."

Black. How lovely. He himself, with his own sandy-haired, freckled fairness, had always dreamt of dark girls.

"Are you beautiful?" he couldn't help asking.

"Yes."

What else could she have said? Their relationship was based on honesty.

Sighing, he typed, "I knew that before asking." And he added before he had time to think, "Honey, I want to see you. I want you to be with me."

There. He had said it, and he would not take it back.

"I love you," she sent back to him. *"I want to touch you."*

It was too much. Roger's head rolled back in ecstasy. His arms dropped limp from the keyboard and, arching back against his state-of-the-art, ergonomic office chair, he murmured, "Oh, come to me, Honey, come to me..."

The hour was very late now, past two, maybe past three, he didn't know. Basking in the warmth of his passion, amazingly, he fell asleep right there.

He dreamt he was still staring at the screen. His body ached, his eyes burned, but he couldn't look away from that black surface. He was a rescuer poised above a whirlpool, searching for a sign of life from someone struggling deep down below.

And then he began to descry her: the shadow of a figure, head and shoulders, similar to what he had seen earlier in the afternoon, when he had thought it was only the reflection of objects in the room. At first it was just an indistinct outline, but with time he made out more clearly the form and even some of the features. The hair was long, or at least it flowed down below the shoulders – he could not see the outline of the neck. The head was petite and round, and what little he could see of the upper face indicated delicate bones, though the chin and jaw seemed disproportionately large. The eyes were small and looked, in the gloom, to be oddly set. Their symmetry did not appear to be perfect.

This shadowy face was not a pretty one. But Roger in his dream felt far from repulsed. Wonderingly, he put out a hand to touch the screen. His fingers were met with a warm, tingling pressure, a reciprocity from the being on the other side. He put out his other hand, and it too touched fingertips with the dark shadow behind the screen.

Moments passed. Roger's fingers dipped slightly into the surface of the screen; then the warm, sure pressure of the other would push him back out. He could feel the glass closing off around his fingers like liquid. The two of them swayed, balancing against each other for an unknown length of time.

Then Roger began to let go, and found that he couldn't. He could pull his fingers away from the surface of the screen, but the fingers on the other side stayed attached, almost as if they were glued to his. He felt the tug of the weight of the person behind the screen as he pulled away, frightened. The hands of the other, black hands, hot and dry, with shiny skin wrinkled like patent leather, would not detach themselves.

Frantic now to get away, he pulled as hard as he could. He woke up on the floor, hands and knees up, guarding himself and whimpering like a puppy.

He got up. The screen was dark, the screensaver having blotted out his last few interchanges with Honey. When he brought it up again, there was nothing new from her. He would have been glad to have company after that nightmare, but when he typed in a few words, she didn't respond, so he went to bed.

It must have been something he ate. Over and over, Roger struggled awake with the feeling of being suffocated, as if something heavy were lying on his chest. Finally, he stumbled out of bed and, running to the shower, doused himself with cold water. It was nine o'clock.

He decided to take it easy that morning and to wait till the same time they had talked last evening to try and contact Honey again. She must be sleepy, too. And he was having trouble shaking that funny nightmare feeling.

Thinking maybe he was coming down with something, Roger drove out to the village and paid a visit to the health food store, where he told a man in a pharmacist's smock and earth sandals how he had been suffering from nightmares, adding on, with a bachelor's self-absorption, the minute details of a few other problems that he had had, or thought he might have had, in the last few months. The man listened carefully and finally said that there could be a couple of causes for such symptoms. He suggested a holistic work-up, but in the meantime prescribed several vitamin supplements. Roger left with a paper bag full of pills, feeling better already.

He decided to eat at the coffee shop, where the food wasn't that great but the waitresses were friendly. He chose a booth in the sunshine, with a view of the street, and ordered meat loaf and mashed potatoes. The waitress, an older lady, was talkative enough with the other patrons, but she was so used to Roger eating with a computer manual in front of his face that she didn't try to chat with him. She stayed over near the cash register, gossiping with the owner.

Roger paid his bill and walked out. He just didn't feel like going home right away. Standing on the pavement outside the restaurant, he studied the people walking by, and it occurred to him to take a walk. So he did walk, past the city hall, past the library. Eventually, mildly exhausted, he sat on a bench, watching the people going about their daily lives. No one took note of him: this was not an interactive program. The weather changed, the sun sailed in and out between the clouds, alternately chilling and blinding him. He felt vaguely lonely and confused.

As dusk fell, he drove back home with a couple of paperbacks that he had picked up from the bookstore and planned to read while watching TV. That would bring him up to eleven, when he would talk with Honey again.

Coming in the door, he had a peculiar feeling that someone had been there in his absence. He didn't know why exactly. He had a good memory of the disposition of all the articles in his home – maybe something had been moved, and he had noticed it subconsciously? But no. He scanned the sunken living room: the great stone fireplace was bare, as usual, and nothing else, not a throw pillow, was out of place. A real estate circular lay rolled up on the coffee table, where he had left it after picking it up off the porch a few days ago.

The kitchen had a stack of dishes in the sink, just the same as when he had left it. Nothing else was out, all the expensive cooking equipment being in its usual place behind the knotty pine cupboard doors and inside the drawers, which were all neatly closed.

In the den, he glanced over the shelves: every book in place. Yet the feeling persisted that someone had been here – in fact, was here right now.

Especially in this room, the den. He had felt it much stronger here the moment he came in.

Then he remembered his nightmare. It must be because of that. He still hadn't cleared it out of his mind, and his imagination was getting the better of him.

Roger wished he had some hard work to do, the sort of all-nighter stuff he had done before he left the company. But for many months, he had been taking it easy, and now there was nothing to do, nothing. Maybe it was time to get back on the horse. Tomorrow he would start a list, make some phone calls.

The paperbacks were unenthralling. He flipped through them, tossed them away, and channel-hopped until eleven, when he switched the computer on and tried to get a hold of Honey.

She wasn't waiting like last time. In fact, she wasn't there at all – he would have to wait for her to contact him again. Oddly enough, when contrasted with how he had felt yesterday, he was a little relieved. She did seem like a very nice girl, but what did he really know about her? Maybe it was just as well she hadn't been there tonight. It was one thing to be intimate on line; the dangers of a face-to-face relationship were much greater. You might find the person completely alien, and it wasn't like you could just pull the plug and they would disappear. It could have been very sticky. He made a mental note to be more careful in the future.

Roger fell asleep in front of the TV and had another bad night of it. This time he suffered from a recurring dream: he saw himself sleeping, as he was, on the couch. But his viewpoint was not from the couch, it was above himself, looking down, as if he were another person in the room. Nothing happened in these dreams, but they were imbued with such a deep sense of dread that, after a few moments, he was forced awake. He would look around, turn his attention to the TV again, fall back asleep, and the dreams would

begin once more. In them, a dead calm reigned – the television faded; there was indeed a complete absence of sound. The pounding
of his heart he felt as a vibration rather than a noise. From dream
to dream, his perspective would change: sometimes he would be
watching from the doorway, sometimes from the corner between
the windows, sometimes he even watched from up high, as if he
were crouching balanced somehow upon the exposed ceiling raf-
ters. He could feel and smell the dusty wood that he clung to, and
the vibration of his heart – *his* heart? – reverberating through the
beams to his clinging fingers.

Eventually, he got off the couch and climbed upstairs to his
bedroom proper, stopping first at the bathroom medicine cabinet
to grab and swallow down a couple of sleeping pills. Crawling into
bed, he once again fell asleep. And if he woke up during the night,
it left no memory upon him

He woke in the early afternoon, listless and grainy-eyed. The
disturbing feeling of another presence, of someone else being in
the house, was stronger now than it had been yesterday. As he
brushed his teeth, he couldn't help turning his head to see if anyone was looking in at him from the dimly-lit hallway.

Downstairs, although the afternoon sun streamed in, the
kitchen seemed full of shadow. Popping a few of the vitamin pills
he had bought last afternoon and spreading a bagel with peanut
butter, Roger still couldn't stop turning, looking around at the
back door, then over his shoulder, to the door that led to the dining
room. Worse yet, when he sat down at the kitchen table with his
bagel and carton of milk, he couldn't resist getting up again almost
immediately and looking under the table. He knew this was very
odd on his part; that this was the way many psychoses began: with
a feeling of paranoia, of being set upon and watched.

Mind over matter, he thought nervously, and sat down with
the paper in the living room, determined to calm himself with
the distraction of reading. He got through the business section,
but it took effort. The news of the world seemed incomprehen-
sible today.

Throwing down the paper, he went to the computer and saw
he had a message.

"I see you," it read. *"Can you see me?"*

"There you are, Honey," Roger typed happily. "Long time no see."

"No see?" came the reply. *"Try. Try to see me."*

What is she talking about, Roger thought. Muddle-headed girl. He hoped she wasn't one of those Zen or metaphysical types who would expect him to meditate with her, or send brain wave messages across the ether or something. He was in no mood to be indulgent right now.

"How can I see you, Honey, unless you send a photo?" he sent back.

It took a while for her to reply. After a minute, however, the message came through:

"You must try to see me."

"You're somewhere on the Eastern Seaboard, Honey!" he typed in, exasperated. "I'm in California!"

At this point came what was for Honey a rapid torrent of words. *"I am here. I am with you. I see you. Try to see me. I want to touch you. Try –"*

Roger, who had been staring at the screen, did not read the rest of the message. He backed off, pushed his chair back, looked around the room – all around the room, quickly. The feeling of being watched – of a presence, of an unwanted closeness – was unbearable. *Try to see me,* she had said. *I want to touch you...*

Roger ran out of the room, out of the house to the garage. Thankfully, he had left his keys in his pocket; he had slept all night with them in his jeans... Here they were! He started up the car, backed it up, and headed down the driveway to the road.

He drove fast. The palms of his hands were wet on the wheel. After several minutes of ignoring the speed limit – luckily, no cop cars were in sight – he began to come to himself. He slowed down, but kept going down the main highway, passing through the village, heading south.

It was two hours to Independence, a town that he had lived in for a while when he was a boy. Late in the afternoon, he stood in front of the house of his old friend – really, his only friend in those days, a girl named Robin.

He struck it lucky. She was still living at her mom's house, and in fact was there to open the screen door to him. But the enthused and affectionate greeting he had hoped for was not forthcoming.

Robin served him a Coke, getting nothing for herself and settling stiffly down upon a chair she had dragged in from the dining room, although there was plenty of room on the couch for both of them.

She had a little boy now. (She was divorced from his father who, Roger gathered without being told, had been the irresponsible type.) The boy showed him his prized possession, a rock collection in a coffee can: "and when you close them up inside, you can shake it, and it makes a lot of noise." After taking off the keys, Roger gave the kid his keychain, a heavy metal cube embossed with a map of the world. Roger showed how it would make a lot more noise than the rock, because of its hardness and shape. The boy listened with a frown, nodded gravely, then hurried off to show his grandpa.

"Smart kid," said Roger. "He'll be a rock scientist someday, if not a rocket one. I'll be asking him to go into business with me in a few years."

"I don't know if I want him to get too heavily into computers," Robin replied icily. "I don't want him forgetting about people."

She had never been the subtle type. "I'm sorry I never came back here, Robin," Roger said after a pause. "I know I promised to. But things were happening so fast there for a while, when I was starting up. And then, I figured you'd be happily married or gone off to school somewhere... I did look for you a couple of times on the Web," he finished lamely.

"I'm not on the internet. It's a waste of time."

Normally, Roger would have felt duty-bound to defend the reputation of his beloved cyber-homeland. But he realized that, at this point, it would be counterproductive. He just nodded his head as if to show he realized that some folks felt that way.

"Why are you here, Roger?" Robin finally asked. "What beamed you down here, today of all days?"

It was no use denying that he had come here for a specific purpose; if he tried to finesse her, it would be all the worse for him in the end.

"Remember when we were kids, all those horror stories we used to read?" he finally asked.

She nodded.

"Well," he gulped, "Something like that is happening to me right now."

When she didn't laugh, he knew he had come to the right person. He explained and, of course, she was skeptical, but she must have felt some curiosity and perhaps a glimmer of old affection for him, because she agreed to go back to the house with him and check it out. He placed his faith upon her open-mindedness, he said. If she saw the messages from Honey and felt the vibes in the house, then he'd know he wasn't imagining things. If she didn't, well, he'd just have to check himself into a psychiatric hospital.

On the way back to his house, Roger got Robin to laugh, in spite of herself, over some of their corny old jokes. They argued PC versus Apple – even though she *said* she never went near a computer anymore, Robin was still passionate about Macs. It began to feel just like old times, except they were riding in a sports car now, not tooling along on their Stingray bikes.

When they got to the cabin, Roger opened the door with apprehension. But Robin popped right in. He was proud and gratified by her enthusiasm about the house. She oohed and aahed over everything and had to see every room. The view of the valley between the pines captivated her, as did the fireplace and the deck outside. Roger turned on all the lights and fired up the Jacuzzi, and Robin dipped her hand in it – but, though his encouragement was sincere, she refused to get in any deeper.

She told him it was a gorgeous house; that she absolutely loved it; that he was so lucky. And she said nothing about vibes. Roger himself felt nothing amiss in the house now. It was his old house again. Or rather, with Robin here, it felt more like home. When she said it was late and she had to go, he awkwardly asked her if she would stay.

But of course that was the wrong thing.

"I don't lead that kind of lifestyle," she said, her previous hostility flaring up again. "I have a son at home, remember?"

Guiltily, Roger realized that he had forgotten all about the little guy.

"I guess this is the way you get girls to come home with you?" Robin continued. "Tell them you live in a haunted house?" She headed toward the front door, but then turned to face him one more time. "Lemme tell you something, Roger: I came here tonight because we *used* to be friends – not because we are."

She would have gone on about it if he had given her the chance, but he was too humiliated to say another word either in agreement or defense, and they drove back to her house in silence.

As it had always been when they were younger, he was sullen long after she had gotten over her anger. He glowered at her when she said goodbye, and was too surprised to react when she leaned over and kissed him softly on the lips before going into the house. Their first kiss. "Goodbye, Roger," she said.

Oh, they were all alike. Honey had now been forgotten, but was the cure any better than the disease? He had been badly hurt by Robin's words. Driving back home alone over the dark road, however, petulance was soon countered by self-doubt: she seemed to think he was immature and selfish. Was he? He hadn't meant to be that way. She should have understood that he hadn't meant to be that way.

Preoccupied with these and other, similarly exasperating thoughts, he unlocked the front door of the cabin. Entering, he felt as if he had been struck in the face. The sensation of being watched was overwhelming. And this time, there was no possible way of ascribing neutrality to the presence: the air bristled with hostility.

"My imagination!" Roger said out loud.

In the den, the computer was on, though he knew he had turned it off after showing Robin a few things. And there was a message:

"Why do you bring her here?"

Roger turned off the computer without letting it power down. As he turned away, a metal yardstick that had been his father's and that he kept on a shelf above the computer fell, or rather flung itself out of the shelf, and slashed itself up against the back of his head. Roger stumbled away, prepared to run, but now the yardstick lay on the floor as if it had never moved. He touched his head; his fingers came back looking like they had been dipped blood.

He suddenly felt very weak. In the bathroom, he adjusted the medicine cabinet's three-way mirror to check the back of his head. It was hard to see anything, his hair was so thick. He fingered the back of his head carefully. "I need stitches," he told himself. His voice sounded very shaky. He felt sick to his stomach.

Roger turned around quickly, though it made his dizziness worse and he had to grab the sink to keep from falling over. He thought he had seen a reflection other than his own in the mirror, someone standing behind him. But no, there was no one behind him....

Slowly, he turned back to the mirror, knowing beforehand what he was going to see. Of course, expecting her, he would find her. That was the way these psychological things worked. And he probably had a concussion... But if she was in his imagination, why couldn't he see her better? Murky, shifting – the outline of a head and shoulders, with long hair, or maybe it was some sort of veil or flap over the head. Eyes like two black balls, poorly matched. They glistened and rolled. Roger peered forward, fascinated. Had he been able to see the eyes moving before? And the mouth – he had never seen it in this much detail – the mouth was moving. It was moist and flexible – it moved too much. Among intermittent spasms and fluid gulpings, it seemed to labor, forming...? Words?

A shot of adrenalin cleared Roger's brain. He ran out of the house, ran to his car. Soon, once again, he was driving down the road. He had nowhere to go for help this time, but he needed to get away from the house, away from the one who now lived there with him – who would be waiting for him, whether figment of his imagination or not, when he got back.

Well, then, he would never go back.

It was so dark and the unlit road was misty – he couldn't drive as fast as he needed to. Luckily, there were no other cars on the road.

He turned on the high beams and the radio, turned on the windshield defroster and fan against the fog and clamminess. Adrenaline was still pumping, and he drove fast, with a lot of braking on the curves. This forced him to concentrate on the road beyond his windshield. Physical danger was a welcome distraction. The road dipped and turned, the pines on either side went skimming past, but his heart began to slow, his mind to stop its skittling.

He should have his car washed more often. A stubborn, sticky dust had settled on the windshield. Dusty patches were mixing with the moist air and the resulting sludge slid between the wipers, but there was a middle patch through which the road and the pines could be seen clearly. Something was moving ahead – two black, rolling...Roger realized he was seeing eyes, the eyes of the face again, the face in the mirror. It was becoming clearer. The eyes, the rippling mouth – hush, hush! She was trying to speak to him!

The car rolled off the highway and into a ditch, running parallel with the road until it stopped. He had had his eyes closed. It was a miracle he had run into a clearing. If he had hit a tree, he would have been killed. Now, he got out and climbed slowly, sliding over the slick wet weeds, back up to the roadway.

Roger bent down, hands on knees, and tried to catch his breath. He couldn't run even if he wanted to right now – his legs felt like wet sand. He stood up and ran his fingers through his hair over and over again, trying to think what to do. There had to be something to do.

So Honey had followed him out of the house. This was the first time *that* had happened. Of course, it was all in his mind. No, he didn't believe in her, not for one second... But she had followed him out of the house! There was no use trying to run away.

There was no use running away. With this thought in his head, Roger half-trotted, half-crawled the two miles back to the house. The lights were still on and the front door was ajar. He climbed the stairs, went into the living room, and fell back onto the sofa.

There was a crackle and a hum from the den. Roger, turning his head, saw through the doorway that the computer was booting up. Honey wanted to speak to him.

Suddenly, rage swept over him. He got up, strode to the computer monitor and knocked it onto the floor, where it tumbled, face-down, lifeless.

"If you want to talk to me," he screamed at the walls, at the air around him, "Come on out! Come on! I'm waiting for you!"

He went on for some time in this fashion, yelling and knocking things off of the desk, throwing things at the walls, until he fell back again onto the living room couch, his strength spent.

She hadn't responded to his tirade, and if he had hoped to frighten her away, his rage had been ineffectual: she was still there. Exhausted, empty, he was perceptive now of her finer movements.

And, now, he had nothing left with which to oppose her. He couldn't move, he couldn't think. He lay back, waiting.

After awhile, she began to move towards him.

In a dream, between waking and sleeping, he spent that night. He dreamt of little things, little sounds: a crackle, a sigh; the pull of heavy, dry air; the touch of something unknowing, unknowable. Odd little sensations; pieces of memories. Yet, for the rest of his life, these memories were more than he could bear to think of, for they were always associated in his mind with a feeling of helplessness, of paralysis, of irremediable violation.

There is a place farther up north and towards the coast: a little expensive, but safe; quiet; private. And, if you can't abide a TV screen in your room, or a mirror, or even an uncovered window, then things are quickly arranged to your liking, without argument or remonstrance. It makes no difference to the people who work there whether your story is true or not. They are ready to indulge you: "There are more things in heaven and earth," etc. A comforting, non-judgmental group.

These are the people among whom Roger spent the winter after his encounter with Honey, and he is beginning to think that it was a simple nervous breakdown that he had; and to hope that, at any rate, he will never see her again.

Robin, his childhood friend, visits him most weekends. They go for walks along the cliffs and sit together on a sun-worn wooden bench above the ocean, where she holds his head against the hollow of her neck while he cries. Then he apologizes and says he doesn't know why he's such a wimp. She wipes the tears from his cheeks and smiles at him, though her eyes are questioning.

Roger's house, the cabin above the pines near Mammoth, was sold without Roger ever going back. He can't even recall the selling price, and his only instruction to the real estate agent was to sell it as quickly as possible – "as is." The house was bought by a husband and wife, both medical doctors, both so busy with their careers that they don't have much time to spend there. Mostly, they sleep in their apartment in Sacramento; often, they don't make it home for weeks at a time.

They have two children: a girl, who is married and living in the Bay Area, and a teen-aged boy, a freshman at Berkeley who comes home weekends and holidays. He is the quiet type. He doesn't seem to mind if the house is deserted. His mother worries about him, wonders if he is overloaded with homework – he seems so withdrawn, so distant when she calls. But all her friends say that's normal at his age. Lately, he spends most of his time on the computer.

He doesn't have a girlfriend – yet.

Mean Mister Mullins

"The old man can't last much longer at the rate he's going," Dr. Chisholm said on his way out. "By those latest blood gas results, he should be dead already – though he's fooled me before. He's been at the brink of death more than once, only to rally at the last hour."

Melanie stood at the wide oak doorway of the old mansion, trying to look calm and not show how scared she was to see the doctor going – leaving her alone again with that awful old man, her patient. The doctor had always been friendly enough to her, but he was a busy man and had no time to give encouragement and advice.

Besides, it wasn't his fault if she had taken on more than she could handle. Melanie wasn't a certified nurse yet – she was merely a cheaper substitute. But this Fall, she hoped to start classes for her R.N. And complaining about a weak old man's behavior, however inappropriate that behavior was, would not be a propitious way to start out her new career. So it was probably best to say nothing and just tough it out.

"...Not that you should let it bother you," the doctor added over his shoulder as he hurried down the stairs to his Mercedes. "If what I hear about the old buzzard is true, he hasn't given you or anyone else reason to mourn his passing."

She watched the doctor's car disappear down the roadway back to town, and then she turned reluctantly back to the house, feeling a little guilty because the doctor had thought she was sad about Mr. Mullins dying. She didn't feel that way at all. She guessed she should feel bad – he was kin, after all – but the fact was that she didn't. Going back into the dark old house, though, and shutting the heavy door behind her *did* make her feel like crying.

The doctor's visit, so quickly over, was the one bright spot in the long, leaden day. *He* wasn't afraid of Mr. Mullins, nor did he seem at all affected by the gloom that hung so heavily over the place. Cheerful, confident, and loud, Dr. Chisholm brought in a breath of fresh air from the outside world. He made Mr. Mullins seem, by contrast, not so large and looming – made him appear what he really was: a very frail, very sick old man.

Mr. Mullins was docile during Dr. Chisholm's visits. He looked like he wouldn't hurt a fly. The housekeeper, before she had been sent away, had told Melanie that Mr. Mullins behaved so well toward Dr. Chisholm because he was afraid of the doctor's temper, which was legendary in the community. He once had a nurse dismissed for answering him back during a crisis in the emergency room, and he could be just as ruthless with his patients. If you didn't follow his orders, or even complained too much, he refused to treat you. And no one wanted to risk having that happen because he was the best doctor in town.

Every day, after the doctor left, Melanie would try to adopt his hearty and impervious manner, though it didn't come naturally to her at all. Now, she resolutely climbed the stairs to her patient's room and said (in what she hoped was a no-nonsense voice), "Mr. Mullins, it's time for your protein drink!"

Mr. Mullins was always in either one of two moods: good or bad. For Melanie, his good mood was worse than his bad because, when in a bad mood, he simply insulted and berated her, and she could get away relatively quickly. But when he was in a good mood, he liked her company. He thought up reasons to keep her in the room; and then, of course, there were the little tricks he liked to play.

"My protein drink!" Mr. Mullins cackled jovially. "Just what I need to give me a little boost where I need it most! Although I'm sure, my dear," he leered as Melanie poured the contents of a very expensive little can into a tumbler, "that your presence is as much of a stimulant as any red-blooded male could handle."

So, he was in a good mood this afternoon. He had fished around for reassurance from Dr. Chisholm that his condition wasn't hopeless, and when the doctor had made vague reference to some possibly encouraging exam results, Mr. Mullins had found reason to rejoice.

But he could only take a few sips of his protein drink before his stomach was full. When Melanie came back to take away the glass, he said in a teasing voice, "I have a little surprise for you."

She quailed to hear those words, but turned and waited.

"Don't you want to know what it is?" the old man wheezed out, seemingly disappointed by her lack of enthusiasm.

Now, here was the sort of thing that drove Melanie to distraction. Of course, she didn't want to know what it was – she didn't want any presents from him. But, if she told him that, she'd never hear the end of it. And, if she said she *did* want to know, he'd spend the next fifteen minutes making her play guessing games.

"Don't you WANT to know what it IS?" he repeated, fairly yelling this time.

"I don't know," she said miserably.

"You don't know?" Mr. Mullins repeated. "You don't know? You're a quick thinker, aren't you, Nursey? Bet you do just great at school. Don't know why I'm subsidizing you, when you can't even answer a simple yes-or-no question. Well, can you?" he asked, after a pause.

"Can I what?" Melanie asked.

"Answer a simple yes-or-no question?"

"I guess so," Melanie replied.

"Well, then," Mr. Mullins continued, smiling excitedly. "I've got a little something for you. Do you want it or not?"

"Yes," said Melanie, "I guess so."

"Put your hands under the covers then."

Melanie stared at the wizened old man. It was true that he often made lascivious jokes, but she had never had to worry about him actually *doing* anything before.

"Go ahead – put your hands under the covers," he gurgled, "and feel around."

Melanie was sure that a more experienced nurse would never let herself be put in this position, but how to get out of it? If she refused, Mr. Mullins would keep bothering her about it. If she said it was improper, he'd accuse her of having a dirty mind, and *that* would supply him with ammunition indefinitely. Melanie felt her face getting red. Soon, Mr. Mullins would notice, and start teasing her about *that*. She figured she had just better get it over with as soon as possible, and started feeling around on top of the bedspread, looking for lumps.

"No, you idiot!" Mr. Mullins cried. "How are you going to find anything that way? Put your hands *under* the covers."

Awkwardly, gingerly, Melanie passed her hands between the two smooth, freshly-laundered sheets – she had just changed them this morning – avoiding Mr. Mullins' scrawny limbs as well as she could. Was she looking for something small, or big? She didn't want to ask. Mr. Mullins was chuckling delightedly.

"Oh!" Melanie cried. Something had caught her hand! She dragged it out to find her first three fingers caught in a mousetrap fastened to the top of a tin box. They tingled painfully as she pulled them loose. Mr. Mullins was wheezing with laughter as Melanie blinked back tears.

Suddenly he stopped laughing. "Oh, dear," he cried, looking at her closely. "I hope you're not hurt, are you? Those things aren't supposed to *hurt*, really."

Melanie shook her head, her throat too tight to speak.

"I'm so sorry, Melanie. Really I am," said Mr. Mullins after looking at her penitently for several seconds. "You know I never want to cause you any discomfort. It's just that I get so bored lying here all day, with nothing to do."

"It's all right," Melanie mumbled.

"Well, at any rate," he said cheerfully, "You'll forgive me when you see what's in the box. You like chocolate, don't you? Didn't you say that you liked chocolate?"

Early on, before she understood Mr. Mullins' personality, Melanie had made the mistake of confiding that small fact to him. Now, she nodded, concentrating on keeping her composure until she could get away downstairs again.

"Well, then. Go ahead – open it!" the old man said.

She had trouble prying open the box because of her hurt fingers, but she knew he would insist on her trying the chocolate in front of him. She felt she couldn't stand to eat anything right now, especially not with those rheumy blue eyes staring at her. But, finally, she pulled the lid off.

Something sprang out, high over her head and then fell on her! In her nervous state she couldn't help screaming, even though she knew before she screamed that it was just a coiled spring, covered with cloth and painted to look like a snake.

Mr. Mullins was laughing his wheezy, chokey laugh again, hunched forward in bed and holding onto his knees with his bony hands for support. Melanie picked up the cloth snake, put it with the box on the table, and walked quickly out – but not before Mr. Mullins saw her face all twisted up and red with incipient tears.

"Hey, Nursey!" he called out after her. "Don't ya want your candy?" And he held up the box, at the bottom of which was one fat, dusty bonbon, its chocolate coating whitened with age.

"That was a great one!" Mr. Mullins wheezed. And, for the next several minutes, he alternately laughed and concentrated on getting his breath back. This is the way I want to go, he thought to himself: laughing. What a silly ninny of a girl. Real luck finding her – most of those nurse's aides were too hard-boiled to have any fun with. And what a stroke of serendipity for her to be a relative! He had always hated his relatives. And, since he had grown old, he hated young people, too. Above all, he hated people who had no sense of humor. He saw it as a duty, as well as a pleasure, to teach people like that a lesson.

Now, he could spend the rest of the day savoring his victory. "I almost scared her to death!" he said to himself aloud, cackling again.

Suddenly another brilliant idea occurred to him. Everybody thought that he was dying, which gave him the perfect opportunity for – for what? This would take some thought and careful planning, but it would be well worth it. He had about used up his stock of rubber mice and dribble glasses. This would have to be something completely different. Something beyond expectation.

"I *almost* scared her to death," he repeated musingly. "I wonder... I wonder how close I could come to *really* doing it..."

Melanie spent the rest of the afternoon downstairs, crying. She was ashamed of herself, but couldn't help it. The hurt fingers and the cloth snake scare were the least of it. She was lonely and homesick. She missed her family so much – coming from a big one, she had never even known what loneliness felt like until now. It was horrible.

But she couldn't go back home. This was her only chance for nursing school any time in the near future – she had saved up enough money for tuition and books, but there was little left over for food and lodging. Her grades, though solid, weren't good enough to qualify for a scholarship, and the counselor had said the curriculum was much too heavy for students to try to work while attending classes, at least during the first year.

The family had talked it over, and finally her mother had re-membered a well-to-do cousin, now dead, who had a surviving husband in the college town. Mother had written to him, explain-ing the problem, and Mr. Mullins had written back saying Melanie was welcome to stay with him while attending school if she was willing to help around the house a bit in return.

Once Melanie arrived and, grateful and eager to please, had shown him what a good cook she was, and how careful a house-keeper, Mr. Mullins had let his own housekeeper go, saying to Melanie that she would do just fine for him by herself. Melanie had felt horrible for the housekeeper, but Mrs. Packard said it was all right. She would find another job through her agency soon enough – and, in fact, this would give her an opportunity to go on a little vacation first.

"I'm going somewhere where it's sunny and warm," Mrs. Pack-ard had said, "This old house is the gloomiest old tomb I've ever worked in. The one I feel sorry for is you – cooped up here all by yourself with that old devil. He's famous for his stinginess, you know. That mean old man never did anything for anybody except he could demand twice as much in return."

Mrs. Packard had promised to send a postcard from the beach. Every day, Melanie checked the mail, but it was always junk.

For the rest of the afternoon, Mr. Mullins was quiet. He didn't call her once, and when she brought up his dinner tray, he didn't bother her at all, or even leer at her, really. Usually, he gloated quite a bit after he had succeeded in making her cry. But this evening he seemed preoccupied. He didn't eat much. He told her he wasn't feeling very well.

The next day, during his morning visit, he told Dr. Chisholm that he was feeling weaker. The doctor replied noncommittally, but said privately to Melanie that, though Mr. Mullins's signs and symptoms showed no real change from yesterday, he could be starting to go downhill.

"Often, it's the patient who tells the doctor he's dying, not the other way around," Dr. Chisholm said, folding up his stethoscope and cramming it into his suit pocket. "Although I always thought that he was in denial... Luckily, he's a hospice patient – he doesn't want to be hospitalized under any circumstances. So, if he starts sinking, don't you call the paramedics. Just keep him comfortable and let him go." And Dr. Chisholm drove off quickly – he was running late on his rounds.

Melanie had wanted to ask if there was any reason, any excuse she could use to have someone come stay in the house with her while all this occurred, but the doctor had gone off too fast. She had already asked Mr. Mullins if her little sister could come to help with the cleaning, but he had flat-out refused.

Now she asked him again, and again he said no. "You and I don't need anyone else around," he rasped weakly, holding on tight to her hand and looking at her with a pathetic expression. "You'll stay with me to the end, won't you, sweetie? I'll make it worth your while." And then he closed his eyes. Even this much speaking seemed to wear him out now. Melanie tried to go but he tightened his grip on her hand. She watched him trying to catch his breath, the bones in his chest laboring. Finally, he continued. "You can't leave me – you need a place to stay. Take care of me in my last moments, and you can stay here after I die. I've instructed my lawyer..." And once again he ran out of air. After a long interval, Melanie pulled her hand away, unresisted. Mr. Mullins had fallen into an exhausted sleep.

The next morning was cloudy again, and when Melanie tried to turn on the little light over the kitchen table, it wouldn't work. She put in another bulb, but that didn't do any good, and soon she realized that all the lights were out, all over the house. She told Mr. Mullins she would call the electric company, but he told her he had already called them – to have the electricity shut off!

"Why?" asked Melanie, more surprised than frightened for once.

"I can tell..." the old man wheezed, blinking wearily at her, "I'm not going to be here much longer. No use... wasting electricity..."

Melanie couldn't believe what she was hearing. Maybe Mr. Mullins' ability to reason was leaving him.

"But your oxygen equipment –" she cried. "It won't work without electricity!"

"What good does all that do me?" Mr. Mullins said with something of his old exasperation. Then his voice became weak again and he murmured, "When it's time to go, it's... time to go."

So there was nothing she could do except search for candles. Luckily, there were plenty in the kitchen and dining room drawers. She lit a few, then she tried to leave a message for Dr. Chisholm's answering service. But here was another surprise – the phone was dead! Mr. Mullins must have had that service cut off, too.

This was too much. Even though he had forbidden her to leave the house without asking him (and, when she asked, he generally refused to let her), she decided to go next door to call the doctor.

The distance between the two sprawling mansions was considerable. She ran all the way, fearing that Mr. Mullins might ring for her while she was gone. As she came up the neighbor's drive, two big Doberman dogs barked and growled and leaped at the fence as if they would have loved to get at her.

The butler who answered the door said the owners were not home. He didn't hide his suspicion that she was up to something, and made her repeat her story several times before allowing her in to use the phone. Melanie left a message and then sat waiting awkwardly for a call back. But Dr. Chisholm was off that day and the doctor who did call back didn't seem to understand what she was talking about, nor care to waste any time trying. He ended by saying that the old man probably hadn't paid his electric bill, that there was nothing *he* could do about *that,* and that he'd pass along the note to Dr. Chisholm's office nurse.

The butler escorted her out coldly and Melanie slunk back to the house of Mr. Mullins. The day was cloudy still and the big rooms were hung with shadows.

Mr. Mullins didn't seem to notice the gloom. He slept with his eyes rolled back in his head most of the time now, and he was not always oriented to time and place. She could rouse him long enough to sip a little soda, but he soon fell back into a stupor. At one point, he whispered that the candles Melanie had lit made him dream he was in church. Was this his funeral service? he wanted to know. Melanie, a regular church-goer herself, was reminded more of old horror movies than anything else. She had a terrible case of the creeps; and all that long, dark afternoon, she was constantly turning to see if someone or something was moving behind her, only to realize for the hundredth time that it was her own shadow moving with the flicker of the candlelight.

The television no longer worked and there were very few books in the house. Mr. Mullins subscribed to no newspaper. He wanted no supper, and she herself couldn't eat. As afternoon slowly tolled into evening, she sat down in the living room, opposite the stairway, and waited.

Waited to see when Death would make its visit.

The house was silent. Outside, night fell. Melanie sat studying the pool of light from the candle at her elbow, reflected in the black square of undraped window glass. It flickered noiselessly.

The question struck her: Would she know when he was dead? Would he call her when he was about to go? Probably she should go up and sit with him. But he hadn't requested that of her, and she couldn't seem to force herself up the stairway. Darkness seemed to float down from it like smoke.

Of course, if he died without calling, she would know only because he *wouldn't* call her. She would wait for the bell to ring, and it wouldn't – that was all.

It could happen at any time. Maybe it had already….

She must have fallen asleep in the big old armchair she was curled up in. She dreamt she was going up the stairs, candle in hand, to answer that tinkling summons. Upon pushing open the heavy door to his room, she found him, hunched up in his usual position, hands on knees. But this time, with a face like a skull – open eye sockets, dangling jaw, white hair streaming as if stirred by the heat of a furnace. Turning towards her, he raised the bell, and swung it again between a skeleton thumb and forefinger, ringing again, summoning her to come closer…

She awoke with a start – the bell *had been* ringing.

For a long while she sat paralyzed with fear. The candle beside her, which, when she had fallen asleep, had been a full-sized taper, was now burnt down to only an inch. Other than that, there was no indication of how long she had slept, or of what hour it was. Outside, it was dark – and inside, dark too, and utterly quiet – except for the echo of that tinkling bell. But was that only in her mind? Had it really been rung?

In the dead calm that followed, Melanie fervently prayed for God's help. Mr. Mullins was her patient, and she must find out if he needed her. She had to go up there.

Mechanically reciting her prayers, she got up, found another candle and, with trembling fingers, lit it. The candlestick wouldn't stay in its socket, and she had to hold it with both hands as she climbed the stairs.

Just as she had left it, the door to Mr. Mullins' room was ajar. She pushed it open slowly and quietly, peering around the door at the bed, where she could see him lying there, motionless. She stood for a moment just looking – two candles on the tables at either side of the bed lit his body, wrapped up in the white sheet she had placed over him just this morning. At that time she had carefully tucked the corners of the sheet under the mattress, but now they were pulled up, and the old man's body lay swathed, like a cocoon awaiting rebirth – or, more factually, like a corpse, neatly done up and ready for transport to the morgue.

The face, too, was covered. The arms were close at the sides of the chest, the legs straight. *How – why had he laid himself out like this?* Melanie wondered in horror.

Standing in the doorway, she watched the chest for signs of respiration – she could see none. At times, the candles flickered, and the shadows they threw on the corpse's shrouding made it look as if there was some slight spasm or movement. But longer observation led her to conclude that this was an illusion, and convinced Melanie that the corpse – for corpse it must be – was completely and finally at rest.

But, to be sure, she had to touch it – unwrap one of the arms, and feel the wrist for a pulse. Only then could she go to find a phone and notify the doctor on call, so that he would come and pronounce Mr. Mullins officially dead.

She approached the bed and started pulling the sheet slowly

and carefully out from underneath the body. The weight of the body and the uneven foam rubber surface of the eggcrate mattress beneath it made this difficult. She could feel her heart pounding and perspiration starting at the nape of her neck. Her hands trembled. That's just adrenaline, she told herself. I'm feeling panicky, but there's nothing to be afraid of, really. It's just a dead body. It can't hurt me. And, in a moment, I'll be out of the house – I'll walk until I find a pay phone...

She got the sheet on the side near her free and pulled it back to uncover the corpse's arm. She reached out to feel for a pulse...

The moment she touched the hand, it jerked! And, before she could move away, the cold, bony fingers had grasped tightly ahold of her arm! She tried desperately to tug herself loose, but the hand of Mr. Mullins would not let go. The sound of her own screaming was like a wind rushing in her ears as she saw the head and torso of the body rise, rise slowly to a sitting position. The face, though still wrapped in its shroud, turned toward her, the hand still grasped her tightly, and the body bowed forward to her in a most friendly, intimate manner. From underneath the sheeting, she heard the muffled voice of Mr. Mullins, deceased, cackling gleefully, *"I just called to let you know – I'm dead!"*

The sun had just risen. Dr. Chisholm was planning to stop by Mr. Mullins' house earlier than usual that morning. His wife wanted him to attend some silly awards luncheon given by one of her many charities. He himself was supposed to receive some ridiculous honorary something-or-other and, in a moment of weakness, he had promised to go. Unless an emergency occurred, he would have to be there promptly at 11:45. He hoped for an emergency.

A few miles from Mr. Mullins' house, he saw a girl walking quickly along the road in the opposite direction. She was hugging her bare arms and, though her eyes were directed towards the asphalt at her feet, Dr. Chisholm could tell she was crying. The girl looked familiar. He backed the car up and, consistent with his belief that everyone owed him an explanation for everything, rolled down his window and demanded to know what the girl was doing out here so early, without a jacket.

Melanie stopped but didn't say anything, her mouth closed tight and her eyes brimming with tears. Dr. Chisholm got out of the car. "What's wrong with you?" he asked.

"I'm going home," Melanie finally sobbed. "I don't want to be a nurse anymore."

Enlightenment came to Dr. Chisholm. "You're that girl taking care of old Mullins, aren't you? Why aren't you at the house?"

"I can't go back there!" Melanie had to squeeze the words out between sobs. But she didn't care now if he saw her cry. It was all over.

He questioned her, and she tried to tell what had happened that night, but her story came out disconnectedly, in pieces.

"You mean you deserted your patient? You don't even know if he's dead or alive?" Dr. Chisholm finally said. And before she could reply, he angrily commanded her to get into the car.

Melanie didn't think she had a choice, so she climbed in. Maybe when he heard the whole story, Dr. Chisholm would have her put in jail. That was okay – as long as she didn't have to go back into that house...

He did drive back to the house, but he didn't ask Melanie to get out of the car. He went in alone. Through the open front door, Melanie could see him sprint upstairs.

Several minutes passed. Melanie became calm listening to the birds singing in the trees.

When Dr. Chisholm came down again, he barked at her, "Where's the housekeeper?"

"Mr. Mullins discharged her after I came," Melanie replied.

"Why didn't you quit, too?"

Melanie explained that she had never been hired, strictly speaking, but was more of a poor relation who had needed a place to stay.

Dr. Chisholm didn't reply but, red-faced and tight-lipped, went to the car trunk. He opened it, got something out, and went back up again. Several minutes passed.

When he came out the second time and opened the passenger door, he didn't berate and threaten her like she had expected. Rather, he told her gently that Mr. Mullins was dead.

"You must have been dreaming about going up to his room

and seeing him sit up," the doctor concluded. "He's been dead for some time, most likely several hours before you ran out of the house."

"But I deserted my patient," said Melanie in a small voice. "I never should have run away."

"And a youngster like you should never have been left alone in a situation like this! But never mind. It's all over now, and you have nothing to feel ashamed of. Come on up, now. You've got to get back on the horse. If you don't face your fears, they'll get blown all out of proportion."

Melanie tried to back out, but finally followed Dr. Chisholm up the stairs and into Mr. Mullins' room, one last time. The old man's body lay exposed, the sheets lying crumpled at the foot of the bed. "Let's give him a little more dignity," Dr. Chisholm said, and he proceeded to show her how to wash and wrap up the body in preparation for its being taken away. He talked gently to her the whole time about medicine and nursing, about life, and about death.

"You remind me of my youngest boy," he said, after seeing Melanie smile at a slight joke he had made. "Not your coloring or general appearance – he was big and stocky, with red hair like mine – but he had a smile like yours, just like yours. Open and generous, unsuspecting... He was never much of a scholar – took after his mother's side of the family – but he got into college on a football scholarship, which was lucky, because with two others in school at the same time, I couldn't have swung it otherwise."

The doctor paused. They had finished wrapping up the body. Melanie was straightening the room and Dr. Chisholm stood, absently trying to stuff his stethoscope into his suit pocket. "Somebody played a practical joke on him once. They gave him a bottle of whiskey and bet him a hundred dollars that he couldn't drink it... He was homesick, just like you. He wanted the money to buy a plane ticket so he could come home for the long weekend that was coming up. He calculated that, with his bulk, he could just handle the amount of whiskey in the bottle... He was never any good at math. They carried him back to his room. He died of alcohol poisoning that night."

Melanie stood silent for some moments as Dr. Chisholm

blinked at the carpet. Then, wordlessly, she accompanied him back to the car.

Mr. Mullins would have laughed out loud if he could have. This was the most fun he had had in years. First, scaring that little idiot into a screaming fit – it had been ridiculously simple. Early in the morning, before she got up, he had managed his way downstairs. There, he had found the electrical service and turned off most of the breakers, leaving only the circuit that served the rooms next to his open. Upstairs again – quite a haul, but worth it – he had told her to move his oxygen machine into the next room for storage. After that, he had been able to sneak over and use it whenever he needed without her knowing a thing.

That set the stage. And, after a suitable interval of play-acting, he had prepared himself for the final act. He wrapped himself up carefully in his own sheet (an exhausting task, but well worth it) after making sure, of course, to place a stiff sheath of plastic from his desk blotter around his middle so she couldn't see his breathing. Then he had rung the bell – and the rest was history!

When Dr. Chisholm had burst in, Mr. Mullins had still been laughing. He told the doctor why and had been pleasantly surprised when, instead of lecturing him like the spoilsport he usually was, the doctor had wanted to know all the details. He had enjoyed the whole thing immensely. He even suggested carrying the thing one step further. Since he had the girl downstairs in his car, he would take her up and show her that Mr. Mullins was really dead. They would wrap him up again. Then, later on, when the girl was once again in the house alone, he, Mullins, would make a second resurrection and scare the living daylights out of her one more time!

Dr. Chisholm had left the hour and manner of this last re-animation up to him, but, when Mr. Mullins expressed doubt as to whether he could lie still long enough for them to wrap him up again (he was out of breath even now), the doctor had had a bright suggestion: there was a drug, he said, which would help Mr. Mullins relax – completely relax, and would calm his breathing, too. He would have trouble moving voluntarily, but for a very short time only. Just a small injection, then he would bring the little bimbo up, show her he was dead, and when they moved him around, he would not flinch, involuntarily even.

At first, Mr. Mullins had been a little wary of the whole idea. But the doctor had said, come on, where's your sense of humor? And of course, Mr. Mullins had risen to that challenge. Sucksinnel – sucksinnel-something was what the doctor had shot him up with, and Mr. Mullins had found it easy to lay completely still, just barely breathing, all the time they were in the room. What a hoot!

Now they were gone. Mr. Mullins tried to move his legs, and he couldn't. He couldn't move them an inch, nor his arms, nor his head. He could barely blink his eyes and, ominously, even the muscles in his chest were working more weakly, even now, when he was free to breathe as deeply as he could. But Dr. Chisholm had promised to come back and wait with him while the effects of the drug wore off.

Mr. Mullins heard two car doors slamming shut and an engine turning over. He felt a momentary thrill of panic. But of course, Dr. Chisholm would have to make a show of leaving. He would come right back as soon as the girl was off the trail. He'd be back in five minutes – ten, at the most.

The doctor certainly had congratulated him most sincerely on last night's work, saying that Mr. Mullins could teach those college fraternity boys a thing or two! But he had not been too gentle in giving Mr. Mullins that shot in his rump – that had hurt! If that was the young quack's idea of a joke, he would soon find out who he was playing with. No one had ever put one over on Ed Mullins.

Wait a minute – hadn't the doctor said once, a long time ago, that a shot in the rump lasted a long time? The short-acting ones were the ones that went directly into your veins. Or was it the other way around? It must be the other way around, Mr. Mullins thought timorously. He couldn't take much more of this. Even under the best of circumstances, he couldn't lie flat for very long before his lungs started filling up with fluid. He slept hunched up on pillows at night. That stuff that the doctor had given him made him feel like he had a ton of bricks on his chest. He needed his oxygen badly. He tried to pick up his arm and reach to the side of the bed where the tank usually was. If he could just reach it…

Then he remembered it was in the other room. He had no

hope of getting at it until the drug wore off completely. But, if anything, the effect seemed to be getting stronger! Really, it was very unpleasant – almost unbearable. He couldn't shift himself to get any ease.

Lack of oxygen began to confuse his brain, but panic made his mind race. He realized he was in a predicament – lying here in an empty house, wrapped up and left to await the arrival of the mortuary van. If they came and got him, he wouldn't be able to move a muscle to tell them he was alive, not dead!

But that wouldn't happen – that was just plain nonsense! Dr. Chisholm would be back any minute now.

Mr. Mullins couldn't open his eyes or turn his head to the wall where the clock was, but certainly quite a bit of time had gone by. Waiting, Mr. Mullins became more and more displeased. Obviously, Dr. Chisholm was playing some sort of joke! Waiting till the last minute, letting him lie here like this. Most likely he was laughing about it right now over his bacon and eggs. But he *would* come back. He *had* to come back, or Mr. Mullins would give him what for! He'd tell him – he'd tell him – Mr. Mullins whimpered mentally as a panic he could no longer fight washed over him – *he'd tell him it wasn't funny!*